Her beauty was delicate, but there was nothing fragile about it.

And she was not as cool and serene as she pretended to be, he decided. Her eyes, dark and restless, gave her away. There was passion beneath the cool exterior. And he wanted to be the one to discover it. It occurred to him that it had been a long time since he had wanted anything quite so badly.

"Bon soir." Insolently he reached for her hand instead of waiting for her to offer it. "So you *did* remember that you'd promised me the first waltz."

"I did not promise, Monsieur Blanchard. You demanded."

"So?" A wealth of insinuation swung with that single word. "And you always give in to demands?" His tawny eyebrows curved upward wickedly. "I shall have to remember that."

"On the contrary." Temper darkened her eyes. "I do not deal well with demands at all…!"

Dear Reader,

In Nina Beaumont's new historical, *Surrender the Heart*, a brash American and an independent Frenchwoman make a dangerous bargain. He will court her to keep away unwanted suitors, and she, in return, will allow him the chance to seduce her. But the two are unprepared for the passionate love that develops between them in this sizzling story set in nineteenth-century Paris.

In *Bogus Bride*, by Australian author Emily French, a spirited young woman must convince her new husband that although he had intended to marry her sister, she is his true soul mate. And in *Knights Divided* by Suzanne Barclay, a medieval tale from one of our most popular authors, a young woman finds herself embroiled in a maelstrom of passion and deceit when she kidnaps the rogue whom she believes murdered her sister.

And in our final selection for the month, Judith Stacy's heartwarming Western, *Outlaw Love*, a Federal Marshal on the trail of a gang of female outlaws doesn't realize that the woman he's falling in love with is their leader.

Whatever your taste in reading, we hope you'll find a story written just for you between the covers of a Harlequin Historical novel. Keep a lookout for all four titles wherever Harlequin Historicals are sold.

Sincerely,

Tracy Farrell,
Senior Editor

Please address questions and book requests to:
Harlequin Reader Service
U.S.: 3010 Walden Ave., P.O. Box 1325, Buffalo, NY 14269
Canadian: P.O. Box 609, Fort Erie, Ont. L2A 5X3

Nina Beaumont

Surrender the Heart

Harlequin Books

TORONTO • NEW YORK • LONDON
AMSTERDAM • PARIS • SYDNEY • HAMBURG
STOCKHOLM • ATHENS • TOKYO • MILAN
MADRID • WARSAW • BUDAPEST • AUCKLAND

ISBN 0-373-28962-6

SURRENDER THE HEART

Books by Nina Beaumont

Harlequin Historicals

NINA BEAUMONT

is of Russian parentage and has a family tree that includes the Counts Stroganoff and a Mongolian khan. A real cosmopolitan, she was born in Salzburg and grew up in Massachusetts before moving to Austria, where she lived for twenty-five years.

Although she has relocated to the Seattle area, her European ties are still strong, so she plans to stick with the exotic settings she has had the opportunity to get to know firsthand.

Books and music are her first loves, but she also enjoys painting watercolors and making pottery.

To Lorna and Ed Hudgens—
thank you for making me part of your family.
My heartfelt thanks to:
my editor, Tracy Farrell, and she and I know why;
my writer friends, Sonya Jorgensen, Suzanne Neel and
Mike Miller, for their brainstorming help
when I was in need.

Chapter One

Paris, October 1855

"Ariane, if you don't take that bored look off your face, you're never going to get a husband."

Ariane de Valmont barely managed to suppress the temptation to roll her eyes in exasperation. Curving her mouth into the semblance of a smile, she shifted so that she faced the stage more fully. Perhaps, she thought, *maman* would not be able to see the expression on her face quite so precisely from this angle.

She refused to be amused, even though the catchy tunes of the Offenbach operetta tempted her to tap her foot and the antics of the very human Greek gods frolicking around on the stage were hilarious. Instead, she let her gaze wander around the audience.

The theater, charming despite its overabundance of gilt decorations and red velvet, was full and the lights had been only partly dimmed in deference to the fact that the audience itself was as much part of the entertainment as what took place on the stage. The ladies, either alone or in the company of parents, chaperons or, since this was Paris, after all, lovers, occupied the boxes. The men, who were either unattached or pretending to be so, were in the stalls. She might be the only one whose mood was not in tune with the gaiety that seemed to pervade the theater like the opulent scent of a sensual perfume, Ariane noted sullenly, but she was certainly not the only one whose attention was elsewhere than on the stage.

Smiles, flutters of fans, flirtatious looks flew back and forth with dizzying speed. It was just like a horse fair back home, she thought with a sniff. Men came from all around the area with their horses, the manes and tails braided with bright-colored ribbons, hoping to attract a rich buyer. The only difference here was that the price for a wife who was blue-blooded and rich or for a beautiful, accomplished mistress was infinitely higher—for the buyer and the seller both.

The thought that she was no different from them all did not improve her mood one bit. Her father had dragged her to Paris to make a broodmare out of her, she thought grimly. All her father cared about were male heirs for the Valmont fortune.

So, here she was on display, her fair hair carefully coiffed and wearing a highly fashionable and extravagantly expensive gown of pale lavender silk. The thought alone of just how much the haughty Parisian dressmaker, who had descended on their château with her army of seamstresses for a whole month, had cost, soured Ariane's mood still further.

She had tried to point out to *papa* that they would be far better off if they used the money for repairs on the stables. But he had merely given a disparaging wave and reminded her that they had plenty of money. She had not bothered to mention that the only reason they did was that she spent her time diplomatically circumventing every decision he made about how the estate was to be run.

Tucking her chin into the palm of one hand, she looked down at the stalls. The men, she decided, were as given to smiles and flirtatious glances as the women. Her eyebrows, which were shades darker than her golden hair, curved upward in a discreetly derisive gesture.

They all seemed to be wearing either elegant black and white evening dress or uniforms decorated with such quantities of gold braid that she was sure they would not have been out of place on a stage. Their sideburns were lavishly curled, their mustaches raffishly twirled, and they all looked as if they had never done an honest day's work in their lives. How could her father possibly expect her to choose a husband from such a sorry collection of fops, she asked herself irritably—even if she had been disposed to want a husband at all?

Suddenly her gaze stumbled and came to an abrupt stop.

It was his hair that caught her attention first. The tawny mane with just a touch of curl brushed his shoulders in contradiction of every fashionable dictate, making him look like a lion in the middle of so many motley tomcats. And the color! It was streaked in a dozen different shades of blond—from the color of pale, sun-bleached wheat to a deep honey color. Although she was not aware of it, her fingers curled with the unconscious desire to touch it.

Her gaze followed the straight, clear lines of his profile, which reminded her of faces she had seen on Roman coins. She had always wondered what a profile like that looked like from the front.

As if he had divined her thought, he turned slightly

and looked up directly at her. Not even thinking to look away or disguise her perusal behind her fan, she kept her gaze on his face, wishing that she could see the color of his eyes.

Ariane did not know it, but her eyes lost that studiously bored look, the corners of her mouth tipped up in the barest hint of a smile and her stiffly held shoulders softened enough for her mother to slant her a look.

Comtesse Marguerite de Valmont saw the expression on her daughter's face change and smiled. Leaning back in her gilt and red velvet chair, she allowed herself a small sigh of relief. It would be all right after all, she thought, and turned her attention toward her husband.

The Greek gods capering on the stage coaxed an absent half smile onto Christopher Blanchard's mouth, but most of his attention was on the people in the audience. He'd lived in too many places where your chances for survival rose in proportion to your ability to judge precisely and instantaneously the people you were dealing with. And from his own childhood experiences in Paris twenty years ago he knew all too well that Parisian society could be quite as deadly as any gold town in California, if perhaps more subtly so. And yet, he thought, it was this very Parisian society that his father had pined for all his life.

Chris had been in Paris a week, long enough to acquire an exquisitely tailored wardrobe and to comprehend that the main motor of Parisian society was the pursuit of pleasure, money and power.

He had also ascertained that Comtesse Léontine de Caillaux, his father's sister, still lived in the same severe mansion that he remembered all too well. And he had discovered that the money from the sale of the gold mine, which he and his father had jointly owned, had gone to buy shares floated by an investment bank that belonged to his half brother.

His roving gaze paused as it brushed a woman attractive in the way of a full-blown rose. She was leaning against the balustrade of her box, her crossed arms beneath her breasts unapologetically emphasizing her creamy bosom. Meeting his gaze, she plucked a flower from the bouquet that lay in front of her and slid it over her mouth in flagrant invitation.

"Suzette Lavalier is one of the most expensive courtesans in Paris," his neighbor murmured. "But rumor has it that her skill is worth every franc and more."

"Actually my taste runs to women who have not been sampled by half the male population." Chris grinned at Roger de Monnier. He felt comfortable in the younger man's company although their acquaintance was only a few days old. "I'm not nearly old enough to need a woman's skill." His grin grew just a shade wicked. "And besides, I like to think that I have skill enough for both of us."

"I'm certain you won't have a problem finding what you want." He smiled back at Chris, wondering if there was some way he could duplicate the American's not-quite-civilized aura that seemed to attract so many inviting female stares. "Paris has something for every taste."

"I don't doubt it."

As they both turned back to face the stage, Chris felt a tingle at the back of his neck. He tipped his head up and to the side and unerringly homed in on the eyes watching him.

The eyes were dark, although he could not quite discern the color at that distance. They belonged to a face with the tiny, perfect features of a porcelain doll. Yet there was strength there beneath the delicate beauty—even a touch of imperiousness. She might look like a soft Aphrodite who would come easily to a man's bed, but he suspected that she was a proud Athena instead. She would fight surrender, he mused, but if conquered, she would give delight beyond measure. And right now she was looking at him with undisguised interest.

He felt the jolt right down to the pit of his belly. A jolt that spread a heat not unlike the fire of whiskey on an empty stomach.

His gaze drifted down to her mouth. The corners tilted upward in the merest hint of a smile as she continued to look at him with an openness and a concentration that another man might have found either unnerving or ill-bred. Chris, on the other hand, found himself inordinately pleased and decided to answer in kind. Instead of the discreet bow that convention would have demanded of him, he tilted his head back in a gesture that was more a challenge than a decorous greeting.

He watched the young woman's mouth turn serious again. Her eyebrows drew together and her eyes narrowed slightly, but she still did not look away. No, she kept watching him, and under her gaze, he felt the heat in his belly spread. Well, well, he thought as his mouth curved, perhaps his stay in Paris would bring him a few new, pleasant memories to replace the old, ugly ones.

Ariane watched the stranger tip back his head. She was not well-versed in the games men and women engaged in, but she understood a challenge better than most. Although she frowned, wondering just what it was that he was challenging her to and why, she was distracted by the sheer, untamed beauty of the man. The movement of his head had his incredible mane of hair rippling back so that it caught the light and she found herself wondering—consciously this time—what it would feel like to run her fingers through it.

When she saw his mouth tilt upward in a smile that managed to be both boyishly charming and insolent, the horrible thought that he had read her mind had her stiffening. Still, pride would not allow her to look away.

"Roger, do you know the girl up there?" Chris did not shift his gaze away from her face as he spoke. "The golden-haired one in the lavender gown."

Roger de Monnier leaned forward, and recognizing the young woman, lowered his head in a well-mannered bow.

"That is Ariane de Valmont. Comtesse Ariane de Valmont. She and her parents have come to Paris for the season," he said. "She's older than most of the debutantes, apparently. God knows why her parents kept her buried in the country for so long. No hint of scandal though," he hastened to add. "Would you like me to present you?"

Roger felt a flicker of regret. He had been rather taken with the young countess himself, but now, seeing the way she and his new friend were staring at each other, he had no illusions about his chances with her.

"I would like that." Chris sent his friend a quick smile before his gaze returned to the young woman.

"Chris?"

"Mmm?"

"She is a young lady of good family." Roger gnawed at his lower lip, not quite sure how to phrase what he wanted to say without insulting his friend. "And this is not—" he coughed discreetly "—the American West."

Slowly Chris turned to face him fully and Roger almost recoiled at the way his pale green eyes had cooled. "I—I didn't mean—"

"Don't worry, *mon ami*. I may be an uncivilized American in your eyes, but my parents were easily the equals of anyone here tonight and more. I know what conduct your society demands—" he paused and raised a tawny eyebrow "—on the surface."

"I meant no insult."

Chris relaxed and smiled. "Then I will not take it as one."

In unison, both men turned back to the stage where the singers had arranged themselves for the finale of the act.

Damn, Chris swore at himself. Why had he let Monnier's words get to him like that? He had been so certain that he no longer cared what they thought of him. Wasn't that why he had come here? To put all those old ghosts to rest? To exorcise all the old memories?

All these years he had told himself that none of them mattered any longer. Now he realized that he had been lying to himself. The memories still hurt. He still cared.

Applause surged up in a wave as the curtain came down, but most of the audience was already engaged in orchestrating the intermission.

Ariane had carefully kept her gaze on the stage for the past minutes. Now, as the audience began to chat and move around, she allowed her eyes to drift back over the stalls. The blond man's seat was empty and she suppressed the sting of disappointment, assuring herself that she cared nothing about his whereabouts.

"I think I'll go visit Justine de Monnier in her box," she said, turning toward her mother. But she saw that her mother was not listening to her. Instead, she was looking up her husband with undisguised adoration, hanging on to every word of whatever it was he was saying to her.

Shrugging, she rose, but before she could move away from her chair, her father shot her a displeased look.

"Sit down, Ariane," Pierre de Valmont said. "I've told you that one stays in one's box at intermission to receive visitors."

"If everyone stays in their box, then who are the visitors?" she asked with a feigned artlessness.

"Don't be impudent. Now s—"

A knock at the door to their box interrupted him.

"You see," the Comte de Valmont said, pleased, his irritation with his daughter forgotten.

Ariane returned to her chair with a huff. "If it's that pudgy little duke with the pig's eyes," she retorted, "I—"

"Will be polite," her father finished firmly and invited the visitors to enter.

As the man with the mane of tawny hair stepped into the box, Ariane's mouth went dry.

Chapter Two

He was even taller than Ariane had imagined, his shoulders uncommonly, almost indecorously broad. His severely elegant evening clothes were perfectly tailored, but that only seemed to call attention to the aura of wildness that clung to him. Certainly he did not look even remotely like the idle young men she had met in the past week.

Ariane stared at him, hearing neither the babble of pleasantries as her parents greeted Roger de Monnier nor the shocked gasp in the box adjacent to theirs.

"May I present my friend, Christopher Blanchard." Although it pained his Gallic sensibilities, Roger said the name as Chris had told him it was pronounced in America. "He comes from America."

"You are an American? How interesting." Marguerite de Valmont smiled vapidly. "We had a visitor from America recently. Where was the gentleman from, *chéri?*" She looked up at her husband.

"Where was he from?" Valmont passed the question on to his daughter.

"Virginia, *papa.*"

"Ah, yes," Valmont said. "A very pleasant gentleman. He purchased several of our horses." He rubbed his hands lightly as he remembered. "*Une bonne affaire.* An excellent deal."

Yes, Ariane thought with a touch of acrimony, it *had* been an excellent deal. But only because she had spent the week haggling with this very pleasant gentleman over one card game after another.

"And where are you from?"

Pierre de Valmont's voice had the interrogative tone typical of fathers of unmarried daughters, reminding Chris of Roger's words. It occurred to him that in California, a question like that would be more likely to elicit a challenge to a fight than an answer, but his voice showed no trace of irritation when he spoke.

"I've moved around a great deal, but I've lived in California for a number of years now."

California? The image of desert and ocean and hot sun was so real that Ariane could almost feel the heat on her bared shoulders. Was it the hot sun which had made his hair that fabulous color, which had bronzed his skin? The men of Provence, where she had spent most of her life, were a handsome lot, but she had never seen a man of such pagan beauty. Suddenly painfully aware that she had been staring, she looked away.

"Are you in Paris on business or pleasure?" Valmont inquired.

"I have interests here that require looking after. But I am certain that being in Paris will also be a pleasure."

Valmont nodded, marginally relieved. After all, a man who had business interests in France was most likely not a complete barbarian, even if his shoulder-length hair and insolent eyes made him look like a Viking intent on plunder.

His gaze drifted to his daughter and he swore to himself. It was the very devil to guard the virtue of a daughter—especially when the daughter had more intelligence and energy than was good for her. Too bad her intelligence had not extended to choosing a husband from one of the many perfectly acceptable sons of the other landowners.

Well, he thought, he was going to make sure that she had a husband before they left Paris. A husband who would give her the sons to inherit the fortune he had built. With a sigh, he returned to his duties as host.

Ariane held herself aloof from the conversation, irritated at the way her parents were quizzing this man. The American was not very loquacious, she remarked, responding to questions in faultless French, but volunteering no additional information. Paradoxically, she found his reticence annoying, although she deplored those self-important mentions about lineage or wealth that most other men made.

"We are looking forward to seeing you at our ball." Roger turned to Ariane. "My sister Justine has spoken of little else since she made your acquaintance the other evening."

"And I am looking forward to seeing her." And she truly was wanting to see again the young girl who was everything that she was not—tall and willowy, with hair the color of pitch, and perfectly at ease in the whirl of balls, carriage rides and flirtation.

He was watching her, Ariane thought, as she kept up the stream of polite chatter. She could feel it as surely as if he were touching her. He was challenging her again, just as he had before. Only this time, she understood that he was challenging her to look at him because he knew perfectly well that she was avoiding it.

She was being rude, she knew, but that thought disturbed her less than the thought that he might think her a coward. Or worse, that he was laughing at her.

Taking a deep breath, she turned toward him. His eyes, which were the clear, cool green of a mountain stream, held a faint amusement that had her forgetting her unsureness, her embarrassment in the face of the surge of annoyance.

He knows just how attractive he is, she thought with an instinctive understanding that went far beyond her experience. *He is so aware of the power of his charm that he expects all women to fall at his feet.* But despite her irritation, she found that she could not remove herself completely from his allure.

"What do you think of all this, Monsieur Blanchard?" She made a small circular gesture with her fan. "How does it compare to California?"

"Paris is Paris, of course," he said smoothly, "but people, in essence, are the same everywhere."

"Do you really think so?"

The sharp inquiry in her tone pleased him far more than docile agreement would have. "You don't?"

"Actually, no." Her eyes moved over him boldly, as if her uneasiness of a few moments ago had never been. "I somehow doubt that you are *anything* like anyone I have met in Paris." Her shoulders moved in a delicate shrug. "Or elsewhere for that matter."

"Is that a compliment or an insult?" He grinned, making it perfectly clear that he considered it the former.

Unable to resist, she grinned back. "I'll let you know as soon as I've made up my mind."

Helpless, Valmont watched Ariane flirt with the large, handsome American. She was truly impossible, he thought. He had never seen her quite as animated with other, more suitable men.

"Shall we have some champagne now?" Valmont signaled to the waiting footman to fill the champagne flutes.

"To a pleasant stay in Paris for all of you." Roger de Monnier raised his glass. "And a long one."

"I'm looking forward to it," Chris said, his eyes not moving from Ariane's face.

Ariane lifted her glass and sipped, watching the American over the rim of her flute. His eyes of that unusual transparent green were lit with male interest. In the past week she had been the recipient of enough such looks to be able to identify it. But while she had easily shrugged off the interest of all those insipid, dull young men, she suddenly found herself unwilling to look away from this man's eyes, which held heat and challenge and that maddening trace of amusement.

Chris watched her, waiting for her to flutter the golden-tipped eyelashes that fringed her fabulous eyes, which were the rich color of amethysts, or send him a flirtatious smile, or hide coquettishly behind her fan. But she did none of those things. Instead she kept watching him, her eyes and mouth serious, as if she were measuring him. It occurred to him that he had never seen a woman with such a capacity for stillness before.

"And you, *comtesse?* Are you looking forward to it?"

His voice was soft and insinuating and, despite her lack of experience, Ariane recognized the ripple of excitement that traveled down her spine for what it was. She smiled, for the first time in weeks feeling no rancor that her parents had dragged her off to Paris.

"Yes," she said, "I am."

"I'm glad to hear that."

A melodious gong sounded, signaling the end of intermission, and Chris stood and bowed over the hand she held out to him.

"The first waltz tomorrow night," he murmured, just loud enough for her ears. "The first and the last."

"I'll have to check my dance card." She tipped up her chin. "I don't know if they're still free."

"The first and the last waltz, *comtesse*." His smile was very white and very wicked in his bronzed face. "Some things are not negotiable."

Ariane felt her pulse skitter as he held her eyes for a long moment before he turned toward her parents.

"I thank you for your hospitality." Chris bowed over Marguerite de Valmont's hand.

As he turned away, his gaze brushed over the woman staring at him from the adjacent box. And all the old, ugly memories came flooding over him.

"What insolence," Ariane said to no one in particular when the box door had closed behind the two men. Shrugging with a not quite successful attempt at nonchalance, she turned back toward the audience. "But at least he's not boring."

"Really, Ariane," Valmont said, "I fail to understand you."

"Don't worry, *papa*," Ariane said without looking at her father. She knew just what kind of face he was making. "I'm not planning to marry the man."

"Good God," Valmont sputtered. "I hope not. Not when you have men like the Duc de Santerre dancing attendance on you."

Chris sat staring into a glass of brandy he had yet to touch.

Nothing had changed, he realized. The moment he had

seen Comtesse Léontine de Caillaux in the box, he had been catapulted back in time.

He had stood, his small, sweaty hand in his father's larger one, looking up with longing at the tall, fair-haired woman who resembled his father so strongly. She had smelled like some kind of flower and he had desperately wanted her to stroke his cheek with her soft hands, just like *maman* had always done before she had gone away to live among the angels.

But she had not touched him. She had not even really looked at him.

"I don't know what you could be thinking of to subject me to the presence of your filthy, little bastard," she'd said. "Really, Charles, apparently living among those savages in America has made you forget good manners completely."

He remembered the sharp sound of her voice as if it had been yesterday. And he remembered the sick feeling in his stomach as he had tried to understand why she looked at him with such disgust.

And he discovered that now, twenty years later, the memory still hurt.

"May I abduct your daughter?" Justine de Monnier's chocolate-colored eyes twinkled as she floated up to the Valmonts in a fussy gown of pink satin and cream-colored lace. Barely waiting for the Valmonts' reply, she tucked Ariane's arm into hers and strolled off.

"I'm going to tell you who *everyone* is." With a co-quettish smile Justine acknowledged a greeting from one young man and then another without missing a beat.

Her eyes amused, Ariane's eyebrows curved upward. "Is the ball going to last a week then?" Justine's words should have irritated her, she thought, since she cared nothing about who "everyone" was, but somehow the younger girl's enthusiasm was infectious.

Justine's laughter chimed. "Only the ones who are *someone,* of course," she clarified.

"That's good to hear, but couldn't we sneak into the game room instead?"

"That would be very naughty of us." Justine giggled. "It's frowned upon for unmarried young women, you know."

"I know." Ariane sighed at the thought that even this diversion was closed to her. At least on those rare occasions when she had found herself at some festivity at home, she had seldom had a problem finding a lively card game—if worst came to worst, in the stables.

"Oh!"

Ariane heard the soft gasp and glanced at Justine, who had snapped open her fan with an elegant flick of her wrist and was fluttering it daintily. Ariane wondered how many hours in front of a mirror it had taken the girl to achieve such perfection. Justine's eyes had become as round as coins and Ariane automatically followed the direction of her gaze.

When she found her own gaze trapped by Christopher Blanchard's eyes, she felt like a fly that had inadvertently walked into a honey pot. She told herself that the small flicker in the pit of her stomach was not excitement but dismay.

"Do you see that man with Roger?" Justine's voice was just short of reverent. "The one staring at us so shamelessly." Her breath caught in an excited little hiccup. "Oh, *mon Dieu.*" She pressed her hand against her bosom. "Where did Roger find him and who is he?"

"I don't know where your brother found him, but his name is Christopher Blanchard and he's an American."

He was still looking at her as if challenging her to be the first one to look away, so she stared back, unwilling to lose this small battle.

Justine's fan went suddenly still and dropped several inches, revealing her Cupid's bow mouth, which was slightly open in surprise. "You know who he is?" She moved closer and gave Ariane's arm a small pinch under the cover of her fan. "You're staring."

"I know." Annoyance stirring, Ariane did not move except to raise her chin another notch. "It's a contest."

Her face remained composed, but her eyes grew turbulent. Her fingers on her lace and ivory fan tightened, but she did not notice. But she was very aware that the blood had begun to rush in her veins as quickly as a river swollen with the spring rains.

His image had floated through her dreams last night, but the reality of the man, so large and bronzed, so very male, had her heart drumming. *It is nothing remarkable,* she assured herself. *It is no different from the way your heartbeat picks up the moment before you take up a hand of cards when the stakes are high.* At the moment, the fatal precision of her observation escaped her.

A moment later her view was obstructed by the pudgy figure of the young Duc de Santerre.

"I am enchanted to see you here tonight, *comtesse.*" His beatific smile had his almost colorless eyes disappearing into the folds of soft, pink flesh. "May I have the honor of dancing the first waltz with you?"

"I'm sorry, *monsieur le duc.* I am promised." Her father's instructions forgotten, the words slipped out as if they had a will of their own. Because she felt sorry for him, she gave him an especially warm smile. "One of the others perhaps?'' she said rashly, regretting her words the moment they were said.

The young duke's eyes disappeared again as, delighted at his good fortune, he watched Ariane write his name on her dance card. He opened his mouth to say something, but he saw that she had raised her head and was looking across the ballroom. He hovered over her a moment longer before he understood that he had been dismissed.

Her eyes trapped in the American's gaze again, Ariane barely noticed as Santerre drifted off. He inclined his head slightly as if in acknowledgment, and she saw that his eyes were amused and knowing.

Damn him. He knows that you saved the first waltz for him. You should have given it to Santerre.

Why cut off your nose to spite your face? Santerre's conversation would put an insomniac to sleep and he'll step on your toes besides.

And the American? What will he do to you?

As if to answer her question he moved then, striding across the ballroom toward her with a singleness of purpose that had the clusters of chatting people parting to let him pass. She stiffened her spine against the flutter in the pit of her stomach, admitting to the uneasiness, but not to the excitement.

She was truly lovely, Chris thought. She was tiny, her soft curves just on the verge of lush. And her skin! He had once seen pearls of that same color—a translucent milky white with just a blush of pink.

Her white gown, adorned only by tiny bunches of silk violets the exact color of her eyes, was almost severe in comparison to the creations decorated with lace and ruffles worn by the other women. And she stood very still, even when she was speaking, as if all that was going on around her concerned her not at all.

Her beauty was delicate, but there was nothing fragile about it. And she was not as cool and serene as she pretended to be, he decided. Her eyes, dark and restless, gave her away. There was passion beneath the cool exterior, he thought. And he wanted to be the one to discover it. It occurred to him that it had been a very long time since he had wanted anything quite so badly.

"Bonsoir." Insolently he reached for her hand instead of waiting for her to offer it. "So you *did* remember that you'd promised me the first waltz."

"I did not promise, Monsieur Blanchard. You demanded."

"So?" A wealth of insinuation swung with that single word. "And you always give in to demands?" His tawny eyebrows curved upward wickedly. "I shall have to remember that."

"On the contrary." Temper darkened her eyes. "I do not deal well with demands at all."

"And to what then do I owe your—" he paused "—unusual acquiescence?"

Ariane knew that he was trying to provoke her and, determined not to be bested, she decided to answer him in kind.

"To the fact that your conversation is more amusing the Santerre's." She let her eyes move over him in a casual but thorough sweep. "And you look as if you will exhibit a certain grace on the dance floor."

Justine let out a small, shocked gasp, but Ariane did not hear it as her own breath caught when Chris threw back his head and laughed. This was not a polite society laugh or a mocking chuckle, but a rich sound of amusement that was as physical as a touch. People around them stared, but Ariane did not notice, for she was fascinated by his laughter and by the way it made the bronzed skin of his throat ripple.

His mouth was still curved in a smile when his eyes returned to hers. "I am enchanted."

It took some effort, but she managed to pull away from his magnetism.

"By what?" She frowned, bristling less at his words than at the amusement in his eyes.

Chris watched, fascinated, as her fabulous eyes iced over, even as they retained a heated flicker of anger.

"How do you do that?" he demanded softly, forgetting completely that she had asked him a question.

"Do what? What are you talking about?" Her brisk, impatient tone softened as she saw that the amusement in his eyes had fled and been replaced by heat. How could eyes of that cool green color carry such intense heat? she wondered.

"How do you make your eyes go as cold as an arctic night and yet the fire is still there?" He curled his hands into fists to keep them at his sides.

She stilled at the sound of his voice—low and yet somehow urgent. A shiver glided over her skin as if he had touched her. For a moment, she merely looked at him, unable to speak. Then forcibly shaking off the feeling, she tilted her chin. "I don't know what you're talking about."

Her stormy eyes challenged him and Chris felt the blood begin to pound in his veins. Had he ever wanted a woman so quickly, so urgently? Yes, she was lovely, he thought, but it was not just her beauty that lured him. Far more, it was her spirit—and the unbridled passion he sensed within her. He pulled in a deep breath and managed a casual smile. "I'll explain it to you some other time."

"Monsieur Blanchard—" Ariane drew herself up to her full height and cursed silently that she did not even reach the American's shoulders. "I do not believe there will be some other time."

"Oh, on the contrary." He lowered his voice to a murmur. "I promise you there will be."

"That sounds suspiciously like a threat."

"Not a threat. Even uncivilized Americans do not threaten beautiful young women." He smiled. "It's a promise."

He wanted to lock her in a room and make love to her until she was out of his system, Chris thought, feeling his body tighten. It occurred to him that one did not need a great deal of imagination to construe a desire that strong as a threat.

"I have had quite enough of your promises, Monsieur Blanchard. And your demands." She started to turn away. "You will excuse me."

The words were scarcely out of her mouth when the musicians began to play the lilting introduction to a Strauss waltz.

"I believe this is my dance, *comtesse*."

Chapter Three

Even as Ariane turned away from him, Chris took her hand and, with his other hand at the small of her back, maneuvered her toward the dance floor so elegantly, so deftly that she knew there was no way she could escape without making a scene.

Despite the difference in their height, there was no awkwardness as he whirled her around to the three-quarter time of the dance. On the contrary, they moved together as if neither of them had ever danced with anyone else.

As much as Ariane disliked the empty chatter at social gatherings, she had always loved to dance. Now the pleasure of moving in time with the music made her forget her annoyance—almost.

"You're enjoying yourself," Chris said. "Why don't you give in and smile?"

She tilted her head back so that she could meet his eyes. The amusement was there again and it touched off her temper as surely as a match touches off a flame.

"I do not relish being manipulated, *monsieur*. Or laughed at."

"I'll admit to the manipulating, but I was not laughing at you."

"Weren't you?"

"No." His eyes turned suddenly serious. "I know how much mockery can hurt. Firsthand."

"You?" Ariane was so surprised at his words and at the way the amusement had drained out of his eyes so quickly that she missed a step. "I cannot believe that."

"Well, it's true," he said brusquely, a little appalled that he had shared that long-ago hurt with her.

"I can't quite imagine anyone daring to mock you."

Annoyed at himself, he shrugged. "It was a long time ago."

Ariane understood childhood hurts—after all, she lived with some of her own. Feeling his discomfort at the confession he had made, she said nothing. Instead, she shifted the hand that lay lightly in his palm and gave his hand a squeeze, accompanying it with a smile.

The touch she gave him was so brief that Chris wondered if he had imagined it. But he knew that he had not imagined the smile of extraordinary sweetness that curved her mouth and was reflected in her violet eyes.

When the dance ended, they found themselves near Justine and her partner.

"Just a word, Ariane," Justine called out. Then, leaving her dance partner with an apologetic gesture, she moved over to her new friend and, under the guise of adjusting the tiny bunch of silk violets that was fastened above Ariane's ear, she pulled her a step away from Chris and whispered, "Be careful. He's gorgeous, but get rid of him quickly and don't dance with him again. People are staring."

"What was that all about?" Chris asked, when Ariane

turned back to him and placed her hand on his proffered arm.

"Apparently we have made a spectacle of ourselves." Her shrug was more exasperated than rueful. "She told me to get rid of you and warned me not to dance with you again."

Had someone asked him, he would have denied that his nerves had tightened. "And are you?"

"Going to get rid of you or going to dance with you again?" Her mouth was serious, but her eyes were smiling.

"Both, either."

They began to walk toward the part of the ballroom where her parents were seated.

"I don't take direction very well. Especially from children." Ariane shrugged. "Justine thinks she knows everything, but she is only a child."

Chris smiled. "While you are veritably ancient," he teased.

"You have no idea how true your words are." His smile was so charming, so infectious that Ariane smiled back, forgetting her earlier irritation. "That's why I'm here, after all. In Paris, I mean." She made a face.

"You see, I've reached the age of twenty-five and my father is appalled that he does not yet have a son-in-law and a horde of grandchildren."

Chris felt a tightening in his belly at the thought of her with another man. It was on the tip of his tongue to ask if she was planning to provide her father with what he wanted when he realized that they had reached the far end of the ballroom. He bowed politely toward the elder Valmonts before he turned toward Ariane.

"Thank you for the waltz, *comtesse*." This time he did not reach for her hand, but waited politely for her to offer it to him. "May I look forward to dancing with you again?" he asked when she did.

Ariane felt the pressure of his fingers on hers. As he lifted his head and met her gaze, she read the challenge in his eyes that told her that the touch had not been accidental. She could feel her father's displeased gaze on her, but the temptation of the dare this man offered was stronger.

"You may."

He retained her hand a moment longer than convention allowed, but she had no desire to pull her hand away from the warmth she could feel despite her gloves. Again there was that brief pressure and she suppressed a shiver of excitement just as he finally released her.

She should not want to dance with him again so badly, she thought, as he walked away, but she did. It was only because his amusing, impudent conversation was such a pleasant change from the inanities she had been hearing, she assured herself. And at the moment she believed it.

Several moments passed before she realized that her father was speaking to her.

"I'm sorry, *papa.*" She turned to him and put a soothing hand on his arm. "What were you saying?"

"I don't want you dancing with him again," he repeated petulantly. "We didn't bring you to Paris to fall into the hands of some—some adventurer," Valmont continued. "I want you to have a good, French husband."

"*Papa*—"

"I want your promise, Ariane, that you will do as I say." Because he had drunk enough champagne to make him feel expansive, but not enough to sour his temper, his tone wheedled rather than commanded.

"I am here in Paris, *papa,* because you wished it."

She gave her father a direct look and felt a little spurt of guilty satisfaction when he lowered his eyes. "The least you can do is let me enjoy myself."

She turned away, refraining from adding that she planned to leave Paris as unencumbered by a husband as she had arrived.

"Ariane—"

The Comtesse de Valmont tucked her hand into her husband's arm and screwed up the courage to speak. "Leave her be, Pierre," she whispered. "The more you storm against him, the more attractive he will seem to her." She remembered quite well how her own father had stormed against the feckless, volatile Comte de Valmont.

Ariane stared after Christopher Blanchard's retreating figure, a plan forming in her mind.

And she was not the only one who stared after him.

It was too much to be borne. The Marquise de Blanchard closed her eyes. The moment she had seen him she had known with an absolute certainty that this man was Charles's son. Oh, he was taller and broader, but the handsome features were too similar to her husband's to be anyone else. The man whom she had loved. The man who had left her for another woman. She had never forgiven him for being either.

Hatred, old and new, was bitter on her tongue as she approached him.

"You are Charles de Blanchard's son. Do not bother to deny it."

The voice behind him was soft, but it dripped ice and venom in equal parts. Instinctively knowing whom the voice belonged to, Chris turned around to face the woman whose stubbornness and pride had condemned him to being a bastard. Reminding himself that he was a grown man and that his existence had, after all, condemned her to being an abandoned wife, he bowed.

"I would not think of denying the truth, *madame la marquise.*"

"You know who I am?" Her small, round black eyes, which gave her the aspect of a plump bird, narrowed. "How?"

"My father had a miniature."

"He kept my portrait?" Her thin mouth, the only thin feature she possessed, curved in a triumphant smile.

"He kept a portrait of his children." Chris kept his voice carefully neutral. "I suspect your presence there was incidental."

The smile froze briefly to a grimace before it disappeared.

"What are you doing here in Paris?" The *marquise* heard the ebony slats of her fan groan under the pressure of her fingers and forced her hands to relax. "If you have come here to embarrass me, embarrass my children, I shall—"

"I advise you not to threaten me, *madame la marquise.* It is not something I take kindly to."

"I will do as I please," she said, choosing to ignore the steel beneath the mild tone. "*I* do not take kindly to the presence of my husband's bastard son, fathered on a woman of easy virtue."

His pale green eyes iced over so quickly that it took all her control not to step back before the cold, dangerous fury she saw there.

"Be grateful, *madame la marquise*—" although his tone was almost without inflection, he managed to make the title sound like an insult "—that we are in public and that I do not choose to make a scene." He paused for a moment to make certain that he had been understood. "I will not be that lenient again."

Slowly Chris turned away and went in search of brandy to wash away the memory of his mother's tears and all the old childhood hurts that were suddenly clogging his throat.

With an outraged gasp Odile de Blanchard watched Charles's bastard turn his back on her. Catching sight of her country cousin, Pierre, across the room, she hurried toward him to tell him just who his daughter had been dancing with.

Ariane had always prided herself on her ability to give her attention to more than one activity at a time. So while she whirled around in a succession of waltzes and polkas and quadrilles, while she carried on one conversation after another empty of everything but a little light flirtation, her mind clicked away efficiently.

Deciding that she did not have the patience to wait for the last waltz, she took advantage of the intermission between sets to look for Roger de Monnier. He was talking to his sister, she saw. Well, it could not be helped, she thought, and it really did not matter. Justine would know soon enough that she had no intention of taking her advice.

"May I interrupt?"

"You're not interrupting, Ariane." Justine hooked her arm around Ariane's. "In fact, we were just talking about you."

Ariane raised her eyes heavenward. "I can imagine."

"I apologize for what I said, but you have no idea how people talk here in Paris."

"Well," Ariane said, "they're going to have to talk some more." Giving Justine's arm a pat, she turned to

Roger. "Would you give Monsieur Blanchard a message for me, Roger?"

"Of course." Roger smiled brightly. Perhaps he would have a chance with the young countess after all.

"Please tell him that I would like to speak to him during the next intermission."

"But—" He threw a helpless look at his sister.

"Please, Roger."

With a bow Roger left the two young women.

"But Ariane, don't you understand—"

"I understand perfectly." Ariane smiled. "But let me explain so that *you* do." Seeing yet another eligible young man bearing down on them, she deliberately turned away, pulling Justine along with her.

"I am here in Paris because my parents decided I could no longer do without a husband. But I have no intention of saddling myself with one. Thus it is of no import whether people gossip about me or not. Do you understand now?"

"You don't want a husband?" Justine stared at Ariane with something resembling horror. "Ever?"

"Ever."

"I don't understand."

"Justine," she said with a touch of impatience. "I am twenty-five. I've lived as I please for a long time and I have no intention of changing that."

"Oh, pooh." Justine wiggled her fingers as if she were chasing a pesky fly. "The empress was twenty-six when she married, and from what one hears, she lived as she pleased and she still does."

Ariane shook her head. "I want my life to stay just as it is. I love my home, my land." Her eyes softened as she thought of the endless fields. "You have no idea how beautiful it is." For a moment she considered explaining how she had made a moderately prosperous estate into very wealthy one, by running it behind her father's back, but she rejected the notion. It was not something Justine would understand.

"And I have no desire to have a husband who will only want to mold me into an obedient wife." Never, she thought, never did she want to be like her mother, who had no life but what her husband chose to give her.

"But what does Christopher Blanchard have to do with all this?"

"I need a smoke screen, Justine."

The girl sighed dramatically. "I don't understand a word."

"Don't worry." Ariane patted Justine's arm. "The main thing is that Christopher Blanchard understands." It occurred to her that she was playing with fire, but, intent on her purpose, she pushed the thought away.

Chapter Four

Chris watched Ariane from the edge of the dance floor, as he had been doing all evening. When her dance partner bent down and whispered something into her ear, he clenched his fists at his sides. When she lifted her face toward the baby-faced young man, revealing her radiant smile, he barely managed to prevent himself from barging onto the dance floor.

Pulling in a deep breath, he cursed himself for a fool. Perhaps it had been simply too long since he had had a woman, he thought. Perhaps he should take Roger's advice and see what Suzette Lavalier or one of her colleagues had to offer.

"What's the matter, Chris? Aren't you enjoying yourself?"

"Of course, I am." Forcing himself to relax, he turned toward Roger. "Why do you ask?"

"Because you're scowling like the very devil." He grinned despite his misgivings. He had seen the direction of Chris's gaze.

Shrugging, Chris said nothing, but his eyes returned to the dance floor.

"I have a message for you. From Ariane de Valmont."

"Indeed?" His heartbeat leaped at Roger's words, but his indifferent tone gave no hint of his sudden turmoil. If her message was to cancel the dance she had promised him, he swore to himself, she was in for a surprise.

"She would like your company during the next intermission between sets."

"What does she want?"

"I am not her confidant." He gnawed at his lip, wondering if he should dare Chris's anger again.

"Don't worry, Roger," Chris said, feeling his friend's discomfort. "You've done your duty and you can believe me when I tell you that I have never forced my attentions on a woman."

"The question of force never entered my mind." Roger smiled ruefully. "Ariane de Valmont is an inexperienced young woman, unused to society. She is no match for a man like you—"

Chris shot him a black look.

"A man like you—" Roger continued unperturbed "—who draws female stares as a magnet draws pins. A man who has enough charm to talk his way into any bed."

"Should I be flattered or insulted?" Chris's brows took on a mocking curve. Then he glanced across the ballroom, where Ariane stood surrounded by several young men while her parents looked on proudly.

"Don't worry, Roger. I think the young Comtesse de Valmont can take care of herself just fine."

"I got your message," Chris said when he collected Ariane after the set had ended. He touched her elbow and soft flesh made his cool restraint disintegrate. "If you are going to tell me that you've decided to get rid of me after all, don't."

Ariane stopped in the middle of a movement, her eyebrows rising at the vehemence of his tone. "And if I was?"

"I shall—"

"More threats, Monsieur Blanchard?"

Chris understood desire. He understood how to gratify it and how to keep it in check. But he was appalled at the unfamiliar, turbulent feelings that were racing through him. Even more, he was appalled at how effortlessly they eluded the control he had honed so carefully. He gave Ariane a searching look. Her mouth and her eyes were serious, but there had been a definite smile in her voice. The unreasoning sense of relief he felt at that unnerved him still further.

"No." He softened the curt answer with a smile. "No threats."

"Good." Ariane's nod was all coolness and composure, but as the unexpected heat curled through her, unfamiliar and a little frightening, she looked away from his charming, lopsided smile.

He was altogether too beautiful, too charming, too virile, she thought. And much too sure of himself. How many women had fallen victim to him? she wondered. Did he, like Don Juan, need a servant to keep a list of his myriad conquests? Well, she was forewarned, she told herself. She would use him for her purpose, but she would not succumb to that charm he dispensed so facilely.

"What do you want from me then?"

Ariane's gaze skidded up at his directness. "For the moment, your company."

"My name is on your dance card. So impatient?" His lifted eyebrows insinuated more.

"Are you trying very hard to be disagreeable?" she demanded.

"No. I just don't believe in wasting time nor in beating around the bush." He paused. "Well?"

"Presently." Ariane lifted her hand in a gesture that requested patience. "I am not beating around the bush," she explained not quite truthfully. "I merely do things in my own good time."

She was hedging and she knew it. But now that he was standing next to her—so large, so handsome, so utterly male—she found that her stomach was quivering. And what had seemed so reasonable, so expedient just a little while ago was suddenly madness.

"Agreed." Apparently the young countess did not intend to send him to the devil, so Chris reined in his impatience. Tucking her hand into the crook of his arm, he directed their steps toward one of the rooms off the main ballroom, where light refreshments were being served.

As they strolled by, a door opened and several footmen carrying huge trays full of empty bottles emerged. The door remained open, revealing a room hazy with smoke, quiet but for the sound of hushed voices, the occasional slap of cards and the gradually slowing clack of the ball on the roulette wheel.

Chris slowed his steps to match Ariane's. When he heard her wistful sigh, he could not resist a grin. "Don't tell me you're a gambler."

"I don't mind a good game of cards." She grimaced inwardly at her prim tone and the lukewarm understatement.

"So the countess has a weakness for games of chance." He laughed, pleased.

"No, cards," Ariane corrected as they began to walk again. "I cannot abide games of chance."

"That's a very fine line you are drawing."

"Not at all." She warmed to the subject, forgetting that young, unmarried countesses did not gamble. And if they did, they certainly did not talk about it. "Cards require skill. In games of chance you are completely dependent on what luck may deal you."

"Don't you believe in luck?" Chris had had too many close brushes with disaster not to. Besides, the blood that ran in his veins was half-Russian, so he came by his belief in the vagaries of fortune honestly.

"Of course I do. Only fools believe solely in their own abilities." She grinned. "On the other hand, only fools depend on their luck to help them every time."

"Lovely, charming, witty, a gambler and a philosopher to boot. Unbelievable." He shook his head. "Now are you going to tell me why you wanted to speak to me?" he said, his impatience getting the better of him.

Ariane took a deep breath. She supposed it was as good a time as any.

"Are you looking for a wife, Monsieur Blanchard?" She met his eyes and held them.

Struck dumb for a moment, Chris only stared at her. There was no facetiousness or coquetry in her eyes. Instead they held only a mild inquiry, as if she were asking a shopkeeper about the relative merits of two bolts of cloth.

"No, actually I am not," he replied, wondering what her game was. She continued to look at him with her eyes of that startling violet color so that he felt compelled to elaborate. "I have no need for an heiress, nor does a man of my station need to make a dynastic marriage.''

''There are other reasons to choose a wife.''

He slanted her a look, not certain if she was flirting or being outrageous, but her gaze still appeared to hold no more than polite interest.

''Pledging my heart forever holds no appeal for me. In fact, I find the thought of my happiness being dependent on another person quite appalling.''

The memory of his father, prostrate with grief at his mother's death, nudged him. Chris had no intention of ever opening himself up to that kind of vulnerability. Ever.

''Excellent.'' Pleased and relieved, she smiled. She could not have wished for a better reaction, she thought. ''Nor am I looking for a husband. I, too, find the institution of marriage quite hideous. Unfortunately, my father is deaf to reason, so I would like to enlist your help.''

''My help?''

She nodded. ''Could I interest you in the role of suitor to throw him off the scent, so to speak? You pretend to court me until others lose interest and my father decides to let me go home. I give you my word,'' she continued quickly, ''that there are no hidden traps here.''

Her smile was so dazzling, her eyes so sincere that for a moment he found himself speechless. Because his reaction troubled him, he drew back into himself and raised an eyebrow.

''And what is in it for me?''

Vaguely dissatisfied with his flippant question, Ariane shrugged. ''The same, I suppose. The moment word gets around that you're rich—if you are indeed rich—you'll have to beat off all the daughters of impoverished counts and dukes with a stick.'' She did not add that she suspected it would be no different if he were as poor as the proverbial church mouse.

"Ah, yes?'' His mouth curved in a smile Ariane might have recognized as predatory if she had been more experienced—or known him better. "Is that all?''

"Isn't it enough?''

"No.'' He smiled. Now that the first shock was past, he was beginning to enjoy himself. "What else do you have to offer me?''

She stopped and gave him a long, serious look. He was smiling that lethal smile of his, and she needed to remind herself that she had sworn to be immune to it. But there was something in his pale green eyes that had not been there before. She did not know what it was and that alarmed her as much as the fact that, whatever it was, it seemed to touch her where she had never been touched before.

"I'm not very good at games,'' she said. "Why don't you tell me what you want.''

"And here I thought I'd be a gentleman and let you offer first.''

"A gentleman?'' Her tone was bland, but the curve of her eyebrows left no doubt as to her meaning.

"You wound me.'' He touched his hand to his heart. "And here I thought my manners were impeccable.''

Because the curve of his tawny eyebrows was cynical and the tone of his voice just bordering on insolence, she discounted the flicker in his eyes that she might otherwise have interpreted as hurt.

"Your manners *are* impeccable, if you wish them to be,'' she added, thinking of his bold touch earlier that evening. "But I have the distinct feeling that the real you lurks somewhere beneath those manners and is not quite civilized." She thought of her first impression of him as a lion among tomcats, and before she knew it, the words had found their way to her tongue.

He threw back his head and roared with laughter, cementing that impression thoroughly.

His laugh was so luxurious, so full of life that Ariane could not suppress her smile. "Good. Now that I seem to have complimented you so lavishly, perhaps you will tell me what it is *you* want from me."

"A sporting chance of seducing you." He spoke lightly and the smile that still played around his mouth was easy.

"What?" Ariane stopped so suddenly that her crinoline swayed like a boat in distress.

Her exclamation had the chatter around them stilling as all eyes turned toward them.

"You heard me." Chris covered her hand, which still lay on his arm, with his and gave it a small tug. "Come along now and keep your voice down unless you want to create a scene."

Skillfully, he navigated them through the crowd. Deciding to forgo refreshments, he guided her onto the gallery that ran around the main staircase. The moment he closed the door to the ballroom behind them, Ariane snatched her hand away from his arm and spun around to face him.

"How dare you?"

He leaned against the marble balustrade, which was richly veined in reddish brown and black, and crossed his ankles, the very picture of relaxed, self-confident masculinity.

"I thought you appreciated direct speech." The corners of Chris's mouth twitched with suppressed amusement. "Was my impression mistaken?"

"I do appreciate direct speech. But I do not appreciate indecent proposals." She pushed away the uncomfortable suspicion that she sounded priggish.

"I didn't ask you to become my mistress, Ariane," he said softly, "although that thought has its own appeal. I asked for a sporting chance to seduce you. There is a world of difference between the two." He allowed his mouth to curve fully. "If you like, I'll explain it to you."

"I'm not a child."

"My thought exactly."

"Don't be coarse." She glared at him. He looked so at ease, so sure of himself, and her insides felt like a mass of not-quite-settled aspic.

"I have no wish to entrap you. I have no intention of using flattery or wine to get you into my bed." He leaned forward a little. "Look, it's like a card game with two players doing their best with their skill—" he paused for a heartbeat "—and their luck."

His wicked grin infuriated her. "I am not interested in your games."

"Oh, but Ariane, they are such pleasant games." His smile warmed. "You have just finished telling me that you are not looking for a husband. What good reason do you have then to deny yourself a little pleasure? Pleasure should be taken when it is offered. Life is too short for anything else."

Damn him, she thought, he knew far too well just how attractive he was. His velvet voice alone was enough to conjure up all manner of delights.

Bracing herself against the impossible images that assaulted her, her voice was cold. "Your conceit is gargantuan. Pleasure, indeed. How do I know that it will be a pleasure?" She tilted up her chin, defying him, but even more defying her own terrible premonition that he spoke the truth.

"I guarantee it, *comtesse.*"

In one swift, supple movement he straightened, captured her hand and brought it to his lips.

"I guarantee it personally."

She tried to free her hand, but Chris did not relinquish it. Instead, keeping his eyes on hers, he began to remove her glove—slowly tugging it off finger by finger, making as sensual a ritual of it as if he were divesting her of some intimate article of clothing.

Ariane forgot to breathe as he slipped the glove off and tossed it aside. Then he raised her hand again and pressed his mouth to the center of her palm.

Chapter Five

Heat. That was all Ariane could think of as Chris's mouth pressed against her palm, as his breath skimmed over her skin like a hot desert wind. When he touched the tip of his tongue to her hand, she jolted as if she had been burned. And, indeed, an unfamiliar ache swept through her like a firestorm.

"Don't." Her voice was so low and smoky that she barely recognized it, and something resembling panic licked at her nerves.

"Don't what?" Chris asked.

His lips shifted seductively over her skin as he spoke. She knew that she should pull her hand out of his grasp, but it was as if she had lost command over her body.

"Don't do this," she managed.

"This?" He traced the width of her palm with his tongue. "Or this?" Moving his mouth downward, he nipped at the fleshy pad beneath her thumb.

She managed to suppress the soft sound that rose in her throat, but she was helpless to prevent the sinuous curl of heat that spread through her to pool in her belly. The desire to close her eyes, to savor this new sensation was so strong that she almost gave in to it. But some last shred of wariness had her bracing against it.

Yet it was that very tension that had her fingers spreading and pressing against his cheek. The slight abrasiveness of his skin tempted her beyond measure, making her want to rub her fingertips against it to acquaint herself with this new texture.

"Go ahead," Chris murmured, fascinated by her expressive eyes, which were able to conceal neither the curiosity nor the temptation. "It is not forbidden to touch."

His words pulled her back from the sea of sensation where she had been foundering.

"Let me go." The words that had been meant as a command came out sounding like a plea. Anger at her own weakness flared within her. Anger—and the traitorous desire to take the words back.

Slowly, his eyes on hers, he lowered her hand and released her.

Fighting an unreasonable sense of loss, Ariane grappled for the right words.

"Is this how your game of seduction is played?" Alarm, masked by indignation, colored her words.

"Would you care to be more specific?"

"Insidiously." She filled her lungs with air in the vain attempt to soothe her raw nerves. "Unscrupulously."

Even as she said the words, she understood that her accusation was excessive, but she was trembling. Trembling, damn it! And she had sworn long ago that she would tremble for no man.

"I played my hand with the cards a kind fate dealt me." He shrugged, trying to rid himself of the sharp desire to feel her fingers on his skin again. "You are making me responsible for your own weakness."

Ariane stared at him, appalled at his nonchalant words. How could he be so indifferent when he had turned her world and her vision of herself upside down with a few words and a touch?

Forcing herself to move, she paced a few steps away and linked her hands to steady them. A measure of self-control returned, reminding her that it was not her wont to blame others for her own mistakes.

Why was she having this absurd conversation? she asked herself harshly. What had possessed her to pick the most dangerous man she had ever seen for her scheme? Why had she not asked someone safe, someone like Roger de Monnier, or one of those baby-faced young men she had danced with?

But she hadn't asked someone else, she reminded herself. She had asked the insolent, beautiful American. And she could not back away now, any more than she could have backed away from a wager or a card game simply because she had discovered too late that the odds were against her. Her pride would not allow it.

The turmoil in her eyes made Chris want to reach out and reassure her that he meant her no harm. Even though it occurred to him that his notion of harm was possibly very different from hers, he pushed away from the balustrade, his hand raised in a placating gesture. Before he could take more than a single step toward her, she whirled around to face him.

"Yes, my weakness. That is exactly the point, Monsieur Blanchard." The fact that her voice was even, showing little sign of the agitation of a moment ago, settled her nerves still further. She was in control, she told herself. And she would stay in control. "You have challenged me to a game where you have an unfair advantage."

The cool determination on her face made him wonder if he had imagined her confusion, her vulnerability a moment ago.

"If you think so," he answered, "then perhaps we should lay down some rules."

"It is not a question of rules," Her voice was brisk. "The fact remains that you have challenged me to a game where you are apparently quite expert, while I have never played it before."

"Never?" His body stirred at the thought. "I can hardly believe that you have never engaged in a little harmless flirtation."

She lifted an eyebrow. "Your demonstration just now had nothing whatsoever to do with harmless flirtation."

"I'm flattered."

"That was not my intention." Because his velvet voice, coupled with his charming half smile, had her stomach fluttering, her tone was sharper than it might have been.

How could he have thought the little spitfire vulnerable? Chris asked himself. His conscience appeased, he prepared to enjoy himself.

"So tell me, *ma chère comtesse*—" he relaxed back against the cool marble "—have you been kissed before, or has no man braved your fury?" He grinned. "I do not ask because I am indiscreet. I merely want to know how high are the walls to be scaled."

"Your effrontery appears to be truly boundless."

"Assuming that as given, why don't you answer my question."

Because his cheeky grin made her want to smile back at him, she took refuge in a haughty look.

"Yes, I have been kissed before." Clumsy kisses, she thought, or bland ones or simply dull ones. Before she knew it, her gaze had drifted down to Chris's mouth. His kiss would be— Oh, God, if his mouth had created such delicious sensations when he had touched it to her palm, what would it feel like if he kissed her?

Suddenly aware of the direction of her thoughts, her cheeks flamed, but she did not avert her gaze, not even when she saw the knowledge in his eyes.

"Go ahead, Ariane." Slowly he pushed away from the balustrade again and took a step forward and then another. "Go ahead and satisfy your curiosity."

"I don't know what you're talking about."

"Liar." He took another step toward her. "Kiss me. Don't say you don't want to."

"No." That one small word seemed to cost her all her breath.

"Afraid?"

"Cautious."

"One could think that you believe me a wolf in sheep's clothing."

Ariane gave Chris a long, slow look before she shook her head. "No. I don't think you would ever bother disguising yourself with sheep's clothing." Giving in, she grinned. "At best you're a wolf wearing a scrap of some poor sheep's pelt who was too imprudent or too slow getting away."

He laughed. "You have a wicked tongue, Ariane."

One association led to another and his laughter died as he imagined taking her mouth, twining his tongue around hers, tasting it, feeling her passion come to life.

The heat in his eyes was so intense that Ariane would have sworn that she felt it on her skin. "So I've been told." Her voice had grown softer and softer until she had only mouthed the last word.

They stared at each other, breath uneven, pulses racing.

"So where do we go from here, Ariane?" Chris asked when he was certain he could speak without babbling like a fool.

"I don't know." Her teeth worried her lower lip. "I still need help—yours or someone else's."

"Mine," he said quickly, not recognizing the sharp emotion that sliced through him as jealousy.

"Yours," Ariane agreed. With him, at least, she would know just where she stood.

"Even though I'm the big, bad wolf." A corner of his mouth lifted.

"But I'm not Little Red Riding Hood." She smiled, regaining her confidence now that she had seen that this time he had been as moved as she. Surely this had been only a random moment where they had unwittingly gotten under each other's skin. "Nor one of those imprudent sheep."

"And the other?" he pressed.

His gaze was so serious, so intense that she felt the dangerous breathlessness return. It occurred to her that perhaps the moment had not been such a random one after all, but she pushed the thought away, unwilling to believe it.

"And here I thought you were a gambler, Ariane. A risk taker," Chris goaded, the urgent beat of his heart at odds with his flippant words. "A chance," he said softly. "That's all I'm asking for." His voice lowered, grew huskier. "Surely you would not deny a man a chance."

Ariane's head made one more attempt to remind her that she was a reasonable person who had never made a decision without carefully weighing both sides of an issue. A sensible person who had never taken a risk that could not be calculated. But now her heart was pounding so madly, so loudly that she heard nothing else.

"All right, Monsieur Blanchard. A bargain. You play the suitor and in return I shall give you a chance." She lifted her small hand against his triumphant smile. "But not a chance to seduce me. That is just a prettier word for the strong forcing their will on the weak."

"Then just what is it that you are offering me?"

She took a deep breath and ignored the feeling that she was making a terrible mistake.

"I am offering you the chance to persuade me that a taste of that pleasure you guaranteed personally is an experience not to be missed."

Because the flare of excitement was strong, he wanted to reach for her, touch her. Because it was too strong, he did not. He had never been a man to be ruled by desire, but for the first time in his life he understood the true temptation of a woman.

"That sounds fair enough."

"How good of you to think so, Monsieur Blanchard."

When she held out her hand to him, not languidly as women present their hand to be bowed over or kissed, but thrust straight out like a man's, Chris's eyebrows lifted in surprise.

"Is the custom of sealing a bargain with a handshake unknown in California?" she demanded, feeling foolish with her hand thrust out in front of her.

"Of course not." Belatedly, he took her hand in a firm grip. "Forgive me. I have never made a bargain with a lady before." He grinned wickedly. "At least not a bargain like this one."

"Monsieur—"

Chris shook his head. "Why don't we put Monsieur

Blanchard to rest? Or don't you think that we are well enough acquainted for you to call me by my given name?''

''I don't think—''

''Say it.'' Suddenly it was important to him to hear her say his name. Not merely important, but crucial, as if that would, in some odd way, turn a bargain made half in jest into a promise. At the moment it eluded him why he should find promises so desirable, when he had always assiduously avoided them.

Still holding her hand, he took a step and then another until they stood so close together that his body pushed her crinoline back so that her skirt billowed behind her. So close that he could feel the light, tempting press of her body against his.

''Say my name, Ariane.''

She should be frightened, Ariane thought. He was so tall, so broad that her world was suddenly completely circumscribed by his body, whose power was not disguised by his elegant evening clothes. His fingers circled her hand so relentlessly that she might have been manacled to him. But it was his eyes where the true danger loomed—his eyes, so intent that they seemed to consume her.

''Christopher,'' she whispered obediently, spellbound by those cool green eyes that held more heat than a thousand fires.

''Chris,'' he corrected.

She smiled. ''That suits you better.''

''So?''

''Christopher belongs in a stuffy drawing room. Chris belongs among mountains and deserts and beautiful, empty valleys.''

Chris chuckled at the precision of her observation. "Is that a polite way of saying that I don't belong here?"

"It's not an insult when I say that. On the contrary." She smiled ruefully. "I don't particularly belong here myself."

"It depends on how you define 'here.'" Slowly he loosened his grip on her hand and placed it palm down against his chest. Then, using thumb and forefinger, he tipped her face upward. "You belong here perfectly." He lifted his other hand to lie against the nape of her neck. "Perfectly."

He remained very still, his touch so light that they both knew all Ariane had to do was step away.

But she did not step away. She had been waiting for this moment, she realized, ever since she had seen him in the theater.

"Now we will seal our bargain my way."

Despite the command in his voice, Chris lowered his head slowly. Then he touched his mouth to hers.

Not wanting to frighten her and knowing well just how much a little control could intensify pleasure, he reined in the impulse to take her mouth fully. Instead he tasted his way along her lower lip, adding only an occasional flicker of his tongue.

Even when her lips parted beneath the light pressure of his, he did not take the invitation. Instead he continued to tantalize, to tease, allowing himself no more than a brief foray to taste her.

Ariane felt heat blossom within her. It poured through her veins until she was suffused with it. Until she was light-headed with it. And still he did not kiss her, but continued to brush her mouth with his as if he was interested in no more than a casual game.

Her hand was still lying on his chest just over his heart

and when her fingertips picked up his quickening heartbeat, she knew that the same heat that curled through her like a living, breathing entity had taken possession of him as well. But he continued with the maddening game, even as his heart began to pound heavily against her fingers.

She opened her eyes to find him watching her. How could he be so controlled, she thought, when she could feel the drumming of his heart? How could he be so controlled when she was melting with the need to taste him?

Lifting her other hand, she threaded it in his hair. She felt the leap of his heart and the answering thud of her own.

"Now," she whispered against his mouth.

The tug of her fingers on his hair and her breathy invitation had his control crumbling like a house of cards. As he took her mouth fully, he heard a sound that he only vaguely realized came from his own throat. Now that he had surrendered, he plunged into the kiss like a man on the brink of starvation.

For a moment Ariane went still as he invaded her mouth. Voracious, his tongue explored and probed. Unbearably aroused, even more by the sensation of being wanted so badly than by the kiss itself, she moaned.

Her moan pierced his consciousness, which had been clouded by his passion. Oh, God, he thought as he pulled back. He had fallen on her like a wild animal. When she moaned again, his eyes flew open.

As he looked down at her, her eyelids rose to reveal eyes dark and unfocused with arousal. Ridiculously grateful that he had not frightened her, he lowered his mouth to hers again.

She waited for the passion to blaze again, but she

found that everything had changed. The fire and flash of a moment ago were gone and in their place was a steady, bright flame. Where he had plundered, he caressed. Where he had demanded before, he offered. Where he had taken before, he gave.

Minutes passed that seemed like hours as they feasted on each other, breaking away only because their breath had become as ragged as if they had run for miles.

As Chris lifted his head, the stunned look in his eyes matched hers. He had not expected such hunger, such need. Nor had he expected a pleasure so sweet, so sharp.

They stared at each other, trying to come to terms with their feelings. If they heard the opening and closing of the door, neither one gave a sign. Even when the indignant voice sounded, they moved apart slowly, choppily, like windup dolls whose mechanisms had begun to run down.

"Monsieur!" The voice sounded again.

Only then did Ariane recognize her father's voice.

Chapter Six

As Ariane turned around to face her father, the warmth and pleasure that were drifting through her began to fade. With something resembling panic she struggled to hold on to these sensations that she had never experienced before.

"*Monsieur,* unhand my daughter." Pierre de Valmont's voice quivered.

Ariane saw the telltale glazing of his eyes that preceded one of his rages. "*Papa,* please—" Moving forward, she stretched her hand out to him. She was not afraid of his rage, but she was afraid of ruining the last of the pleasure that was still drifting through her like the echo of a lovely melody. "Please."

His daughter's plea penetrated that place inside his head that sometimes seemed to take over. Her voice was soft and submissive as it should be. He focused his eyes on her face and the fear he saw there soothed him.

"You will come with me now." He strode toward her and held out his arm.

Ariane obeyed him, grateful for the support of his arm and hating herself for needing it.

"You will stay away from my daughter, *monsieur*," he said. "Stay away."

When they reached the ballroom door, Ariane stopped and turned to look over her shoulder.

Chris was standing there as she had left him—his hands by his sides, his eyes still stunned. Perhaps, she thought, the odds were not against her after all.

Ariane took a deep breath the moment they were seated in their carriage. There was no sense in prolonging it, she thought. If he was going to fly into a rage, he would do it whether they were in a carriage or in their apartments.

"*Papa*—" she began.

He interrupted her. "Your conduct was inexcusable, Ariane. You made a spectacle of yourself." He leaned forward. "But that isn't the worst of it."

"What do you mean?" She flinched back from the smell of alcohol on his breath.

"Do you know who this man is?"

She shook her head and lifted her shoulders in a shrug. "I know as much as you do."

"What?" he screamed. "You know?"

"Pierre, *chéri*—" Marguerite de Valmont's hands fluttered ineffectually. "Please." She touched her husband's arm, but he shoved her roughly into the corner of the carriage. Softly, she began to cry.

"What are you talking about, *papa?*" Ariane demanded loudly, knowing that it was important that she keep her father's attention focused on her. "Know what?"

"That he's a bastard," Valmont shouted. "He's Charles de Blanchard's bastard."

Ariane stared uncomprehendingly at her father for a moment before she made the connection.

"The Charles de Blanchard who was married to Cousin Odile?"

"Yes. Don't you understand?" He gestured with his fist. "He left her for another woman and this man is their child."

He was still glaring at her, but she saw that the unreasoning rage had passed.

"But, *papa,*" she said, "that was at least thirty years ago."

"So?" he growled. "Odile still remembers very well that she and her children were abandoned. And we cannot afford to insult her. She will be invaluable in introducing us to the right people."

"Papa—"

He silenced her with a gesture. "All that aside, someone of his parentage would not be a suitable husband."

"Papa—"

"The discussion is over, Ariane." Valmont subsided against the cushions of the carriage and, forgetting his daughter's presence, tugged his wife out of the corner where she was still sniffling and put his arm around her shoulders.

Ariane watched her mother smile tremulously and go into her husband's arms with no hesitation, his roughness of a few moments before already forgotten.

Her stomach twisting, she looked away. She would never allow herself to love a man, she thought. Never.

Chris swore under his breath as he nicked his chin. Reaching blindly for the soapstone to stop the small trickle of blood, he managed to send a glass tumbling into the washbowl. The sound of breaking glass had him swearing again. Damnation, he seemed to have two left hands today—both apparently equipped with five thumbs.

Sam, who after twenty years was more companion than servant, looked up from brushing a suit, his thick black eyebrows raised in surprise.

Chris met Sam's gaze in the mirror and suppressed the urge to growl. He was in a foul, edgy mood after a restless night full of dreams. Shadowy dreams that he could barely remember and explicit dreams that even now had his body stirring.

She was crowding him. Not a moment seemed to go by that he did not find himself remembering something about her. Her lovely face. The texture of her skin. The look in her extraordinary eyes when she had suggested her outrageous bargain. And then there was the taste of her mouth.

Suddenly he snapped back to reality and found Sam's fingers circling his wrist.

"What the hell are you doing?" he demanded.

"Your eyes got all dreamylike. Wouldn't want you to cut up that pretty face of yours." Sam grinned. "Why don't you let me finish doin' that?"

Chris frowned, but did not protest as Sam took the razor.

"You sure did a lot of dreamin' last night," Sam said conversationally, bending his knees to accommodate the difference in their height. "Lot of talkin', too."

Chris slanted a look up at Sam, a glimmer of humor entering his eyes for the first time that day. "Are you trying to tell me something, Sam, or ask me something?"

"Both, I guess." Sam grinned again. "You took to speakin' Frenchie halfways through the night." Adroitly he scraped away the last of Chris's beard. "She must be somethin', this Areeann, huh?"

"Something," Chris agreed, deciding that this was possibly more apt than any description of Ariane he had come up with.

"Some female company'll do you good." Sam pronounced sagely. "Maybe you'll sleep better at night."

"And then again maybe not." Chris thought of the odd bargain he had made with Ariane. Somehow he did not think that it would allow him to sleep better anytime soon. Not unless he got very lucky. And if by chance he did, he would definitely not be spending his nights sleeping.

He frowned at his reflection in the mirror. What the hell was Ariane de Valmont doing in his dreams anyway?

Why was he dreaming again now? He'd kept dreams at bay for so long. He shivered. Even now, twenty years later, he shivered at the memory of the nightmares that had begun as his mother had lain dying.

But he had fought them, he reminded himself just a little desperately. Fought and obliterated them. He'd freed himself from all the fears, all the emotions. Now he didn't need anyone anymore and he was determined to keep it that way.

Chris placed his card on the silver salver offered by the majordomo. While the majordomo strode off, another liveried footman showed him into a small salon. The room was elegantly furnished, but its empty feeling led to the assumption that it had no other purpose than to function as a kind of waiting room for visitors.

Minutes passed—five, ten, fifteen. Although Chris had spent most of his life in places where niceties like engraved cards and gloved servants and silver salvers were the exception, he understood the rules of society well enough. And he understood that the Marquise de Blanchard was keeping him waiting in order to humiliate him.

He remembered a room much like this one. He'd sat there, expectant and excited as he waited with his father for his aunt, Léontine, to receive them. Then he'd sat there alone, fighting angry tears, after his aunt had had him removed from her presence. The old memories tugged at him, but he pushed them away. He was no longer a small boy who could be hurt by petty meannesses, he told himself. He was a man who had made something of his life.

With every appearance of equanimity, he extracted some papers, as well as a small notebook and pencil, from the inside pocket of his navy blue frock coat and began to make notes for the business meetings that he had scheduled in the coming days.

Almost half an hour had passed when yet another footman came to tell him that the *marquise* would see him now. Chris gathered up his papers without hurry, drawing a disapproving glance from the servant, and followed the man.

The drawing room was overheated, overstuffed with excessively fussy rococo furniture and smothered in heavy velvet drapes, whose only saving grace was their brilliant azure color. The sweet, heavy scent of patchouli lay over the room like a pall. Chris remembered his father's simple tastes and decided that it was no wonder that he had fled.

The Marquise de Blanchard sat on a fragile, gilt armchair as if it were a throne, the passionate hatred in her eyes belying the arrogant coolness of her features. A short, jowly man stood behind her, his hand curved on the back of the chair, his dark coloring and the embonpoint that strained his waistcoat making it obvious that he owed his appearance only to his mother.

"I thought I made it quite clear last night that I wanted nothing to do with you," the *marquise* began without preamble, not even bothering to wait until the footman had closed the door behind him.

"Your effrontery in calling on me is quite staggering." She paused. "Almost as great as your effrontery in daring to use the Blanchard name." Contemptuously she tipped her plump chin toward the salver where his card lay.

"I regret to disappoint you, but although my birth was not sanctioned by marriage, my father adopted me. It is all quite legal. As for calling on you, it would not have been my choice to do so, *madame la marquise*," Chris said, lifting one broad shoulder in a lazy shrug. "It was, however, your choice whether you choose to receive me or not."

"You should have him thrown out on his ear, *maman*." The lines of ill-temper around Maurice de Blanchard's mouth deepened. "You have absolutely no reason to acknowledge him like this."

"Do I assume correctly that this is my half brother?"

Maurice straightened as if he had been prodded with a hot poker.

"What excruciatingly bad taste to even mention that we are—that we could be related," he corrected quickly. "But what can one expect from a man raised among savages?"

"An interesting concept." Chris's mouth curved in a derisive smile. "It could be worthwhile to debate which one of us was raised among savages." Ignoring the *mar-*

quise's outraged gasp, he continued. "As far as the question of our being related is concerned, perhaps you should ask—" his cool gaze flickered briefly to the *marquise* "—*madame votre mère* if we are."

Although she understood his implication perfectly, it was that transient look that the *marquise* found truly insulting. Jumping up, she advanced toward him.

"I will not endure your vulgarities any longer, *monsieur*." She waved at him with a heavily beringed hand. "State your business and decamp."

"I am here at my father's request."

The *marquise* gave a snort of a laugh. "The wretch probably wants to mend his fences, as he did after his—" her small mouth curled "—mistress died."

Chris stiffened. "I beg to correct you. After my mother's death, my father wanted to mend his fences with his sister. *Only* with his sister."

"And whom does he want to mend fences with this time?" She laughed.

"I must disappoint you, *madame la marquise*," Chris said softly. "My father died four months ago." Grief welled up within him to clog his throat, but he kept his expression tightly controlled. This he would not share with them.

"Charles is dead?"

Chris felt absurdly touched by her stricken whisper. Words of condolence rose to his lips, but before he could speak, he saw the look in her small, black eyes sharpen.

"You said you were here at his request. Did he leave—"

"Was there a—" Maurice stepped from behind the chair.

"No." Chris looked from the *marquise* to her son. Neither one showed even a perfunctory sign of grief. He could have forgiven them that, he thought. After all, his father had wronged them both. But he could not forgive the gleam of cupidity in their eyes.

"That is no more than was to be expected," the *marquise* snapped. "He probably didn't have a franc to his name." Feeling the unsteadiness of her hands, she linked them tightly to stop the hateful trembling. That one moment of hope could redeem a lifetime of humiliation tinged her next words with an extra dose of acid.

"What are you doing here then?" she demanded. "Making a collection so that you can have masses said for his black soul?"

Chris tamped down the anger that rose within him—anger not for himself, but for the gentle man who had been his father. Yes, he had had his faults. Yes, he had committed his sins. But surely he had not deserved this crude vindictiveness.

"If my father did not have a franc to his name, then it was only because he signed all his property over to me when his health began to fail," he said, keeping his voice neutral with some effort.

Suddenly the acute instincts that had enabled him to hold his own and better in a hundred rough-and-tumble card games had him lifting his head like a wild animal scenting danger. The tension in the room had changed, intensified. There was more than simple greed here, he thought. There was the smell of a card player down to his last chips who had drawn a poor hand. There was the smell of desperation.

"He requested only," he continued without missing a beat, "that I travel to France to inform his wife and children of his death."

"How very generous of him," the *marquise* mocked.

"No, *madame la marquise,* only foolish." Suddenly

Chris felt very tired. "You see, he had not given up hope that I would someday find a bond with my—" he paused "—with his legitimate children." He shrugged. "Perhaps he hoped that his death would be that bond."

"Bond?" Maurice shrieked. "How dare you sneak into our home with some flimsy excuse." His fists balled, he moved forward—a prudent two steps only. "You are probably nothing but a common thief looking for a target." His voice rose still higher. "I should have you arrested."

"You would be ill-advised if you did," Chris said softly.

Another insult on the tip of his tongue, Maurice de Blanchard opened his mouth. But the words died on his lips as he saw the warning in his half brother's eyes.

Chris shifted his gaze to the *marquise* and bowed. "I consider my errand discharged and wish you a good day."

Odile de Blanchard stared after her husband's bastard. Oh, how she hated Charles, she thought. For leaving her for another woman and for fathering such a beautiful creature when—her gaze brushed over Maurice—he had given her such a sorry specimen of a son.

Chapter Seven

Chris dismissed his carriage. After the oppressive heat and scent of the Hôtel de Blanchard, he needed fresh, cool air. His cape slung carelessly over his shoulders against the light October drizzle, he began to walk.

The past hour had left an ugly taste in his mouth. He had expected bitterness, but even after his meeting with the *marquise* the previous evening, the personal animosity that he had encountered today had surprised him. What angered him most was that he had permitted himself to be dragged down to their level of making personally insulting remarks.

Well, it couldn't be helped, he thought. He had never been a man to whine over mistakes made. Mistakes were something to be corrected, and if that was not possible, then you just had to live with them. And the past hour belonged definitely in the latter category.

Blanking out his mind with the willpower he had honed for years like a sharp blade, he covered block after block with his long stride.

Rounding a corner, he found himself on the quay. Aware for the first time of his surroundings, he crossed the road and stood at the low stone wall. Across the gray ribbon of the Seine was the stately facade of the Louvre, to his right the Île de la Cité, the twin towers of Notre-Dame visible over the haphazard cluster of crooked walls and roofs.

It was strange, he mused, how clearly he remembered the city from his stay here twenty years ago. Only now that he was here did he realize how precisely every impression had stayed with him.

He'd come here to prove to himself that the old ghosts no longer existed. And if they did, that they no longer mattered. But they still existed, he brooded. And they still mattered. And he had no idea what the hell he was going to do about it. Thrusting his hands into the pockets of his midnight-blue cape, he stared down into the swiftly flowing water.

"Just where do you think you're going?"

"Out." Ariane finished buttoning her pelisse. "For days I've been trussed up like a holiday goose and displayed like a slave on the block. I need some fresh air." She looked at the reflection of Henriette's broad face in the mirror, and the tug of tenderness had her regretting her ill-tempered words. "I'm sorry." She turned around. "I didn't intend to snap at you."

Henriette put down the tray she had been carrying. "It's not proper for you to go out alone."

"I've been going out alone for years and am none the worse for it." Her eyebrows rose. "No one knows that better than you." Henriette, after all, had been her nursemaid, then her maid and her confidante.

"But not in Paris."

Ariane smiled. "You say that as if the devil is lurking in every doorway."

"Maybe not the devil, but perhaps one of those fops

who brought their cards today.'' Henriette scowled at the cards, which had been stacked on a small silver tray. ''Who knows what's worse?'' she grumbled, giving voice to her French peasant's healthy mistrust of the capital and its residents.

''Don't worry, Henriette.'' Ariane patted her maid's ruddy cheek. ''I'm just going for a walk and no one is going to accost me.'' She grinned. ''I'm sure that Parisian fops do not make a habit of lurking about in the rain.'' She winked. ''It would spoil their pretty curls.''

''And what will I tell your parents when they ask me where you've gone?''

Ariane shrugged and turned back toward the mirror to tie her bonnet.

The older woman sighed, realizing the uselessness of any further protest. Moving closer, she fluffed out the bonnet's bow of violet silk. ''Be careful, then, *ma petite*.''

''Don't worry,'' Ariane repeated. ''With my sharp tongue, I can probably disable one of those fops you are so afraid of at twenty paces.''

Her words reminded her of the previous evening and the American's reference to her wicked tongue. The memory spun further, slipping much too easily past all the defenses she had spent half the night erecting. She remembered how the American had looked at her. Remembered how his mouth had felt on hers.

Fireworks of arousal exploded within her. In her innocence she could not have put a name to it, but she recognized it, for it was the same feverish sensation that had pulsed through her the evening before.

''What is it?'' Henriette demanded, attuned to every nuance in her charge's eyes.

Ariane shook her head and slipped out the door. What

she needed was a gallop through the fields, she thought, but since that was not possible, a brisk walk would have to do.

As she stepped outside, she filled her lungs. But the cool, damp air did nothing to stem the heat that was still welling up inside her. Deciding that the light drizzle hardly warranted opening her umbrella, she set off down the rue de Lille as quickly as the heels on her elegant half boots would allow.

Even from a block away she could smell the tainted scent of the river. Taking a left onto the quay, she crossed the road and stood at the low stone wall.

The drizzle had stopped and the watery sun that was fighting its way through the clouds was reflected on the water. The voices of street criers hawking soap and eggs and fish competed somewhere down the quay. A carriage clattered over the uneven sandstone pavement behind her. As she shifted to avoid being splashed, she saw him.

He was standing perfectly still, staring down into the water.

Her heart began to pound and, without hesitation, Ariane began to walk toward him.

Ariane approached Chris, expecting him to acknowledge her presence with some clever, cocky word, but he did not. Instead he continued to stare down into the swirls and eddies that the river made as it flowed around the stone arches of a nearby bridge. The damp breeze blew the hair that curled just above his shoulders into his face, but he did not seem to notice. She might have thought that he was trying to provoke her with his inattention, but she saw that his full mouth was taut with tension.

"Is something wrong?" She touched his arm lightly.

Chris spun his head toward her, his eyes blank for a moment before they cleared and truly saw her.

"What are you doing here?"

"What a gallant thing to say," she teased lightly.

"My apologies." Realizing just how surly he had sounded, he dredged up a smile to accompany his apology.

She gestured up and down the quay with her umbrella. "I'm going for a walk. The house where we have rented apartments isn't far away." She wrinkled her nose. "Close enough to the river to smell it every time we open a window."

He made no comment, but he continued to look at her so intently that she began to feel like a butterfly that has been pinned to a board. Turning her head, she looked down at the water, where the sun's reflection combined with the movement of the current to form silvery-gold highlights.

"A pity that it smells so foul when it looks so pretty," she murmured. "But—" she moved her shoulders in a philosophical shrug "—there never seems to be anything pleasant or beautiful without a drawback."

"And what is yours?"

The words were clipped and harsh, more an accusation than a question. Ariane slanted a look up at him. His eyes were cool, hard even, and the challenge she saw in them held no hint of the heat that had been there last night.

"Just what do you mean?"

"Do you lie, Ariane? Cheat?" Had he gone mad? What the hell was he doing? he asked himself. But even as he questioned himself, the words bubbled out of him like poison from a festering wound. "Are you cruel, vindictive, malicious? Do you heap dirt on the dead who can no longer hurt you?''

She stared at him, wondering what had become of the smooth talking, casually charming man of the evening before. The man who had flirted with her as if he did not have a care in the world beyond seducing her. Now he stood there with skin taut with tension and eyes as sharp as daggers.

''Whom are we talking about here?'' she asked quietly. ''Me or someone else?''

''Forgive me.'' Chris shook his head, appalled that it had taken no more than a few words from a malicious woman to make him lose the control he prized so highly. ''Please forget I said anything.''

''I suppose that it's quite understandable that you want to know all about the woman you've made an unusual bargain with,'' she said, ignoring his protest.

''Please—'' He raised a hand to silence her.

''I have many drawbacks, I'm sure'' she continued as if he had not spoken, not quite sure why she felt such a strong need to do so. ''But I have always preferred the truth because it's much too difficult to keep one's lies straight. And I don't cheat because it takes the fun out of competition.'' She met his eyes and held them. ''As far as cruel, vindictive and malicious are concerned, it's difficult to be a good judge of one's own character.''

Her words and the seeming sincerity of her tone touched him. Because he did not want to be touched, Chris stepped back behind that shield of skepticism that had always proved itself an excellent weapon.

She might have let it go at that and said nothing more if his tawny eyebrows had not taken on that maddeningly cynical curve. He might as well have said outright that she was all of those base things.

"You'll have to wait until we are better acquainted and tell me." She paused. "You know, some animals are vicious because their life has made them so and some are vicious because they are born that way. It's probably no different for people."

Chris laughed harshly. "As I said yesterday, a philosopher."

Ariane looked at his strong profile. He exuded power and a virility, she thought, and yet it was that trace of vulnerability that he had shown her in the past minutes that gave him a human dimension that she found all too appealing.

"Have I passed the test?" she asked softly, "or was this merely an intellectual exercise?"

He turned toward her. She was looking at him, her fabulous eyes wary and just a little sad. A wave of tenderness flowed through him—so soft and yet so strong that he found himself powerless against it.

"I'm sorry." He shook his head again. "I spent an abominably unpleasant hour this morning and the taste is still in my mouth. Now I've taken it out on you and made you sad." He surrendered to the desire to touch her and lifted his fingers to her cheek. "You are much too lovely to have anything ugly touch you."

She found herself wanting to return his touch. Unsettled by her own reaction, she spoke a little too brightly. "Then you shall make amends by accompanying me on my walk." Without waiting for his assent, she gave his cape a playful tug and began to walk.

Surprised and fascinated by her reaction, Chris stared at her retreating back for a moment. Then he caught up with her with two long strides and offered her his arm.

"Would you like to tell me about this miserable hour you were subjected to?"

He made a dismissive gesture. "I don't want to burden you."

"I meant what I said. I do not make empty offers."

Choosing to misunderstand her, Chris stopped and turned to face her. "Neither do I, Ariane." His gaze made a leisurely journey over her face and came to rest suggestively, invitingly on her mouth. "Neither do I."

This time the smile in his eyes matched the one that curved his mouth. It was the impudent smile she remembered from the evening before. And his velvet voice carried that same sensuous promise that was as tempting as sin. When his gaze settled on her mouth, she felt a flicker of the same traitorous pleasure of the night before when he had kissed her.

Telling herself that she did not want to feel the warmth that was suddenly winding through her, she opted for a cheery smile. "Have it your way. I won't press you," she said, and they continued their walk in companionable silence.

"You really aren't going to press me, are you?" he asked after a little while, surprised at her easy silence.

"Am I supposed to?" She sent him an oblique look.

"Are you a woman?"

"I really hate to disappoint you," she said testily, "but we women are not all cut from the same cloth."

"I didn't mean you were, but there are certain qualities women seem to have in common."

"Yes." Ariane sent him an exasperated look. "We all have a nose in the middle of our face."

Delighted, he burst out laughing. "Ah, I see another philosophical discussion in the offing." He stopped and touched her cheek again. "Whatever we are going to be, Ariane, we are not going to be bored."

"No," she agreed, barely managing to suppress the

desire to turn her cheek into his hand. "We are not going to be bored."

By mutual consent, they turned away from the river and returned to the warren of streets beyond the quay.

"It doesn't seem to smell a great deal better here either." Ariane wrinkled her nose. "But then no place smells like home."

"And where is home?"

"In Provence." She closed her eyes against the sudden wave of homesickness. "There are fields and fields of sweet grass and wildflowers."

Home was such an alien concept for him that it was not anything he had ever consciously missed. But when he heard Ariane speak of her home with such love, Chris felt a flash of envy. What would it be like, he wondered, to feel such kinship with a place? For a moment, he permitted himself to covet such a feeling, but only for a moment. Then he reminded himself that attachments were not for him. Whether to people or to places, attachments only made you suffer in the end.

"And what does one do with fields of sweet grass and wildflowers?"

"One raises horses." She smiled. "There are horses from the Valmont estate all over the world."

"You sound very proud of it."

She nodded. "It's hard work and sometimes it's as risky as a high-stakes card game, but I love it."

Chris stopped and gave her a puzzled look. "You make it sound as if you run the estate by yourself."

"My father thinks he runs the estate." She made a face. "And I spend a great deal of time making sure he thinks that. He does not have—" she paused, trying to find a polite way of expressing his absolute incompetence "—a particularly good head for business."

"And you do this all by yourself?" Even as he heard the instinctive amazement in his own voice, he wondered that he should feel surprise. After all, he had known that very first night at the theater that she was far more than a lovely, desirable woman.

"More or less. Are you one of those men who believe that women were put here on earth to look decorative and bear children?" She sent him a suspicious look. "If you are—"

"I am not, but even if I were, I would not dare to admit it." He laughed. "Not when you have such a pugnacious glint in your eye."

"Are you telling the truth?"

Chris smiled ruefully. "After my outburst earlier, it would be rather shabby if I lied, wouldn't it?"

His eyes were as clear as spring water and Ariane felt her heart leap. There was something in those clear, green depths that she wanted to reach out for. Because she wanted it so badly, she looked away quickly. She could not afford to want anything from any man, she reminded herself. Especially not from this one.

"It appears that I've made an excellent choice for my little subterfuge," she said with a brittle little laugh. "I seem to have picked the only man in Paris who believes that women are allowed to have a brain. I am a very fortunate woman."

It did not escape his notice how she had withdrawn from him with a few clever words. He wanted to reach out for her, to make her look at him. Really look at *him.* But he knew that he would not. And what would be the sense in it? he asked himself cynically. After all, she was only looking for some help in a charade and he was only looking for some dalliance.

"Fortunate?" Suddenly reminded of his interview

with the Marquise de Blanchard, he frowned. "Before you say that, perhaps it would be only fair to tell you just whom you have picked." The knot of tension in his belly was back. "Who knows?" He shrugged. "You might change your mind."

Taken aback by his words and the way she felt the muscles in his arm bunch with tension, she looked up at him, but he kept his eyes straight ahead.

"We have a bargain and I do not welsh." Ariane slowed her steps and waited for him to look at her. When he did, she allowed a suspicion of a smile to touch her mouth. "Especially not on a bargain sealed twice."

"Don't you want to know who I am?"

"I know who you are." As she said the words, it occurred to her that it was a perfectly outlandish, perhaps even a rude thing to say to someone with whom she had had but one real conversation before today. But she *did* know him, something within her insisted. She knew him better than people she had known for most of her life.

"I know who you are," she repeated, as much to reassure herself as to give him an explanation. "You are a man."

She saw the light in his eyes and, interpreting it as amusement, she raised her chin. "An arrogant, insufferable man."

And so much more, she reflected, thinking of his lazy charm and his clever tongue. Thinking of that odd tender moment when he had touched her cheek. Thinking of the barely checked passion with which he had kissed her last night. But all this she did not mention.

"For all you know, I could be a black-hearted rogue." Although her characterization pleased him beyond measure, for some reason Chris felt the need to play devil's advocate.

"A black-hearted rogue would have tried to seduce me by fair means or foul," she said matter-of-factly. "He would not have given me fair warning."

"A ploy perhaps. Besides, I *am* planning to seduce you by fair means or foul."

"Oh, for heaven's sake," she said sharply. "Why are you mouthing this—this drivel?" She lifted both hands in an exasperated gesture. "I am not a child, Chris, who has to be led by the hand. Or saved from myself. I know what I'm doing." Even as she said the last words, she felt a small pang of uncertainty, but she ignored it.

"Do you?" He shook his head. "I don't think so. You don't have the slightest idea whom you picked." He spoke harshly, angry at himself that it would matter so much to him whether the facts of his birth would signify to this slip of a woman. Angry that it would matter so much to him whether the expression in her extraordinary eyes would suddenly change from half-amused annoyance to contempt. "You don't know who or what I am."

"I know that your father is Charles de Blanchard," she said softly.

He found himself staring at her. "You do?"

"Odile de Blanchard was quick to inform my father when she saw me with you. You see, she is his cousin. Only second or third cousin," she added with a mischievous smile, "so I hope you won't hold that against me."

"And you still want to keep our bargain?" He felt a combination of relief and terror.

"It will be a bit tricky to persuade my father, but—" she gestured "—I'll manage somehow."

"And the gossip?"

"I sincerely doubt that people are going to find that worth mentioning." She spoke briskly, realizing instinctively that a proud man like him could easily misinterpret compassion as pity.

"After all, the second most influential man in France is the Duc de Morny, the emperor's illegitimate half brother. Believe me, people are much more liable to whisper about your bank account."

Before she could say anything else, she heard someone crying her name. Reluctantly looking away from Chris, she saw Bertrand, the family's old servant, bearing down on her.

Chapter Eight

Bertrand's sparse gray hair was standing every which way, as if he had repeatedly run his fingers through it. His coat was crookedly buttoned and he was breathing so hard that his breath formed white clouds in front of his face.

"What's wrong, Bertrand?" Ariane grasped the older man's thin arms.

"I was afraid I wouldn't find you, Comtesse Ariane." Bertrand closed his eyes as he tried to pull enough air into his lungs. "The *comte,* the *comte*—"

Ariane tightened her grip. "Is something wrong with *papa?*"

Bertrand shook his head and gulped for more air.

"What is it?"

"When he found out that you had gone out by yourself, he flew into one of his rages."

Ariane's mouth thinned. "Is *maman* all right?"

Bertrand nodded. "I heard something break, though." He touched her sleeve. "Will you come, Comtesse Ariane?" he asked plaintively. "If anyone can calm him down, you can."

"Of course, Bertrand." She gave him a pat on a

rounded shoulder. "Go ahead. Tell them I'll be along directly."

"If it's all right, Comtesse Ariane—" he ducked his head "—I'll wait for you in front of the house."

Ariane nodded. "Go ahead."

"Shall I come with you?" Chris asked politely, although he had already made the decision that he would not let her face this apparent madman alone.

"Oh, God, no," she answered almost absently without looking at him, her mind already on the task before her.

"I cannot allow you to go alone." The words were out before he knew where they had come from. Never before had he felt this need to protect someone.

"Allow?" Her head snapped up. "It is not your place to allow or disallow me to do anything. You will excuse me now." She gave him a curt nod and started to walk away.

"Ariane." He moved after her and curled his fingers around her arm to stop her. "Then I ask you to allow me to go with you."

The impatient reply that rose to her lips was quelled by the look in his eyes. No one had ever looked at her quite that way before—with such quiet determination, with such concern. Through the cloth of her wrap and her gown, she felt his thumb trace circles on her arm and tears stung her eyes at the unexpected gentleness.

"No, Chris." Without realizing that she did it, she placed her hand against his chest to soften her refusal. "He was not very enthusiastic about finding me in your arms last night. If he saw you now, God knows what he might do."

"All right," he agreed reluctantly, already planning how he could circumvent her wishes. "Will you be in physical danger from him?'' He took her arm as they began to walk again.

''No, he has never hurt me. The only one he occasionally hits is *maman*.'' Her mouth tightened. ''But then she is only his wife.'' She shifted her shoulders in a cynical little shrug. ''If he were a woman, people would probably call him hysterical or mad. Since he is a man, they say he has a hot temper.''

When they reached the town house where the Valmonts had rented the second floor, Ariane looked up, half-expecting her father to be hanging out a window, shouting imprecations. But the only one to be seen was Bertrand, pacing up and down in the entry.

''Is the gentleman going up with you, Comtesse Ariane?'' Nervously he twisted his large-knuckled, bony fingers.

Ariane shook her head and gestured him up the short staircase that led inside. When he had disappeared behind a heavy door, she turned back to Chris.

''Are you sure that you will be all right?''

She nodded.

''And our bargain?''

''Since you are harping on it that way, I'm beginning to believe that you would like to welsh yourself.''

''Not a chance.'' He touched a finger to her cheek. ''When will I see you again?''

''I have an invitation for tea at the Monniers' tomorrow.''

He smiled at her prim tone. ''I would rather see you without chattering people all around us.'' He took her hand in his and ran his thumb gently over her knuckles.

''No doubt.'' Ariane chuckled. ''You'll just have to make do with tea and use your imagination.''

''Was that a dare?''

She dismissed his words with a shake of her head. "Not even you are brazen enough to try and seduce me in the Monnier drawing room." Her smile faded. "I must go now."

Chris nodded and released her hand. She had almost reached the staircase when he called out her name.

She looked at him over her shoulder, her hand already reaching out for the newel post, her eyebrows raised in question.

He shook his head. "I just wanted to hear your name." He paused. "And see your face one more time."

The smile she gave him was of such sweetness that Chris felt a moment of regret that he was looking for no more than a little diversion and a little physical release. She might have been worth it.

Still, he stayed for a long time in the cold, damp entry, just in case she needed his help.

"Well, it's about time."

Her father's loud voice greeted her as she stepped into her parents' suite, but Ariane breathed a small sigh of relief. *Maman* was still sniffling softly and a pile of glass and porcelain shards lay in a corner, but she could see that the worst of the tempest was past.

"I will not have this, Ariane." He fixed her with his blue gaze. "It's bad enough that you flit about the countryside at home, but I will not have you prancing around the streets of Paris alone."

It lay on the tip of her tongue to say that she flitted about the countryside on the business that kept him in champagne—and in champagne flutes, which always seemed to end up broken. It also lay on the tip of her tongue to say that she had not been prancing around the streets of Paris alone.

Instead she lowered her eyes and said, "I needed some fresh air."

"Next time you go, take someone with you." He turned away, both his rage and her presence almost forgotten.

It would be simple, she knew, to ignore how easily he dismissed her. To forget his words the moment they were spoken. To circumvent his wishes with a coil of harmless lies for the remainder of their stay in Paris, just as she circumvented his wishes at home. But, Ariane decided, the moment did not seem to dictate what was simple.

She closed the distance between them and her father looked at her, surprised and annoyed that she was not gone.

"*Papa,* I am here in Paris much against my wishes because you wanted it so. I ask you to—" she paused to swallow the bitterness of needing to ask for something so basic "—allow me a modicum of freedom. I am not an irresponsible child."

"All right, all right," he acceded carelessly, having already lost interest. "As long as you comport yourself like a lady. And as long as you give me a proper son-in-law," he added.

"If I marry, it will be a man of my own choosing."

"You *will* marry." His eyes narrowed. "If not a man of your choosing, then a man I—"

"No. I will marry the man I choose." She took a quick breath and decided that this was the perfect opportunity to make the charade she planned possible. "Even if that man is Christopher Blanchard."

Her father moved toward her suddenly, his right hand raised, but she did not even flinch.

"Do not go against me in this, Ariane. I warn you."

He took another step toward her. "Stay away from Blanchard." The warning issued, Valmont turned away from his daughter.

Ariane had to fist her hands in the folds of her skirt to help herself tamp down the anger that roiled within her. But when she spoke her voice was soft.

"Do I not have the same rights as my own mother?"

Valmont spun back to face her. "What are you talking about?"

"*Maman* made her own choice." She paused for a breath before she delivered the final blow. "The Comte de Chevigny would have chosen another man to be his daughter's husband. We all know that. And we know that had he not given in, then I myself would have been a bastard."

She ignored her mother's soft, shocked gasp. "I would have your promise, *papa*, that I will have no less." She took a deep breath. "And I would have your promise that I may continue to see Christopher Blanchard."

His eyes narrowed, his mouth pinched, Valmont stared at his daughter for a long moment. "And how shall I explain *that* to Cousin Odile?" he demanded crossly. "Never mind," he finally snapped. "You have my promise, but do not misuse the freedom you are given. I warn you."

"Thank you, *papa*." Ariane lowered her gaze, knowing that both triumph and animosity would be in her eyes. Slowly she turned and went back to her rooms, wishing that she had been born a man.

Chris had spent an excruciatingly boring half hour. He had been accosted by a curious dowager, two eager mothers of marriageable girls and several young wives with the hungry eyes of women neglected by their men, and he had begun to ask himself why he had subjected himself to this absurd ritual. When he heard Justine's high voice from the adjoining salon and a low responding laugh, he had his answer.

Expeditiously and with little regard for niceties, he extricated himself from a young countess with an open invitation in her almond-shaped black eyes. Picking up a snifter of brandy on the way, he moved to stand in the embrasure of a trio of windows directly across from the door.

Chris's clear, green gaze caught hers the moment Ariane entered the drawing room arm in arm with Justine. It was almost as if he had been lying in wait for her, she thought, as a lion lies in wait for its hapless prey. She braced herself for his approach, but he made no move toward her. He did not move at all. Instead he sent her a lazy, intimate smile across the room that had her pulse accelerating.

"Come away," Justine snapped and jerked Ariane's arm. She would have to speak to Roger, she decided. The American was certainly quite gorgeous in an untamed, uncivilized sort of way, but he was going to ruin Ariane's chances with his openly provocative glances, she thought. It was a pity, but Roger was just going to have to make certain that the American stayed away from Ariane. She sighed as she tightened her grip on Ariane's arm.

Ariane almost missed a step as Justine tugged her in the direction of a small group of fashionable young men.

"What are you doing?" Ariane demanded.

"Steering you away from *le beau sauvage*." She giggled. "That's what they're calling him, you know. And it fits perfectly."

"I don't find that particularly amusing, Justine." Ariane stopped and looked at her friend, who stared back at her as if she had gone mad.

"Just because he openly bends the rules that everyone considers sacrosanct and bends in private anyway," she continued, "is no reason to call him a savage."

"But rules are what makes us different from—" Justine wrinkled her forehead in her attempt to find a proper response to Ariane's protest, then threw up her hands in a helpless gesture "—from savages."

"Of course." Realizing the futility of the discussion, Ariane shrugged. "Where would we be without our corset of rules?"

Oblivious to the irony of Ariane's statement, Justine gave her the approving smile of a teacher pleased with a particularly bright student. Barely pausing to take a breath, she began to give Ariane a lethally concise description of the men in the group. By the time they drew close enough to hear fragments of the lively discussion, Ariane knew the names, titles and prospects of every single one of them.

"—Crédit de Paris—"

"—shares floated—"

"—risen sensationally—"

"I had my broker buy five hundred thousand francs' worth of shares and—"

"—cannot possibly be sustained at this—"

"Blanchard has told me, strictly in confidence, you understand—"

"—a fluke—"

"Don't you gentlemen know that discussing business in a salon is a punishable offense?" Justine's flutelike voice effectively brought the discussion to an end as the men turned toward them.

Frustrated, Ariane suppressed the impulse to throttle Justine. Instead of listening to the pleasant but empty chatter that now began, she would have much preferred to hear more about Cousin Maurice's business.

Subtly she tried to get the conversation back to these apparently sensational shares, but a ferocious pinch from Justine finally persuaded her to give up. She would have to talk to Monsieur Leclerc, she decided. He would know. He might look like a dry-as-dust bookkeeper, but he was the shrewdest broker in Paris. And—she smiled a secret, little smile—he had no problem reconciling her business sense with the fact that she was a woman.

"You will be in Paris the whole season, I hope."

"Your eyes are the color of violets, Comtesse Ariane."

"It is criminal that you have denied us the pleasure of your presence up to now."

"Would you enjoy an excursion to Fontainebleau?"

"Do you ride? I have just bought a lovely, gentle English mare that would be perfect for you."

"Could I interest you in looking at my family's collection of ancient jewelry? The Courtaud collection is world-famous."

The trivialities bubbled around her like a kettle set to simmer. Ariane dispensed appropriate remarks and smiles and wondered how long she could put up a polite front before her eyes began to glaze with boredom.

As one of the young men moved away to fetch her some refreshment, she found herself facing Chris. Close enough to have heard the chatter, he was standing absolutely still—as still as a predator that has scented his prey. And in that very stillness was a power, an excitement that had her heartbeat racing.

His eyes remained on hers, cool and sharp as if he

were gauging her. Pride had her tilting her chin upward, unaware that she was exposing her throat where a pulse beat like a small, caged bird. Then, although his mouth remained serious, she watched the amusement seep into his gaze. Already restless within the circle of the foolish, preening men, Ariane stiffened.

Damn him, she thought as her mouth thinned with annoyance. He was amusing himself at her expense. As angry at herself for her susceptibility as she was at him for his impudence, she began to turn away.

He broke his stillness then and his movement caught her gaze and held it, as lightly, as inexorably as a spider's web holds an unsuspecting insect. He lifted his glass slowly, so slowly that that alone was a provocation and her gaze lifted with it. Just before the thin crystal touched his mouth, he tipped the glass toward her in a silent salute that was as intimate as if they were the only people in the room.

She wanted to turn away. She *had* to turn away. But she remained frozen into motionlessness. Only her eyes moved, to watch him hold the fiery liquid in his mouth to savor it, before he swallowed it down his throat. She saw his eyes warm. An answering warmth coursed through her. She did not know it, but her mouth softened again, growing lush and expectant.

"I hope this is to your taste, Comtesse Ariane."

Ariane started as the voice broke into her sensual reverie. With a bow, a young man whose name she had forgotten held out a cup of lemon-scented tea and a plate of *petits-fours*.

Resolving to ignore Chris for the remainder of the afternoon, Ariane sipped tea and nibbled pastries. The facade of cool control was in place, but behind the facade was a quiet desperation.

Because there was nothing else she could do, she pretended that her heartbeat was no longer racing. She pretended that her breathing was even. And indeed she gradually began to relax as the fashionable young men continued to ply her with compliments and self-aggrandizing statements that barely required more than an occasional smile.

Justine again gave her that pleased teacher's nod and, her duty done, plucked the dashing Comte de Bourges, whose ring she was determined to wear before a great deal of time had passed, from the group. Relieved, Ariane watched her draw him toward one of the bay windows that seemed to have been constructed with dalliance in mind.

Carefully Ariane focused her eyes—and her attention—on the young men who were gathered around her. But no matter how hard she concentrated, she was as aware of Chris's broad-shouldered body as if he were standing next to her and not beyond the circle.

She told herself that she would ignore him, but by and by this promise was forgotten, as she was so weakened by temptation that her gaze was drawn again toward him.

A smile touched his mouth as if to reward her. Their eyes met, but only for a moment. Then his gaze slipped down to her mouth and rested there as a butterfly alights on a flower. Her mouth began to tingle and the physical sensation had her starting out of the daze where he had plunged her.

Without warning, his eyes moved upward to meet hers. The warmth there had turned to the heat of a smoldering fire just waiting to break into flame. He had fully intended to remind her of the kiss they had shared, she realized. His audacity vexed her, but strangely enough the annoyance seemed to remain captive in her mind alone, while her body remained soft and pliant, as if it were just waiting to mold itself against his hardness.

And it was the strength of her mind that she called on now. Fighting both his knowing gaze that seemed to weave a magic spell within her and her own traitorous body, she retreated behind the shield of her intellect. With a gaiety that was just a little desperate, she threw herself yet again into the trivial conversation, determined to show him that she was immune to his sensual games.

But she was not immune. And it was her own pride that made it all the more difficult for her. Her own pride that dictated that she meet him on the ground he had picked and fight him with his choice of weapons.

Chris's gaze drifted to her mouth again. Leisurely it traveled down to the pulse that hammered at the base of her throat, then down still further to brush over the lush curve of her breasts. And at intervals his eyes returned to meet hers—to challenge, to tease, to arouse—and to test his progress.

Her eyes had widened, darkened with a helpless arousal, and his admiration for her grew as he continued with his provocative little game. She was not a woman who would surrender easily, he thought, and the challenge whetted the desire that was already as sharp as the edge of a honed sword.

He wanted her so badly that he could taste the desire on his tongue. The fantasy of himself peeling down the bodice of her gown to bury his face between her lush breasts stirred his blood. The fantasy of himself spreading her soft, white thighs and sliding into her stirred his body.

He had never been a man who looked for immediate gratification. On the contrary, he knew very well how

keenly anticipation could heighten pleasure. So under
other circumstances, he would have continued with this
game for hours. But he knew that there was no way he
could do so and not embarrass himself and his hosts.
She was going to win, he thought. This time. Another
time, he would be the one to reap the rewards of the
victor. He was sure of it.

Leaving her to the flirtatious chatter of the gaggle of
young, fashionable men, he moved away. The sense of
loss that surged through him both surprised him and annoyed him. He was looking for a little lighthearted dalliance, he reminded himself, not involvement. But before
he could stop himself, he had turned back to look at her.

The group around her had shifted so that all he could
see was her spun-gold hair, which was gathered in curls
behind her ears, and the soft curve of her neck. The
thought that those young fops were standing close
enough to look into her fabulous eyes, to breathe in the
lightly floral scent of her skin constricted his throat. With
a silent oath, Chris signaled a servant to refill his glass.

She was melting. Chris's gaze—ever bolder—drifted
over her, its very laziness a provocation. Was he some
kind of sorcerer, Ariane wondered, who, with just a
glance, could light a fire? Who, with just a glance, could
heat her body so that it seemed to have become one
warm, liquid mass? And every time he lit a new fire, he
would seek confirmation of his success in her eyes.

He was seducing her. He was seducing her in the middle of the Monnier drawing room, she thought, remembering her words yesterday afternoon. The words he had
obviously taken as a challenge.

How dare he do that to her? Anger twisted together
with the arousal, creating still more heat. She wanted to

fight back, but what could she do but throw up her chin and meet his eyes, where the lethal heat dwelled.

One of the young aristocrats whose name she could not remember moved between her and Chris, granting her a moment of respite. The air that had seemed to sizzle around her cooled, as a hot summer afternoon is cooled by a sudden shower. Suddenly, without knowing how she could be so certain, she knew that he was gone.

A blanket of coldness seemed to spread over her. She should be pleased, she told herself. Why then did she feel this sense of loss, as if something important, something essential had been taken away from her?

Suddenly the flirtatious chatter became unbearable. Only half-aware of what excuse she used, Ariane moved away from her admirers.

As quickly, as surely as if he had called out to her, she found him. He was standing at a window in one of the small, almost empty salons, the drink in his hand untouched.

Anger vibrating within her, she swept into the room.

Chapter Nine

"I imagine that you're quite proud of yourself. Congratulations." She heard the testiness in her voice and approved of it. It was her own fault that he was playing games with her. After all, she had practically dared him to do it. But if he thought that she was going to accept it with meekness, she was certainly going to set him right.

Slowly Chris turned to look at her. The wave of longing was so strong that he almost reached out to touch her. Because he resented it, because he refused to accept it, his fingers tightened around his glass instead.

"What for?" His surly tone masked the battle going on inside him. "It is yourself you should congratulate." He lifted the snifter and took a long swallow of cognac. "It was you who won after all."

"Me?" Ariane stared at him, unsure how to interpret the frown and the rude tone, which were at variance with the eyes that had heated and darkened with an emotion she could not identify. "But it was you who seduced me in the middle of the Monnier drawing room."

"Did I now?" he asked softly, aroused—and far more touched than he would have admitted—by her open admission. This time he surrendered to the need to touch her, reaching out and running the backs of his fingers down her arm from the edge of her sleeve to her elbow.

Ariane jolted lightly, but did not pull away from his touch, telling herself that she would not give him the satisfaction of retreating.

"I would have said that it was the other way around," he continued, and tortured himself by running his fingers back up the satin skin to the cream-colored lace that rimmed her sleeve. "You seemed to be functioning quite well in the midst of your sea of admirers." Desire swam through his blood, mingling with the brandy, one heating the other. "While I—" He broke off and shrugged.

Tightening her muscles, Ariane struggled not to feel anything as his fingers drifted down her arm. When she failed, she struggled not to show it.

"You started the shabby little game," she managed with some semblance of control. "I did nothing. But you—you knew exactly what you were doing to me."

Chris smiled at her unwitting admission, but the smile faded as he reminded himself that whatever he had done to her, she had done far worse to him.

"Ah, Ariane, but it was I who fled."

And it had been more than just his physical reaction that had caused his retreat, he admitted silently. Just who was she—this tiny woman who made him want so badly? He forced himself to withdraw his hand and, feeling what it cost him to do it, felt fear grip him like icy fingers at the back of his neck.

Relief and disappointment mingled as she felt his hand drop away. She looked at him, her eyes puzzled. "I don't understand. Why did you?"

"I'll explain some other time." He laughed shortly.

"Don't put me off like that," she flared, taking issue

with what she interpreted as dismissal. "I am not a child."

"Oh, I know." A quicksilver amusement that was directed at himself crept into his eyes. "Believe me, I know."

"Good. Then you will explain." Her lush mouth thinned. "You owe me that at least for playing your detestable game with me." The puzzlement she had felt earlier gave way to anger, her eyes darkening to the tempestuous purple of a summer sky just before a storm breaks loose.

Her eyes were dark and passionate and Chris felt the desire, which had ebbed a little, begin to claw at him again. "Don't push me, Ariane."

"Push you? *You?*" She stepped closer to him so that her pale green skirts pressed against his legs. "And how far did you push me back there?" As she tipped her head toward the salon, a flush flowed up her face—anger and embarrassment and the memory of the heat she had felt. "I'll have the explanation. And I'll have it now."

She was so close that he could smell her—that fragrance of flowers and woman. The scent swirled around him until he was caught in it as if it were a vise. Something snapped within him then, blocking any rational function of his brain. He reached out and closed his fingers around her hand.

The surprise that was spiced with fear in her eyes pleased him unreasonably. The desire to draw her hand down and press it against his half-aroused sex was so great that he almost gave in to it.

"Don't tempt me, Ariane," he finally said. "Or I will show you what you do to me with just a look."

Color swept into Ariane's cheeks as she understood what he meant. Her hand was tingling as if she had touched him, and the same tingle echoed within her until every nerve in her body seemed to reverberate with it. Horrified at her own reaction, she took a step back, but the physical distance did nothing to diminish the excitement that skittered through her defiant body. Excitement that made her want to close the space between them, and touch him again.

"They were right," she whispered, appalled at the uncivilized feelings that he seemed to call up within her so effortlessly. "You *are* a savage."

She whirled so quickly that the room was a blur around her. Although the desire to run was strong, her pride was stronger. Slowly, her skirts barely swaying, she walked from the room.

Chris watched Ariane walk away and cursed himself—and her. He had always enjoyed women and he had never had trouble dealing with them, taking and giving affection and sex in a straightforward manner that had made everything simple.

With her nothing was simple. He should just stay away from her, he thought irritably. After all, Paris was full of pretty, willing women. He would be far better off with one of them than with a sharp-tongued virgin with fabulous eyes and enough spirit for two women. He tossed back the rest of his brandy. Then, with a sigh, he moved forward to find her. An apology was the least she deserved.

But she was not in the main drawing room, nor in any of the smaller salons. Seeing Roger, Chris signaled to him.

"Have you seen Ariane de Valmont?"

"I believe she's left. And quite hurriedly, too." Roger

pressed his lips together. "Did you have words with her?"

"Words?" Chris laughed shortly. "I suppose that's one way of putting it."

"Chris, I have told you—"

"Damn it—" He dug his fingers through his hair. "I know what you told me. And it's nothing I haven't told myself." Pushing past Roger, he moved toward the staircase.

Ignoring the glances and raised eyebrows, he half ran through the drawing room. He caught a glimpse of a wide skirt the color of a new leaf disappearing around the wide curve of the staircase and stopped for a moment to call out her name. But the tap of her slippers on the stairs told him that she had not heeded his call. Swearing, he ran down the stairs two at a time.

Her breath catching, Ariane dashed down the stairs as quickly as she dared, cursing under her breath at the way her smooth-soled kid slippers skidded over the polished marble. But she had to get away from here.

That vulgar, ill-bred boor! She huffed a little, as much from annoyance as from the tightness of her corset. How dare he do that to her? First seducing her with his eyes until she could have sworn that she had felt his hands on her skin and then almost making her touch him as if she were a woman of the streets. Even now the heat rose into her cheeks as she remembered how her hand had tingled as if he *had* made her touch him. She told herself—no, she insisted—that it was only indignation, but deep down, she knew better.

"Ariane!"

She jolted at the sound of Chris's voice. She did not want to face him. She could not. Desperate, she speeded up her steps.

She had only a few more steps to go before she reached the foyer. There would be servants there, she thought, so that she would not be alone with him. At the moment it did not occur to her that the presence of servants—or anyone else—would not prevent Christopher Blanchard from doing anything he wanted to do.

Even as the sigh of relief passed her lips, her shoes slipped over the rounded edge of a step, taking her feet out from under her. Ariane clutched at the banister, but it was far too wide for her hand to grasp it and her hand slid uselessly down the carved stone. Her derriere made contact with the marble, and she swore, aloud this time. As she struggled to rise, her crinoline belled up around her, forcing her to concentrate on keeping her skirts down.

"Ariane! Are you all right?" Chris bent down toward her, already reaching out to lift her up.

"Don't touch me," she snarled at him. "Don't you dare touch me." She tried once again to get up, but her lack of success made her feel like a barnyard fowl ineffectually flapping its wings.

The guilt he had felt earlier forgotten, Chris grinned as he saw that the only thing she had hurt was her pride. She was hissing like a kitten that had gotten tangled up in a bolt of cloth, and he took a step back to enjoy the show. After watching her for a few moments, he shifted forward slightly and held out his hand.

"Why don't you call a truce for a minute. You can be as angry at me as you want once you're on your feet again."

Ariane looked at him with eyes narrowed to violet slits. She really hated it, but she knew that there was no way she could get up alone without making an even greater fool of herself. She lifted her hand and gingerly placed it in his.

He tugged her up and gave her a smile that deepened the creases in his bronzed face. Ignoring the smile, she looked down at their still joined hands.

"Don't you dare—" Before she could finish the sentence, he dropped her hand as quickly, as unceremoniously as if it were a hot coal. "Well—" She took a step back, a bit disappointed that he had not given her a reason for more sharp words.

"I don't set great store by refined manners, but I am not generally crude." Chris marked a small bow. "I'm sorry if I offended you."

"If?" She glared at him. "If?"

"I'm sorry *that* I offended you." He raised his hands in a gesture of surrender and sent her a grin that had disarmed legions of women. "Is that better?"

She gave him a curt nod and shifted to continue down the stairs with what she hoped would be more dignity.

"Ariane." Chris's hand closed around her arm to hold her back.

"I told you not to touch me," she snapped, trying to ignore the heat that seemed to flow directly from his fingers into her blood.

Pleased, he had felt the leap of her pulse, but knowing better than most men when retreat was politic, he released her.

"Afraid?" He provoked her.

"You've asked me that before. No," she said, not quite truthfully this time. "I just don't want your hands on me."

He looked at her, chin proud, eyes flashing, and swore to himself that someday soon he would have her begging him to put his hands on her.

"Fair enough."

She frowned at his ready agreement. "Why did you come after me?" she asked. "Was there something you wanted?"

Chris gave in to the laugh that rose in his throat. "Ariane, you don't know the half of it."

"A poor choice of words, I suppose." Ariane felt her mouth begin to curve in answer to Chris's laugh and pressed her lips together to prevent her smile from blooming. It was really too bad that she was no good at holding a grudge, she thought. Especially when someone had as much charm at his disposal as Chris did.

"I don't want to play word games with you," she finally said. "Why don't you say whatever it is you wanted to say and be done with it."

"I wanted to apologize." He grinned. "And I believe I've already done so." His grin widened, deepening the creases in his cheeks. "Would you like me to apologize again or am I forgiven?"

"No." Ariane shook her head. "I don't want you to apologize again."

"That was an answer to only half my question." He smiled.

His slightly lopsided smile was so boyishly disarming that she found herself smiling back fully. "I should be mean and tell you that I haven't. Just to see what you can come up with to make me change my mind."

"I suspect that you are not very good at being mean. I could give you some lessons." He grinned. "Then you can be mean to me and I can show you how creative I can be at getting you to change your mind." He leaned closer, but not close enough to threaten her. "How does that sound?"

A chuckle bubbled up in her throat and, remembering

the deadly boring conversation all those perfectly mannered young men had subjected her to, Ariane decided that a little rudeness coupled with wit was by far preferable to inanity paired with courtliness.

"It sounds like the best offer I've had all afternoon." She paused for a moment, her eyes twinkling. "But then it doesn't take a great deal to outdo a ride on a nice, docile English mare—" she rolled her eyes toward the white and gilt ceiling "—or a tour of the world-famous Courtaud jewelry collection."

The mellow gibe pleased him far more than a breathless compliment would have and he grinned. "I'll work out a lesson plan."

"You do that." She gave him a nod. "Good night."

He did not touch her this time, but his arm shot out in front of her to block her path.

Ariane said nothing, but only gave him a questioning look.

"Fair warning, Ariane. Nothing has changed. I still want to seduce you."

Her heart thudded at his softly spoken words. And at the heat that had sprung into his eyes again. But she had herself under control quickly.

"I never would have guessed." One finely drawn eyebrow curved upward. "But if I recall I told you that I do not believe in seduction."

Her coolness, when he knew that there was so much heat underneath, made him want to take her into his arms and coax some of that heat to the surface. But he knew that this was not the time for it and, for the second time in minutes, he swore to himself that he would have her. And soon.

"Forgive my choice of words." His voice softened,

lowered still further. "Persuasion then. Just some friendly persuasion."

He was standing two steps below her so that their eyes were level. When he saw her gaze skim down to his mouth, he smiled.

"And you, Ariane, in all your innocence, are just as eager to be persuaded and to persuade—" he gave the word a little mocking undertone "—as I am."

"You're quite full of yourself, aren't you?" The words were sharp, but were spoken without heat. "What do you know about me or about what I want?"

"I know that you won't have it easy when you fight me." He paused. "You're going to have to fight yourself, too."

Because the heat was expanding within her, melting her from the inside out, her voice sharpened. "You want, so you take. Is that what you do?"

"It doesn't always work quite so smoothly." Chris grinned. "But basically I believe that life is too short for a great deal of self-deprivation."

"I don't fancy a great deal of self-deprivation myself, but I do believe in self-control." She paused to take a deep breath and reassure herself that she had pulled back from the brink. "And in looking before you leap."

What he saw in her eyes pleased him. Temptation, heat and a wariness that warred with both. He was a man for whom complications were something to be vanquished or ignored, but he had never relished an easy victory.

"You do that, Ariane." He held her gaze. "You look all you want." Then, deliberately, he lowered his eyes to her mouth.

He was going to kiss her. She watched those eyes that were as green as springtime promises wander down to her mouth and she could almost feel his lips on hers. He leaned closer and closer still until she could feel his warmth.

Then, suddenly, the warmth was gone as he stepped back and to the side, giving her room to pass by him.

"I wish you a pleasant evening, Ariane."

He watched the succession of emotions in her eyes—surprise, annoyance and, finally, amusement that held no rancor. His heart gave a funny little thud, as if the beat had tripped over an obstacle and he had to suppress the odd desire to rub his hand over his chest, as if there were a pain there to be soothed.

"I wish you the same, Chris." Her hand on the balustrade, she walked down. At the bottom of the staircase, she looked back over her shoulder to where he still stood.

"And pleasant dreams." She sent him a mischievous grin and headed for the room where the wraps were kept.

Chris swore silently. Somehow—he was not sure how—she had bested him tonight. Then he laughed softly. He might have lost the battle, but he'd be damned if he wasn't going to win the war.

Chapter Ten

"**Y**our mother was quite insistent that you would not mind seeing me on such short notice, *mon cousin*." The Comte de Valmont smiled vaguely, still a little stunned at finding himself expedited here as unceremoniously as a truant schoolboy is sent to the headmaster's office.

Maurice de Blanchard made a disparaging gesture with his soft, plump, perfectly manicured hand. "It is my pleasure to take time for a relative. And it is my business to be at the disposal of a prospective client."

"Yes." Valmont cleared his throat. "Your mother has pointed out my folly at not having purchased Crédit de Paris shares before." He coughed again. "I have decided to remedy this."

If he didn't remedy it, he was sure that Odile would do exactly as she had threatened and make certain that no one received them. He frowned. And all because he had foolishly promised Ariane that she could make her own choices.

"I'm pleased to hear it." Maurice's smooth, slightly bored smile did not reveal his keen interest. "Of course, the shares have risen too far in value to be a true bargain." He gestured his cousin toward a small table where coffee and brandy stood ready. "They have, after all, more than doubled in value from the original price of five hundred francs. But—" he gestured with apparent modesty "—there is every reason to assume that they will rise still higher. Perhaps as high as sixteen hundred."

"Indeed?" Valmont's interest was suddenly piqued.

"One can never know, of course," Maurice said with a small shrug, his well-schooled demeanor managing to positively reek of both modesty and utter confidence. "We do what we can, but shares like ours or any kind of stocks, for that matter, can be a fickle mistress." He allowed himself a small chuckle, intimating that his shares, of course, were quite the exception.

Valmont smiled, falling into the trap as easily as a naive girl succumbs to the wiles of a practiced seducer. What a stroke of good fortune, he thought, his heart racing, just as it did when he heard the clack of dice. "That sounds very enticing, *mon cousin*."

"And what amount were you thinking of?" His nerves were jumping, but his mother's merciless training kept Maurice's smooth smile in place and his hands steady. He poured dark, pungent coffee into the demitasse cups made of fine Chinese porcelain without spilling a drop.

"Your mother was so quick about arranging our meeting that I've not had time to check with Leclerc, my broker, about what can be liquidated for cash. Much of my fortune is tied up in my horses, you know."

"It's fortunate that you came directly to me." Maurice smiled at Valmont over the rim of his cup. "I will be quite frank. Your Leclerc is a stodgy, conservative old bird and he would have advised against Crédit de Paris shares as too speculative."

Valmont shifted.

Maurice caught his movement and smiled. "Don't worry. The Duc de Morny and General Cavaignac are two of my biggest shareholders." He leaned forward and lowered his voice as if he were sharing a secret. "You know how these things work, *mon ami*. After the emperor, they are the two most powerful men in France, and any venture they are associated with is guaranteed to be successful."

"Yes, of course." Valmont tried to remember the figures on those papers that Leclerc had sent a few weeks ago. "I don't know the exact amount, but it should be somewhere in the neighborhood of several hundred thousand francs," he blurted out. "Perhaps even half a million." He smiled. "And then there is my daughter's dowry."

Blanchard picked up his cup to distract himself from the pulse that begun to leap with excitement. A million francs or even two would not cover all those projects gone sour, but even a few hundred thousand would certainly stop a few of the larger holes. When he was certain that his gaze held no more than polite interest, he looked back at his visitor.

"I would like to conclude this business as soon as possible." Valmont laughed, pleased. "If I wait, I will end up paying even more for the shares, eh?"

"Yes, quick action would seem to be required."

"I will be in touch soon."

Outside, he sighed with pleasure at his own cleverness. He had killed two birds with one stone, he thought. He'd appeased Cousin Odile's anger at Ariane's impossible behavior, while increasing his fortune. Whistling, he went down the stairs.

* * *

Several blocks and a world away from Maurice de Blanchard's elegantly appointed office, Ariane sat in a large, dusty room. Every surface, even part of the scratched plank floor, was covered with thick folders and piles of loose papers, but she knew that, if necessary, Monsieur Leclerc would pick out just the file he was looking for within seconds.

"It is a rare pleasure to see you again so soon." Leclerc beamed at Ariane over his spectacles, which had slid down to the slightly bulbous tip of his nose. "If I had known that you were coming today, I would have had the bank draft you wanted ready."

"There's no hurry, Monsieur Leclerc." She smiled. "It appears that it is quite simple to live on credit in Paris, as long as you act as if you have plenty of money."

"Ah, Comtesse Ariane, you have discovered the secret of Parisian society." He smiled at her over his round spectacles.

"I wanted to ask you about something I heard yesterday." Never one to equivocate, Ariane came to the point quickly.

"I overheard part of a conversation about shares floated by the Crédit de Paris. Apparently these shares have risen enormously in value since being issued. Would this not have been a welcome addition to the Valmont investments?"

Leclerc smiled at the politely couched reproach. To another client he would have simply advised against this investment. Because he respected Ariane de Valmont's sharp mind, he took the trouble of explaining.

"Crédit de Paris finances projects in France and abroad—building projects, industry, new inventions. The shares it floats pay for the projects. When and if the projects are successful, the shares increase in value." He paused. "My informants—and they are generally quite reliable—tell me that up to now not a single one of the projects has been brought to fruition."

"Then why has the value of the shares risen so strongly?" Ariane frowned. "Why has it risen at all?"

"Several investors bought huge blocks of shares at the very beginning. One remained anonymous, but the others were the Duc de Morny and General Cavaignac, two gentlemen whose power is so great that it seems to guarantee the success of any venture—at least for a time. So within weeks people were scrambling to purchase Crédit de Paris shares so that they almost doubled in value." Leclerc shrugged. "These things pick up momentum—whether it is an up- or a downswing. And it appears that the upswing will continue as long as people believe the projects will someday be profitable. Or as long as the large investors hold on to their shares."

"Then this is all no more than an elaborate ruse to swindle people out of their money?"

"I cannot prove anything along those lines. And I would not want to offend your cousin in any way," Leclerc said cautiously, "But my instincts are warning me away from these shares, no matter how tempting they look."

Before she could continue, a stoop-shouldered young man opened the door and was unceremoniously elbowed aside as the Comte de Valmont swept into the room, bringing with him the scent of cologne and expensive cognac.

"Ariane!" Valmont frowned. "What are you doing here?"

"I am here about the bank draft you wanted, *papa*."

The convenient lie rose to her lips with the ease of long practice. She was annoyed—at herself most of all for feeling the need to lie—and her mouth thinned.

"I see." Feeling expansive and generous, he patted his daughter's cheek. "And I'm here to make us even richer than we are." He chuckled.

"Leclerc, I want you to liquidate all stocks and investments—the railroads, the shipping stocks, everything—and buy Crédit de Paris shares." He rubbed his hands. "I've just spoken to my cousin Blanchard."

"But, *monsieur le comte,*" Leclerc said cautiously, "to put your eggs all in one basket like that—"

"Leclerc, this business is a sure thing, since Morny and Cavaignac are involved." He frowned. "I don't understand why you didn't tell me about these shares long ago."

"But *papa*—"

"And I suggest that you, young lady, run along. After all, it's your fault that I had to placate Cousin Odile." Valmont wagged a finger at her. "However, it's fortunate that this business will be so profitable." He sent her a charming smile "So I shall forgive you."

Ariane stood up and exchanged a look with Leclerc. He sent her an almost imperceptible nod that reassured her that he would delay until she found a solution. "Good day, Monsieur Leclerc, *papa.*"

It was her fault, she thought as she stepped out into the narrow corridor. If she had not been so insistent on her charade with Christopher Blanchard, her father would not have had to placate Odile de Blanchard by buying her son's worthless shares. What was she going to do? she asked herself as she pressed her hand against her roiling stomach. How was she going to keep her father from ruining them?

The coachman of the carriage she had hired was lounging against the driver's seat. Without waiting for him to come round and open the door for her, she jerked it open and began to wrestle her crinoline inside the carriage with more force than finesse.

"May I?"

She looked up to see Christopher Blanchard smiling at her. Before she could answer, he had put his hands around her waist and lifted her inside.

"You? What are you doing here?" she demanded, ruthlessly ignoring the rush of pleasure. "I should have the driver throw you out."

"Maybe you should." The creases in Chris's bronzed cheeks deepened as he leaned forward and pulled the door closed. "But you're not going to."

"How do you know?" Ariane demanded.

"We have a bargain. Or have you forgotten?" Ignoring the way she crossed her arms tightly in front of her, he instructed the coachman to drive to the Bois de Boulogne.

"I don't have time for this," she grumbled.

"It is fashionable to drive in the Bois. And if we aren't seen together," he continued, his tone friendly and casual, "how will your legions of prospective husbands know that you are being courted by someone with serious intentions?" He waited until she looked at him. "*Very* serious intentions."

"You think this is quite amusing, don't you?" She made a circular motion with her hand.

Chris caught her hand in midmovement and brought the gloved fingers to his mouth.

"It might have been proper to call on you. To leave my card. To wait and see if you decided to receive me—accompanied by an appropriate chaperon, of course."

He felt her discreet tug and, marginally, tightened his grip on her fingers. His eyes on hers, he brushed his mouth again over the soft leather the color of a doe in the spring.

He saw that amusement—and sparks of excitement—were wearing at the edges of the annoyance in her eyes and took ruthless advantage. Keeping his eyes on hers, he skimmed his mouth over her fingers again.

"Now, could I possibly interest you in taking off your gloves?" His voice was soft with invitation. "I would much rather put my mouth on your skin."

Ariane saw the lazy amusement in his eyes, as well as mischief and arousal. It was tempting, so very tempting to do as he asked. But she remembered much too clearly how it had felt when he had buried his mouth in her palm. She remembered much too clearly how his warm breath had caressed her skin. And she wanted to give in to it.

"I'm sure you would." She laughed, only mildly irritated when the laugh came out a little shaky. "May I have my hand back now?"

"This time." Chris held on to the small hand for a moment longer, then shifted forward and placed it in her lap. "No promises about next time, though."

She laced her hands in her lap. He was as tempting as hot, spiced wine on a cold day. Wine that would spread its flavor on your tongue. Wine that would warm your blood. Wine that would rise to your head and make you dizzy.

Suddenly, she remembered her father's visit to Monsieur Leclerc's office. It had completely slipped her mind, she realized. She had been so occupied with Chris's sensuous games, that she had not given it a moment of thought. Her stomach muscles clenched.

"Is something wrong?" When she did not answer, he reached out and laid one hand over her tightly laced ones. "What is it, Ariane?"

"Nothing." She made the disclaimer automatically, because she was not accustomed to sharing a problem to be solved with anyone.

"Talk to me. Perhaps I can help."

Her gaze skittered up to his. There was no teasing in his eyes, none of that flirtatious charm he dispensed so easily. Because there was nothing but the invitation to share something that was troubling her, the story spilled out of her.

"Do you want me to help you, Ariane?" Chris asked her when she had finished. He found himself holding his breath as he waited for her answer. He was asking her to trust him, he thought, and he wanted very badly that she would. He was not sure that he relished the feeling.

She wanted to say no, Ariane thought. After all, she had been responsible for everything for such a long time that the concept of help was foreign to her. She looked at him for a long moment. The clear, green eyes held no amusement now, no teasing light. Perhaps she could trust him. After all, he had openly reached for what other men tried to sneak. He had never been anything but honest with her from the very beginning. And she had no one else to turn to. No one.

"Yes," she finally whispered. "Yes, I do."

"Thank you." He found himself absurdly touched by her words.

"For what?"

"For trusting me. You're not used to asking for help."

"There was never anyone to ask," she said simply.

"Not even your parents?"

"Especially not my parents." She shrugged. "My father knows horses, but he is not a clever businessman. So I just started doing what was necessary." She shrugged. "It wasn't that hard. I was good with figures. The hardest part was making my father think he was making all the decisions."

The matter-of-fact way she spoke touched him far more than tears or complaints would have. "How old were you?"

"Fourteen or so."

"Fourteen?"

"Women get married and have children at fourteen. Why not run an estate?" She bristled.

"Indeed, why not?" Chris smiled. "I can see why you are in no hurry to turn your inheritance over to a husband."

"I will never do it. Never." Ariane balled her fists. "I've worked too hard to let some man squander my money."

"You could marry for love." He teased.

She raised her hands defensively. "And become a woman like my mother? A woman who has no mind of her own, no life, but what her husband gives her? Even when what he gives her is violence?" She shook her head. "God forbid."

Chris frowned at her words, but said nothing except to instruct the coachman to return to the city.

They rode in silence and when the coach had rolled to a stop, he leaned forward. "I will solve your problem for you, Ariane."

"You're very sure of yourself."

"In this case with good reason." He smiled. "You see, I am that anonymous shareholder of the Crédit de Paris."

"You?"

"Apparently my father thought to expiate his sins by supporting his legitimate son's venture." He suppressed a small flash of bitterness that his father had done this at his expense. "And this will give me the leverage I need."

"I don't want to cause trouble between you and your brother." She felt a quick pang of guilt.

"Don't worry." He shrugged. "There *is* nothing but trouble between my brother and me."

She nodded. "Thank you then," she said. She wondered suddenly if he would demand a price for his help and a hint of discontent colored her gratitude.

Because he was watching her very closely, he saw both.

"Ariane, this has nothing to do with our bargain. I don't attach strings to my help."

She saw the truth in his eyes and she wondered if he realized just how attractive that statement made him.

Chapter Eleven

"**Y**ou cannot see the Marquis de Blanchard without an appointment." The young man with the curly blond hair and cool eyes blocked Chris's path.

"Watch me." Chris met the secretary's gaze and moved forward, quickly enough for the hapless young man to realize that he was serious and slowly enough for him to get out of the way. He pushed open the ornate door and kicked it closed with a crash that had Maurice de Blanchard shooting out of his chair.

"Just what do you think you're doing?" The look on Chris's face had him taking a step back. Only the scrape of his chair on the glossy parquet floor prevented him from taking another.

Chris said nothing as he crossed the elegant office. He stopped at the desk and silently, he stared at his half brother, deliberately using his eyes and his silence as the weapons they were. Then, moving forward as quickly, as unexpectedly as a wild animal moves to capture its prey, he slapped his hands down on the highly polished surface of the desk, taking a juvenile pleasure in the way Blanchard jolted.

"Wh-what do you want?" Maurice stuttered. "G-get

out of here, before I have *gendarmes* called to r-remove you.''

Chris let a full minute go by, enjoying watching drops of sweat pop out on Maurice's upper lip.

"Sit down," he finally said, his low voice far more menacing than if he had shouted. "Sit—down," he repeated as softly as before, but spacing the words so that they sounded like the swish of a silken whip. Only when Maurice groped behind him for the arm of his chair and plopped down gracelessly, did he straighten.

"Now, *monsieur mon frère*," Chris sent him a smile that was no more than a brief flash of white in his bronzed face, "we shall talk business." Carelessly pushing aside a heavy onyx tray that held elegant writing utensils decorated with lapis lazuli, he sat down on the edge of the desk, quelling his half brother's protest with no more than a lifted brow.

"I have no business with you." Needing to hold on to something, Maurice's soft hands curled around the lapels of his suit coat. "I refuse to have business with you." His mouth turned down contemptuously. "And don't call me your brother," he added petulantly.

As Maurice began to rise, Chris leaned across the desk and pushed him back into the chair with a single finger.

"I am sorry to disappoint you, on both counts. Believe me, I, too, would have preferred it otherwise."

Maurice de Blanchard gave his lapels a tug and laced his fingers, catching himself just in time before he gave into his deplorable habit of cracking his knuckles.

"I'm told that the Comte de Valmont wishes to purchase Crédit de Paris shares." Chris paused. "My information is correct, is it not?"

For a moment Maurice considered lying, but, deciding

that he would not be able to get away with it, he finally gave a curt nod.

"You will contact Valmont and tell him that, unfortunately, no shares are available for purchase at this time." Chris's voice was conversational, the tone making no demands.

"I cannot do that," Maurice sputtered. "It's not true, and besides—" He stopped himself just in time.

"Besides what?" Chris inquired mildly.

"Nothing," he said sullenly. "I am a man known for my word. I see no reason to jeopardize that just because you—"

Chris played with his cuffs, needing a moment until the urge to haul Maurice across the desk by the front of his coat had passed.

"Allow me to explain it to you." Forcing himself to relax, Chris propped a hand on the desk. "It may be of some small interest to you that I hold a block of, oh, I'd say about four thousand Crédit de Paris shares." He took a moment to enjoy the expression of horrified surprise on his half brother's face. "You have our father to thank for that.

"Now, if I were to, say, put these shares on the market—" he paused for a moment to let his words sink in "—people might start to wonder."

"No one will wonder." Even as Maurice dismissed the words with a gesture, he felt his bowels turn to water. "The shares have been rising continually since they were issued."

"When I was small, I liked to build houses made of cards," Chris said conversationally. "A good house of cards has a nice, wide foundation that looks quite solid. And all you have to do is give just one of the cards a tap—'' he flicked his forefinger against his thumb ''—to bring the whole edifice down.''

"The Crédit de Paris is a reputable institution." The sweat was trickling down his back, and Maurice could feel the blood pumping so hard in his temples that he wondered that his veins did not burst from the pressure. But his training and his hatred of the man who sat with such odious nonchalance on his desk enabled him to regain a measure of control. "People trust me."

"I am sure they do."

"I have friends, powerful friends."

Chris sent him a smile. "I do not doubt it."

"And I have enough shareholders that I do not have to be afraid of a bastard from a country of savages." Despite his contemptuous words, he could smell his own fear even as he spoke.

"There, my friend, you are mistaken. But, by all means, let us try it out." Chris slid off the desk and stood. "The shares will be on the market within an hour and then we will see who is right."

"No!" His hands like ice, Maurice leaped up from his chair. "I mean, it would be a poor deal for you. The shares are still rising and you will lose money." The words tumbled out quickly, desperately.

Chris lifted a shoulder in a casual shrug before he turned and began to walk away.

The nonchalant shrug enraged Maurice as had nothing that had gone before. But even greater than the rage was the fear that was lacing his throat tight. "All right!"

Chris heard the breathless words and kept walking.

"I said, all right." His nerves jumping, Maurice scurried around the desk. "I will do as you ask."

Turning, Chris waited until his half brother had reached him.

"And you?" Maurice asked, despising the fact that his voice was not quite steady. "Will you keep the shares in your possession?"

"For the time being."

"But—"

"I said, for the time being." Chris's voice hardened. "If that's not good enough for you, perhaps you should consider purchasing my shares yourself."

"But th-that is more than four million francs." His jaw slackened.

"Is that too rich for your blood? Too bad." Chris's mouth curved with the suspicion of a smile. "Then you'll just have to make sure that you do not do business with Valmont."

"Is this some kind of plot?" Maurice demanded. "My mother told me that you were sniffing around Valmont's daughter."

Chris was shocked by the rage that welled up inside him at the insinuating look in his brother's eyes. "It would be better for your health not even to mention Ariane de Valmont's name." Because the urge to smash his fist into his brother's jowly face was almost more than he could control, he turned and strode out of the office.

Maurice stared at the door for a long time after it had closed behind his father's bastard. Then suddenly, something clicked in his mind, as a lock clicks when one has found the right key. He threw back his head and began to laugh.

He fairly danced to the ornate walnut sideboard and poured himself a generous measure of fine, old cognac from one of a whole array of Baccarat crystal decanters. Raising the snifter, he toasted himself and his cleverness.

A second swallow began to spread warmth where the ice of fear and humiliation had been before. The bastard had delivered the very weapon he needed into his hands, he thought, gloating, and he would use that weapon against him. The frisson of pleasure he felt at the thought was almost sexual.

He chuckled again. Tossing down the rest of the cognac, he began to plan.

The moment she saw Chris drive up, Ariane dashed toward the entry of the apartment. She was already in the stairwell when she remembered the curious concierge in her little glassed-in cubbyhole downstairs. Retreating into the apartment, she waved the footman away.

The moment Chris stepped over the threshold, she caught his arm. "Were you able to—"

Out of the corner of his eye, Chris saw the far door open. "Everything's all right," he murmured. "Later."

"But what—" She tightened her grip, but with an easy twist of his arm Chris freed himself and moved away.

"Good afternoon, *monsieur le comte.*"

She whirled around, only now realizing that they were no longer alone, just in time to see Chris bow in her father's direction with just the right degree of deference.

"May I speak to you for a moment?" Chris asked Valmont.

Ariane made a sound that could have been either surprise or protest or both. She saw her father gesture Chris forward without even so much as a glance in her direction. Helpless, not quite certain what was happening, she watched Chris disappear into the salon.

Ariane sat as far away as possible from Chris, irritated that she was forced to sit here with Henriette as a chaperon. If they had been alone, she would have given her temper a free rein.

"I'd like an explanation." In an attempt to regain calmness, she laced her hands in her lap, but her demure posture did nothing to soothe her temper.

"Isn't that a little foolhardy?" Chris couldn't resist a grin. "Don't you remember what happened the last time you demanded one?"

Ariane managed to check the sharp retort. "If that is intended to get a rise out of me, I must disappoint you."

"No matter." He shifted his shoulders in an easy shrug. "That will give me all the more reason to try again. I find the thought of getting a rise out of you delightful."

"No doubt." Ariane sent him a cool look. "But to return to our earlier topic—will you please explain what is going on? I asked you for your help, and barely an hour later you're back, asking my father for permission to call on me."

"As if I didn't have anything better to do. Isn't that what you mean?" He shook his head in mock chagrin. "You have a temper like a firecracker," he said. "Actually, I came to talk to you. When your father appeared, I decided that it would be a shame to pass up the opportunity to make it official, so to speak."

"I don't see that that was necessary—" She flared.

"We're going to do this right." He moved a little closer to her and watched her, pleased that she started to shift away from him, pleased that she stopped her own movement and threw her chin out instead.

"I have no intention of sneaking around to snatch a furtive moment with you, Ariane. Besides—" he sent her a winning smile "—our little charade will hardly be believable if I do not have your father's official permission to call on you."

"Well, just make sure that you don't make it too official." Nervously, she picked at the watered silk of her gown. "We wouldn't want to find ourselves pushed into a marriage neither one of us wants."

Chris frowned, unexpectedly finding himself quite annoyed that she thought the idea of marriage to him so distasteful.

He leaned back. "Well, at any rate, as far as the other is concerned, it has been satisfactorily settled."

"Truly? Oh, thank heavens." Relief washed through her, the tension releasing itself in a laugh. "Now everything balances out, just like a well-kept account book."

"What do you mean?"

"This whole business came about because I made my father promise that I could continue seeing you," she explained. "He felt he had to apologize to Odile de Blanchard and she lost no time and coerced him into this business with Maurice. She threatened that otherwise she would make certain that no one received us."

"Why didn't you tell me?"

"Would it have made any difference?"

"No." He smiled. "But it would have pleased me."

"It is not my business to please you," she said huffily.

"Shall I try and please you, then?" he asked, shifting slightly so that he was facing her profile. His gaze drifted over the delicate curves of her face and neck, and he lifted his hand to finger one of the curls that were bunched behind her right ear.

"Shall I tell you that your hair is the color of a pure gold nugget? Or that it has the texture of silk?" He looped the curl once around his finger and drew the strand along her jawline. "Shall I tell you that your skin is like velvet?'' He trailed the lock of hair down the side of her neck and then back up to her chin. ''Shall I tell you that you are so lovely that you take my breath away?''

When she turned toward him, his fingers tightened on her hair as the need to take her into his arms grew stronger. ''Shall I tell you that your mouth is made for mine?''

Ariane's breath caught in her throat as she watched him watch her. Then his gaze dropped down to the strand of hair that he was drawing so provocatively over her skin. She watched his eyes narrow in fierce concentration as he raised the curl to touch it to her mouth.

''Don't. Henriette—''

''Is dozing over her sewing.''

''Chris—''

''Sh.'' Letting the curl fall, he continued the journey along her lower lip with his thumb. When her lips parted, he allowed his thumb to slip inside—just a little.

She should do something, say something, Ariane thought, but her thoughts scattered like a flock of panic-stricken birds as his thumb slipped into her mouth. Lightly it slid along the moist inner side of her lower lip, the sensation so new, so exciting that it robbed her of the power of speech.

His thumb stole further to run over the edge of her teeth and then further still until it touched her tongue.

''Open your mouth, Ariane.'' His voice whispered over her skin like a caress. ''Open for me.''

She watched him draw closer and closer still. There was challenge in his eyes. And desire. And need.

The blood was rushing in her veins like a swift river. She could feel it pulse against her skin. She could feel the heat within her grow and spread. Finding that she needed to touch as well, she lifted her hand and closed her fingers around his wrist. Following an instinct she had not known she possessed, she nipped at his thumb, which was still damp from her mouth.

The fire of desire leaped in his eyes, showering her with sparks. Discovering for the first time just how arousing it was to be desired that way, she kept her fingers curved around his wrist. Her eyes on his, she nipped again, then ran the tip of her tongue over the spot as if to soothe. His pulse throbbed against her fingers, the rhythm quick and strong and inviting.

Needing more, she drew his hand downward so that his fingers slid down to lie against her throat and, tilting her head up to him, offered him her mouth.

Chris lowered his head slowly. Because he wanted to plunder, to devour, he only tasted—a flick of his tongue at the corner of her mouth, at the curve of her upper lip. Even when he finally pressed his mouth fully against hers, he allowed himself no more than the caress of lips against lips.

He was driving her mad with expectation, Ariane thought. He had taken but a taste of her mouth even though she had offered him all that he had asked for with that velvet voice of his. Even now, as he fit his mouth to hers, he did no more than graze her lips with his. And all the time he kept his eyes on hers, that contact as arousing and erotic as the touch of his mouth.

But she needed more. Her hand still circled his wrist and although she did not notice it, her fingers tightened.

If he had not needed all his willpower, Chris might have smiled at her wordless demand. But he was on the razor's edge of madness. Now, he thought, as he took her mouth fully, sinking into the kiss like a drunken man sinking into quicksand.

Her taste spread on his tongue—wild and sweet. More, he thought. He needed more. He lifted his hand to her face. Cupping her chin, he changed the angle of the kiss, deepened it.

The room was still, but for the sound of quick, uneven breathing. Suddenly the sensuous silence was broken as a chair grated against the wooden floor.

They stilled, but remained mouth to mouth for a long moment before they pulled apart.

Ariane looked toward Henriette and was surprised to see the older woman walk to the far end of the room and sit down in the embrasure of a window so that she faced away from them.

Chris curved his hand around Ariane's cheek and drew her head back so that she faced him again. His eyes had darkened, no longer cool like a mountain stream, but hot and bright like fiery emeralds.

"I want you, Ariane. Very badly."

She wanted, too. The admission pushed itself into her consciousness, making shameless demands, and she almost reached for him. But she was accustomed to being strict with herself and doing without, so she shifted away from his touch. She expected a measure of ease, of comfort, but instead an ache took up residence in her heart.

"And being the man you are, you expect immediate gratification." The acerbic words did not soothe the ache, but instead seemed to exacerbate it.

Her words were like the stab of a small, but lethally sharp knife, but his wickedly curved eyebrows hid the pain well. "And just what kind of a man is that?"

"A man who takes what he wants."

"And is that bad?"

"Perhaps not in itself. Not unless what or who is being taken has some objection."

"I am a man of some experience, Ariane." He smiled ruefully, "If you tell me that you were objecting just then, I'd have to call you a liar."

"No, I was not objecting." She wanted to look away, but her pride would not allow it. "But that fact does not mean I was asking for more."

"No?" He shifted closer. "I'm afraid I shall have to call you a liar after all."

Unable to sit still any longer, Ariane jumped up and began to pace. "Why can't you just leave it be?"

Chris rose also, but did not move toward her. "Have you ever wanted something, Ariane? Really wanted something?" He fisted his hands at his sides to stop himself from reaching out for her. "Have you ever wanted something so badly that you wake up in the middle of the night to find that you hurt? To find that you can't breathe for the wanting?"

She stared at him, fascinated and a little frightened both by his words and by the intentness in his face.

"Have you?"

Ariane shook her head.

"Well, this is how I want you, Ariane," he said softly. "So be warned."

"Stop it!" Panic flashed through her as Ariane realized that she wanted him just as badly—only she wanted more. Much more. "All you want is to get me into your bed." Suddenly the thought hurt unbearably that all he wanted from her was her body. "I want this whole charade to stop."

"You started it, Ariane, and now you want it to stop?" His easy, teasing tone masked the sudden desperation.

"Yes." She pressed her hands together, willing her lie to become truth. "Yes."

"Do you?" Now Chris closed the distance between them and lifted his hands to frame her face. "Do you?" Ever so slowly he lowered his head toward her.

His hands cupped her head so lightly that she needed but to step aside to be free of his touch. But she did not.

The needs swirled through her, dark and desperate. *Oh, God,* she thought, *what have I done? What have I—* All thought fled her mind as his mouth touched hers. As her eyes fell closed, her lips parted, inviting, anticipating. She strained toward him, wanting to taste, to savor, but he had already raised his head and shifted away, leaving only his fingertips touching her face.

Chris said nothing as he waited for her to open her eyes. When she did, he saw that they were dark and confused and he ignored the guilt that streaked through him. He watched her eyes clear. Watched the understanding come into them. He waited for the anger, but found sadness instead.

"I'm sorry. I just wanted—" His words petered away.

"To prove that I was lying," she finished. "You did and I was." Defiant, she raised her chin. "I shall try not to be so self-indulgent next time."

"Tell me, why are we compelled to scratch at each other all the time?"

"Isn't that what people do when each one is trying to gain the upper hand?"

"Is that what we are trying to do, Ariane? Is it really only the winning that matters?"

Ariane frowned. "What do you mean?"

"Did our kiss give you pleasure, Ariane?" Chris asked softly.

"Do you really need to ask that?" she asked a little desperately.

"Perhaps not." He smiled. "But I need to hear it. I need to hear the words."

It would have been easy to resist a demand. But the need pulled at her.

"Yes." She pulled in a deep breath. "Yes, our kiss gave me pleasure."

"What does it matter who wins?" He lifted his fingers to her face. "What does it matter, when the pleasure could be like a hundred kisses? A thousand."

His thumb nestled at the corner of her mouth, reminding her of the kiss they had shared.

"Do you believe me?"

Although his words alone had the heat rising within her, the pain of being but a receptacle for his pleasure stole through her as a thief steals through the night. How much worse would it be afterward, she asked herself, when she had given him what she could give no other?

"Yes, I believe you." Her words came slowly, reluctantly.

"But?" he coaxed.

She shook her head. "Sometimes the promise of pleasure is not enough."

"What more do you want?" he demanded, appalled at the realization of just how much he was prepared to give.

"Please, Chris." Ariane stepped away from his touch, raising her hand when he would have followed her. "Enough now."

"Ariane—"

There was something in his eyes that pulled at her, but she closed herself against it. "Go now. Please."

He saw a veil come down over her eyes, as if she had put the fire within her behind lock and key.

"*À bientôt*, Ariane." He bowed, but did not touch her. "Soon."

When the door had closed behind him, Ariane remained perfectly still, wondering if she had already lost. Wondering if she had already given him what she had sworn to herself she would give no man.

Chapter Twelve

With a brief nod, the Duc de Morny dismissed Maurice de Blanchard. Leaning back against a column, he settled down to watch his quarry.

He must be slipping that he had not discovered her yet. After all, he'd been a connoisseur of women even back in the long-ago days when he had been only Auguste Demorny and had lived from card game to card game. Well, he had been busy of late, he mused, making plans for the journey to Russia that he could finally make now that the war in the Crimea was over. The thought of the fortune he stood to make there pleased him as it could please only a man who had once had holes in his pockets.

No matter, he thought. As it was, he could discharge a long-owed favor to Blanchard and pleasure himself into the bargain. He stroked his luxurious mustache. Yes, he decided. She looked fresh and innocent, and she would be a delightful change from the jaded women who moved in court circles. Already he could feel his blood begin to move in anticipation of the hunt.

His dark eyes followed the young countess as she valiantly tried to avoid being trampled by the Duc de Santerre's clumsy attempts at the waltz. The music swirled toward its final culmination. As it ended with a flourish of drums and cymbals, he moved forward.

Chris had had Maurice watched carefully for the past days to make certain that he did not attempt to evade his promise by some trick. Now as he watched Maurice gesture nervously as he whispered in the Duc de Morny's ear, he felt the hair on the back of his neck stand. Like a wolf who scents danger, he knew that this was trouble.

Morny dismissed Maurice with a single gesture, crossed his arms in front of him and leaned back against a column, which looked like the finest Italian pink marble, but was in truth plaster. It occurred to Chris that both the column and the man were perfect symbols for this world of lies and illusions. If he had not been so edgy, the observation might have made him laugh. But right now, he was not inclined to amusement.

The *duc*'s heavy-lidded eyes were half-closed, but he watched the ballroom floor as keenly as a hunter on his perch watches a deer come into his sights. Warily, Chris followed the *duc*'s gaze toward the dance floor and saw Ariane.

Suddenly, he forgot Maurice and Morny and this whole sordid story. She was like a torch in the midst of darkness. Need rose, so sharp that he could taste it, so urgent that it whipped through him like a lightning storm.

Forcing himself to look away from Ariane, he glanced back to where his brother still stood behind the *duc*. He saw the *duc* push away from the column and move onto the dance floor where the dancers had just finished a set. He saw his brother's mouth curve in a cold smile. Suddenly he understood and he spun his head to the side just in time to see the *duc* approach Ariane and her partner. And fiery need turned to icy rage.

"My apologies." Morny bowed to Ariane and turned to the young *duc*. "May I have a word with you, Santerre?"

"Of course." The younger man reddened with pleasure. His name and his fortune were centuries old, but he could only dream of the power that Morny had accumulated. Mindful of his manners, he turned to Ariane. "May I present the Duc de Morny. The Comtesse de Valmont."

"Enchanté." Morny bent over Ariane's hand and applied just a touch of pressure to her gloved fingertips before he released them. "Do I dare to hope that you are not just a transient visitor to our capital?"

"Not transient, but not permanent either. I am here for the season."

"Do I detect a note of disaffection?" He saw the surprise in her eyes and thanked his instincts which had invariably served him well. "But, *ma chère comtesse,* that is something we cannot allow."

"Santerre." He clapped the young man's plump shoulder. "Come see me in my office toward noon tomorrow, won't you?"

"With pleasure." Santerre bowed and by the time he straightened, he saw that Morny had already turned away with the lovely young countess on his arm.

"Tell me, how long will I have to bear the embarrassment of your presence in Paris?"

The last time Chris had heard that stern voice he had been a small frightened boy, and even the knowledge that he was now a man secure in his own power could not prevent the old memories from rushing back. Determined to counteract them, he turned toward his aunt with a slowness that bordered on insolence.

"I'm afraid it will be a while." His mouth curved in a smile calculated to provoke. "I'm enjoying myself too much to leave yet."

"It is too much to be borne." Léontine de Caillaux spoke in a furious whisper. "Everywhere I go, there is talk about you, about your shameless conduct."

"My shameless conduct? Indeed?" His eyebrows rose in a mocking curve. "Then I should fit right in with this society where the empress's best friend thinks it a grand joke to be taken for a streetwalker on the boulevards."

"How dare you?" Her aristocratic mouth curled in a sneer. "But then what can be expected from a bastard?"

"I thought your opinions might have mellowed—" Chris hid the pain under his casually spoken words "—now that the second most powerful man in France is a bastard like myself." He paused. "Please excuse me. It was a pleasure talking to you," His smile was tinged with malice. "Aunt Léontine."

He heard her furious gasp as he turned away and wondered why it did not make him feel any better.

Morny handed Ariane a cup of champagne punch, making certain that his fingers brushed hers—but only briefly. After all, he was a man of finesse and discretion—when it suited him.

"I sincerely hope that you have passed an amusing half hour with me, *comtesse*." He held her gaze with his fine, dark eyes.

Ariane answered him with the noncommittal smile that she had learned served better than a spoken lie.

"Dare I hope that now you will think more charitably of our little world?"

"I never said that I thought of it uncharitably."

"Ah, but you thought it, my dear." He smiled and touched her arm. "And your thoughts are legible in your very lovely eyes—" he lowered his voice "—for the man capable of reading them."

Ariane watched him over the rim of her punch cup, trying to understand the source of her discomfort. The *duc* was charming. He was a handsome man and not even the fact that what had once been a magnificent head of hair had become no more than a fringe of dark curls could detract from it. The admiring looks from his heavy-lidded dark eyes were no more provocative than all the other looks she had received. The flirtatious little touches were no more than what was tolerated in polite society. But there was something about the way he seemed to concentrate every bit of his attention on her that made her think of a hunter looking at a wild animal through the sights of his rifle.

So she was reluctant, he thought as he watched her. All the better. That would give a little spice to the chase—and make the outcome that much more satisfying.

Suddenly Ariane felt a flicker of awareness dance down her spine. Before she had time to examine the feeling more closely, she heard Chris's voice behind her left shoulder.

"I believe that you promised me the next waltz, *comtesse*."

A flash of joy went through her as she turned to look at him. Joy so strong and pure that it easily obscured the thought that he was taking her power away from her again by assuming that she wanted to go with him.

"So I did," she said, falling in with his lie without missing a beat.

"Shall we?" Shifting to her side so that he stood between her and the *duc,* he held out his arm and tipped his head toward the dance floor, which was just beginning to fill again for the next set.

Turning to the *duc,* she sent him what she thought was a polite smile. Because she was a woman without artifice, the smile reflected only her pleasure at Chris's presence. "I beg you to excuse me."

"I would have enjoyed your company a bit longer," he said with the stiffness of a man unused to rejection.

"Another time perhaps, but I like to keep my promises." She suppressed a small giggle, feeling like a child who had gotten embroiled in an unexpected, delightful prank. *"Au revoir."*

Morny stared after them, not quite believing that the chit had actually walked away from him on the arm of a man he had never seen before. His eyes narrowed and he looked around him. Catching sight of Blanchard, he crooked a finger in an imperious gesture of command.

"You commandeered me quite shamelessly back there." That first burst of joy was tempered now by a trace of annoyance, but Ariane still could not prevent her smile.

"I was just doing the gentlemanly thing and rescuing you." Using the control that he had cultivated all his life, Chris pushed aside his anger and sent her a wicked grin. "Or are you trying to tell me that you would have preferred to remain in that old roué's company?"

Managing to suppress a giggle, she lowered her gaze. "You were presumptuous, but I'm properly grateful for the rescue."

Chris threw back his head and laughed loudly enough for the couples dancing near them to look at him.

"Stop it." She squeezed his arm. "You're making a spectacle of yourself. Of us."

As if she had not spoken, he continued to laugh. His head was thrown back so that his sun-streaked hair flowed past his shoulders and she could see the taut golden skin of his throat rippling with his rich laughter. Suddenly her mouth went dry and she could only stare at him, all rational thought driven from her mind.

"Forgive me for laughing, but you looked so unspeakably prim when you said that." He looked down at her.

His words shook her out of her sensual haze. "Well, I'm certainly glad that you're enjoying yourself at my expense." She pressed her lips together. "Besides, you're probably right. I most likely am prim."

"I'm sure you could make a man believe that, Ariane." He grinned again, more easily this time. "But that man isn't me."

She looked at him. The amused eyes, the insolent grin should have angered her, but instead she could feel the heat of a moment ago returning, expanding in her belly. Expanding and creeping upward until she was certain that her whole body was washed with color.

"I've kissed you, remember?" His voice lowered, grew husky. "I've slid my tongue between those lips that you're pressing together so tightly and I've felt you kiss me back."

He felt his body move in response to her closeness and his own words. Even though he knew that it was not wise, he bent his head a little closer to her. "So I know that you aren't prim, Ariane." Her fragrance drifted up to him, driving his arousal up another notch.

He was weaving a sensual web around her, drugging

her, melting her with his words, his voice, the heat of his body.

"Please, Chris." Ariane dragged in a breath in a vain attempt to quiet the tempest within her. Instead, she succeeded only in filling herself with his scent. "Don't do this to me."

He might have pushed her, just a little further, ~~but~~ he saw the trace of fear in her eyes, which had darkened to the color of purple shadows at dusk. Straightening, he shifted so that their bodies were again at the socially prescribed distance.

"Better?"

Ariane gave a choppy nod. "Why do you play these games with me?"

"Games?" His eyebrows rose. "I don't play games with you, Ariane. In fact, I was never more serious in my life."

"Yes, I suppose our little bargain appeals to the gambler in you."

"You would know."

"Oh, I'm not really a gambler." Feeling a little safer now, she relaxed a little. "Yes, I enjoy the occasional card game, but that's because I enjoy sharpening a skill, that's all. My father has more than enough gambling blood for the whole family."

"That's why you make daring bargains with strange men." Chris chuckled. "Because you have no gambling blood."

Before Ariane could answer him, she heard her name being called and saw that Justine and her count were next to them.

"Your father is looking for you," Justine whispered urgently. "He looks angry."

Ariane sighed, thinking for a moment that it might

almost be worth it to take a husband and be rid of her father's moods and whims and rages. But the thought fled as soon as it had come. Nothing was worth giving up her freedom. Nothing.

"Can we find him, Chris? I'd rather get the storm over with."

He nodded and began to ease them toward the edge of the dance floor.

"Why do you put up with it?"

"What do you suggest I do?" Ariane sent him an oblique glance. "For you men it's easy. If you don't like your cards, you fold and look for another game. We women have to play the best we can with the hand we've been dealt."

Silently Chris considered her words. Wasn't that what his father had done? Wasn't that what he himself had done all his life? With a few words she had reduced his life to an exercise in egotism.

She shrugged. "Besides, I could never leave my home. The land may belong to my father, but it is mine as it never was his."

He saw tenderness soften her gaze and understood that it was this love for the land that drove her, even though he could not begin to understand the feeling itself. He owned land, but what did land mean, after all, to a man who had been a gypsy all his life, but a place to stay before moving on to the next?

Suddenly Pierre de Valmont appeared beside them and grasped Ariane's arm so forcefully that she stumbled.

"Just what do you think you're doing?" he snarled.

Chris felt the rage he had felt just minutes ago return. Without thinking beyond the moment, he shoved Val-

mont back with the flat of his hand, moving immediately
to stand between him and Ariane.

"And just what are *you* doing?"

"Get out of my way, Blanchard. This is a family matter and none of your business."

Chris took another step toward Valmont so that their
bodies were almost touching. "Everything about your
daughter is my business, *monsieur le comte*. After all,
you did, if you recall, give me permission to court her."

The icy rage in Blanchard's eyes had Pierre de Valmont taking a step back. "I did, but that does not mean
I gave *you* any exclusive rights. She—"

"She can speak for herself." Ariane slid her hand
between the two men and gave Chris a push back. "And
you can address me directly, *papa*. There is no need to
use Monsieur Blanchard as an intermediary. Now—" as
she lowered her hand, she touched Chris's arm in silent
request "—what is it that you have to say to me?"

The wind taken out of his sails, Valmont stared at his
daughter for a moment before he found his anger again.

"Are you mad, leaving the Duc de Morny standing
there like a schoolboy and going off with Blanchard?
Don't you know who he is? If he—"

She interrupted him. "I've told you, *papa*, that I will
make my own choices. And you promised—" she
caught his eyes and held them "—you promised that
you would respect whatever choice I made."

"But, but," he sputtered. "When the Duc de Morny
shows an interest in you—"

"Monsieur le comte—"

"Stop it, both of you." Her voice rose enough to silence both men. "I will tell you one more time that my
choices are my own, *papa*. If that does not suit you, I
will spend the remainder of my stay in Paris locked in

my room." She let her breath out in a small huff. "Now, if you will both excuse me."

The two men turned to face each other.

"Both Morny and I are bastards," Chris said softly. "But Morny is the bastard brother of the emperor. Do you really think that he would marry the daughter of a count from the provinces, even one with an excellent dowry? He would seduce her, but he would never marry her."

"What about you, Monsieur Blanchard?" Valmont's gaze sharpened.

"I've asked you for permission to court her, haven't I?" Chris's tone was testy.

"I may be her father, but I am also a man and I've seen how you look at her. Are you only interested in seduction, Monsieur Blanchard? Or would you marry her?"

"Yes. Yes, I would." With a start Chris realized that he spoke nothing less than the truth.

"I will remember that, Monsieur Blanchard." Valmont looked at the younger man. "You can count on it."

Chapter Thirteen

Chris jackknifed up in bed, the sweat icy on his skin. Breathing hard, his heart pounding, he stared out into the dim room. The memory of the dream was already slipping from his mind, but the overwhelming panic stayed with him, so real that if he could have moved, could have made a sound, he might have screamed. Slowly, awareness that he had only been dreaming seeped into him. Slowly, his muscles began to relax. Swearing, he tunneled his hands into his damp hair and slumped forward to rest his forehead on his updrawn knee.

"You all right, Chris?" Sam asked softly as he opened the door between their rooms. "You were thrashin' round somethin' fierce."

Sam's voice brought him back a little closer to reality, and he started to raise his head. "I'm all right, Sam." But his head was heavy, so heavy, and he decided it was too much effort to lift it. "Go back to bed."

He wanted to be left alone, he thought. If he could just remember the dream, surely he would be able to deal with it as he had always dealt with everything that had troubled him. He'd pick through it, dissect it and then discard it. The insistent memory of his conversation with his father's sister last night reminded him that he was not as good at discarding things as he had thought.

"Here." Sam stood at the edge of the bed. "I brought you some water." He waited until Chris raised his head and held out a glass. "When you were little, you always wanted water when you'd dreamed bad."

Chris frowned at the reminder, but took the water and downed it. The cool, clear liquid seemed to wash away some of the panic that still tightened his throat. He could breathe a little easier now, but the pressure in his chest was still there.

"More water?" Sam suppressed a desire to brush over Chris's tangled hair as he'd done so often those many years ago, in the months after his mother had died. "Or you be wantin' somethin' else?"

"No. I'm fine." The sympathy in Sam's soft, raspy voice grated on his nerves and his tone was harsh. Straightening, he thrust the glass back at Sam. "Now go back to bed." He lowered his head again, running his fingers through his hair, fisting them, as if that small pain would be able to cancel out the weakness of falling prey to a dream.

Sam stood there a moment longer, remembering the boy who had woken up almost every night screaming from nightmares. He'd conquered the nightmares, but the price had been high—and he was still paying it. He wondered why the nightmares were coming back now. With a sigh, he turned and moved toward the door.

"Sam."

He looked over his shoulder. Chris had raised his head again and Sam saw that his eyes still held traces of his nightmare.

"Thanks."

Sam nodded and closed the door behind him.

Chris swore again and, throwing back the covers, rose and went to the window. He pulled back the heavy brocade drapes and looked outside, not really seeing the wet cobblestones that glistened in the yellowish light of the lanterns.

The dream—he refused to think of it as a nightmare—was still hovering on the edges of his mind. For a moment, he allowed himself to wish that he could just leave it that way. But he was compelled to examine it. Because he knew that his dreams reflected his greatest fears.

The memory eluded him, but the panic he had felt swept back over him in a wave. Although he had braced himself for it, it tied up his throat as if an unseen hand were trying to strangle him.

He did not try to ignore the panic—he could not. But he pushed past it to dig deeper and deeper still into his memory. There had been shadows there and something dark and threatening. Cold sweat trickled down his neck to pool above his collarbone. He pressed his forehead against the cool glass, as a single image began to crystallize—Ariane had been there.

The memory flooded him now, so quickly that he gasped. Thrust back into the menacing darkness of the dream, his first instinct was to block it out again. But he knew from experience that only if he immersed himself completely in the dream first would he be able to shield himself from it.

Pushing forward, he saw her. At first it was only the glint of her golden hair—like the flickering light of a faraway candle. She was afraid and he could feel her fear as if it were his own. He raced toward her, but she always stayed just out of his reach. And when he had finally come close enough to touch her, she disappeared and all around him was the echo of mocking laughter.

He heard a moan and raised his head, only to realize that it had been he himself who had made that desperate sound.

Damn her, he thought, as his hands clenched against his damp skin. If she filled his waking hours, couldn't she at least leave him to sleep in peace?

But, he reminded himself, he'd conquered the dreams once before. All he had to do was to close himself off from feeling too much. Close off that part of him that could be touched. That part that Ariane seemed to touch with no apparent effort.

With all the discipline he had taught himself, he struggled against the feelings she evoked. But an insidious fire burned within him. A fire that begets a hundred new flames as soon a single one is extinguished.

The unruliness of his emotions appalled him. If he could not pluck her out of his mind, he thought, he had to leave Paris. Why should he stay? He'd done what his father had asked him to do. He'd learned the hard lesson that his own ghosts still lived. And what did he care if his brother was running a swindle?

His brother. His brother who had set Morny to stalk Ariane. So he was back to her, he thought. So there was no escape. His presence here had started a chain of events. If he left, Ariane would still be in danger. And, no matter what the cost, he knew he could not leave her unprotected when the fault was his.

Then he laughed softly, mirthlessly, as a man might laugh who finds himself with his back against the wall. Why was he trying so hard to hide from the truth? he asked himself. No, he would not leave. And the need to protect Ariane was only part of it. He wanted her, yes.

But even more—he wanted the softness, the goodness, the purity she could give him. He wanted just a taste of it. He wanted to bask in her warmth just for a little while.

He could live with that, he thought. Relieved, he let his eyes fall closed, not noticing that he had stepped off the edge.

Oblivious to both the fine, cold drizzle and the stench from the river, Ariane sat on the low, stone wall. She'd needed to think, so she had fled from the apartment, which was dark and closed and smelled of old dust and wax just like the family crypt in the churchyard of their village.

She'd heard the words Chris and her father had exchanged at the ball. She'd felt how her heart had leaped when Chris had said so emphatically that he would marry her. And she'd spent several restless nights reminding herself that this was not what she wanted.

She didn't want marriage. Not to anyone. Especially not to him. Oh, she could admit that she wanted him. He made her feel—things. She wanted those things— that heat, that excitement. But she didn't want the manipulation, the control, the violence that she was sure would follow.

"What are you doing, sitting here in the rain?"

Ariane jolted, as much from the absurd thought that she had conjured Chris up as from the sound of his voice.

"I had to get away." Her gaze skittered up to his face, then away. "I needed to think."

"Do you want to tell me about it?" His hands flexed with the need to touch her.

"No!" The single word was a sharp cry that betrayed

her and she tried to undo the damage by repeating it with what she hoped was equanimity.

"No," she said, lifting her chin because she wanted so badly to be brave. But she found that it was painful to look at him now—at the magnificent physical embodiment of what she wanted and could never allow herself to take—and she looked back down at her hands. "You're not my father confessor, after all."

"No, I'm not. And I don't want to be." He sat down next to her on the damp stone wall. "But I'd like to help if I can."

He watched her lift her eyes briefly then and he saw the odd glitter there, as if she were on the verge of tears. But when she spoke, her voice was sharp and brittle.

"Can you make this indolent life that is driving me mad disappear?"

"Is that all it is?" His eyebrows rose. "I was remiss these past few days and neglected you." He grinned. "Perhaps I could have kept you from reaching this dangerous stage of boredom."

Ariane opened her mouth to protest his arrogant assumption, but she made the mistake of looking up at him before she spoke. There was challenge in his eyes— challenge that was both mitigated and exacerbated by the smile there.

"Perhaps." She shrugged. "You annoy me regularly, but you rarely bore me."

"Rarely?" Chris grinned at her less than gracious tone. "I shall not call you on that. For now."

Despite herself, Ariane was responding to his amusement with a smile of her own. "A true gentleman," she said dryly.

"We shall endure the season together." He rubbed

his gloved fingers lightly over hers and found himself wanting more. "And it will pass in a flash."

Ariane nodded, wondering why she did not find the thought comforting.

"So, tell me, has your father become accustomed to the idea of not owning Crédit de Paris shares?" Chris asked.

Ariane shrugged. "I believe he's quite forgotten. And apparently so has Cousin Odile." She frowned. "Strangely enough."

She paused for a moment, worrying her lower lip as she wondered if her question was too intrusive. "By the way, how *did* you persuade Maurice? You never did explain."

"I suppose you could say that I blackmailed him." He deliberately chose the harsh word and waited to see condemnation in Ariane's eyes.

But the look she sent him held only a mild question.

"I told you that I held a solid portion of Crédit de Paris shares." He shrugged. "I threatened to put them on the market. Maurice decided that it was preferable to lose your father's business."

"I'm sorry that you are at odds with your brother because of me."

Chris laughed harshly. "I told you not to worry about that. He hated me long before this."

"Why should he hate you for what your father did?"

"Hasn't anyone regaled you with the whole story?"

Ariane shook her head.

"Then I suppose I owe it to you."

The old, familiar tightness settled in his belly. He had not felt it for many years, but, he thought grimly, he'd been feeling it far too often since he'd been in Paris.

She heard the strain in his voice and she put her hand on his arm.

"You don't owe me anything, Chris." She smiled. "If anything, it's the other way around."

"I'll remind you of that someday." A ghost of a smile touched his mouth. "When it suits my purpose."

"I have no doubt that you will. But I meant it, Chris. You don't have to tell me anything. Besides, I already know that your father was married to Odile."

"Still, I would rather you hear the whole story from me than half lies and innuendos from others." Shifting so that he faced her, he gripped her upper arms. "I want you to be very sure that having my name paired with yours will not suddenly begin to offend you."

"It won't—"

"Listen to me first, Ariane." Suddenly aware that his hands were biting into her flesh, he loosened his grip. "Please."

She retreated before his rigid determination, but the softly spoken plea made the retreat easy and painless.

Chris took a deep breath. "My father was attached to the French embassy in St. Petersburg." Needing to move, Chris rose and began to pace. "My mother was a Russian princess just out of finishing school and engaged to be married."

"When they met it was what the French call an *amour fou,* a mad love, and it made no difference to them that she was barely eighteen and he was thirty-five and had a wife and two children. My father asked his wife for a divorce, but she refused, and that might have been the end of the matter but for one thing." He passed a hand over his face. "My mother was expecting a child.

"My mother's family locked her up in a convent, but history intervened. Tsar Alexander died about the same time I was born, throwing the country into chaos and rebellion until the succession was sorted out, and it was that chaos that made it possible for my father to free my mother from the convent and flee.'' His voice dulled as he continued. ''It was winter and she did not handle the journey well. She never really recovered and she wasn't yet thirty when she died.

''My father never forgave himself. He survived my mother by more than twenty years, but he never stopped grieving.'' Chris stopped to stare into the water, but he saw only his father's face. This was, he reminded himself, why he would never allow himself to care for anyone with the all-encompassing love his father had felt for his mother. ''And the guilt he felt about abandoning his other family ate at him to the very end.''

His story told, Chris fell silent, but he did not look at Ariane.

''What a poor opinion you must have of me.'' She struggled for anger and found only sadness.

His head snapped to the side to look at her.

''You've told me the story of two people who loved each other—perhaps too much. Yes, they hurt others, but they did one thing right.'' She rose and put her hands on his. ''They made a child between them. A child conceived in love.''

Chris stared at Ariane. ''No condemnation? No contempt?''

''No.'' She shook her head. ''But why do *you* condemn them? Do you judge them so harshly that you see yourself as inferior to other people? I would not have thought that of you.''

''No, Ariane.'' He shook his head. ''I have a healthy opinion of the man I am, but I have seen my father's sister and others look upon me with contempt.''

"And you think that I am like that?" She shook her head. "As I said, you must have a poor opinion of me."

"Don't you understand, Ariane?" His hands closed over her shoulders. "How are you going to feel when people start resurrecting all the old stories? How are you going to feel when that starts reflecting on your reputation?"

"For a man who appears to be intelligent, you are acting remarkably stupid." Pushing her way past the sadness, she found the anger and held on to it.

"One." She raised her hand to the middle of his chest and held up her thumb. "I want to get through this season and return home unencumbered by a husband. I do not care a fig for the state of my reputation.

"Two." Her forefinger joined her thumb. "As I already told you, your purse is of far more interest to people than the facts of your birth. And three." She hitched her hand up a little higher and added a third finger. "I do not judge people by what their parents did or did not do. I judge them on their own merits."

As he listened to her storm at him, Chris found the tension he had felt falling away from him. By the time she had finished speaking with a small huff of irritation, he was smiling.

"And just what are my merits?"

"I'll let you know when I find some." Ariane glared at him, finding his smile infuriating. Finding it more infuriating still that she wanted to answer it with one of her own.

"Perhaps I can jog your memory." He slid his hands down her arms and linked them with hers. Slowly, he bent toward her and took her mouth.

Even as she fell into the kiss, she pressed their joined hands against his chest. "Don't," she whispered.

"Why? What are you afraid of?"

"You're out to seduce me." She took a step back and tried to unlink their hands. "Isn't that reason enough to be afraid?"

"But you knew that from the very beginning, Ariane. Are you afraid now because I'm winning?" Something welled up inside him—pride, anticipation, joy. Unable to resist, he lifted their still-joined hands to her face. "Is that it?"

"Oh, go to the devil, Chris." Knowing that anger was her best weapon, her best protection, she threw herself into it and tore her hands out of his. "Is being seduced by you different than being seduced by the Duc de Morny just because you are fifteen years younger and have all your hair?"

Behind its thin disguise of anger, he could feel her fear. He did not understand it, but he wanted to soothe it. He cupped her face and stroked his thumb over the fine line of her cheekbone.

"Morny is a hunter. He would take his pleasure in you, but in the end you would be no more than a trophy. One more woman whom he has bedded. I—"

Ariane felt her heart give a dull jolt at his hesitation. "Leave it, Chris. You don't have to tell me pretty lies."

"Lies?" He frowned. "I would not insult you by telling you lies."

"Then don't insult me by telling me that I will be more than a trophy for you."

What could he say to that? What could he say that would not sound false? So he said nothing. Instead he lifted his other hand so that they formed a frame for her face. Then he lowered his head to brush a kiss over her mouth.

Ariane shut her eyes against the prick of tears. Perhaps

she'd said that she did not want pretty lies, but if he had given her one, she would have taken it and held on to it.

"I won't tell you that you will be more than a trophy," he whispered. "But someday I will show you." He paused, but she remained very still, her eyes still closed.

"I don't want to hurt you, Ariane. And I don't want to take more than you want to give. Do you believe me?"

He might not want to hurt her, she thought, but he would. And as far as the other was concerned, he had already taken far more than she had ever wanted to give. "Yes," she whispered and forced herself to open her eyes. "I believe you."

It would be all right, she thought. Surely to be wanted like this by this man would be enough. And no matter what the pain, she would be safe, she reminded herself. He would leave and she would be safe. He would leave and she would not be in danger of surrendering her heart, her very self to him.

"You're very persuasive." She managed a smile. "But then I've always known that."

"Persuasive enough?" he asked, his mood suddenly lighter.

"Enough for what?"

"To have you go riding with me."

Looking beyond his shoulder, she saw his servant standing at the corner holding two horses.

"Do you mean that?" She could already feel the wind combing through her hair and her spirits lifted. "Oh, thank you."

Chris grinned. "If I had known that it would make

you smile at me like that, I would have suggested it far earlier. Come on." He held out his hand, his heart lifting when she took it without hesitation. "Let's go."

Chapter Fourteen

Squinting against the smoke, Maurice de Blanchard lit a cigarette, although he had crushed one out just moments before. He inhaled the sweet, perfumed smoke greedily, trying to drown out the smell of sour wine, cheap absinthe and sweat that seemed to permeate everything in the tavern—the wooden tables, the walls, the damp, dirty straw on the floor.

A little farther down the long table, several men sat huddled together over their dented metal cups, which were attached to the wall by thin chains. As he exhaled a long stream of smoke, several of them lifted their heads, as reflexively as dogs sniffing the air in front of a butcher shop. The men's eyes were glazed and empty. Only one of them roused himself far enough out of his stupor to shoot him a look that held envy and a mindless loathing. Maurice shrank back against the wall, feeling as conspicuous as if he were dressed for a ball at the Tuileries, although he was wearing the shabby clothes his valet had procured for him.

Silently, he cursed his father's bastard. Nothing had gone right for him since he had shown up in Paris. He'd thought to have a small revenge, but even that had been unsuccessful. So now the bastard had brought him to this.

He'd crept through the Faubourg Saint-Antoine, shuddering at the crippled beggars and stumbling drunks he came upon in the narrow, muddy streets. He had felt his stomach rise to his throat at the sight and stench of the filthy gutters and heaps of garbage that half-naked street urchins and mangy dogs fought over in the hope of finding something edible. And he had been all too aware of the hostile silence that had fallen on the tavern when he had entered it.

The door opened, bringing in a short burst of cold air. Tainted though it was with the smells of the street, it seemed fresh against the air of the tavern, which reeked of alcohol and despair. Heads lifted briefly and Maurice slumped a little in a mixture of horror and relief. The man, his hat pulled down low over his pockmarked face, had to be Rigole, whose services he had come here to buy.

Rigole ordered him over to an empty corner of the tavern with a rude gesture. Maurice chose to ignore the arrogance. Dropping his cigarette on the floor, he followed him. He heard sounds behind him, but in his hurry to reach the man he wished to hire, he did not look behind him at the two men who were squabbling over the half-smoked cigarette.

Maurice cleared his throat, but Rigole ignored him and gestured for wine.

The serving wench, her face young and unlined, but her eyes as old as the earth, shuffled up to them and poured wine into two cups from an earthenware pitcher. Rigole pinched her bony hip, but she only sent him a glassy look and moved away. Shrugging, he took a long drink and wiped his mouth with the back of his hand.

Only then did he turn to his prospective employer, his eyes sly and unsmiling.

"I heard that you might have a job for me."

"Y-yes, I might." Maurice squirmed a little on the hard bench.

"Well, speak up."

"What—" He cleared his throat. "What do you charge?"

Rigole laughed harshly. "For what? A burglary? A robbery? An abduction?" Shifting a little closer, he grinned. "A murder?"

He leaned back and gauged the nervous man in front of him. "You pay for the task and for what it is worth to you." He took another drink. "And I see that it is worth a good sum to you."

"I will not let you extort money from me." Feeling very brave, Maurice straightened. "I will pay the usual rate. No more, no less."

Rigole cuffed him on the shoulder with his meaty fist. "You'll pay because you are greedy to have the job done." A corner of Rigole's mouth lifted in a sneer. "And maybe you should remember where you are, *mon ami*," he said softly. "And that you and the contents of your pockets will reach home only if I allow it."

Maurice paled as he realized the truth of the statement and pressed his thighs together to suppress his sudden need for a privy.

"But don't worry. I am a man of honor." He leaned close. "Now tell me what is this task you have for me?"

Quickly, before he lost his courage, Maurice began to speak.

* * *

"You have no idea just how lucky you are." Justine sighed as she observed herself critically in the lavish full-length mirrors that curved around her in a half circle.

"How so?" Ariane asked. Secretly she shared Justine's opinion, although she was absolutely certain it was not for the same reasons.

"Look at this." Justine picked up a handful of her black curls and glared at her reflection.

"Like the best ebony wood." Ariane sent the girl an indulgent smile.

"Exactly." A line of displeasure appeared between Justine's eyebrows. "Easy for you to smile. You have hair the same color as the gold powder the hairdressers use." She pouted. "And a complexion of lilies and roses, while I look like a blackamoor even if I plaster my face with rice powder."

"Fashions change at the drop of a hat. Besides, I suppose that you know there are worse fates than having a less than fashionable haircolor." Ariane felt her tolerance of her friend's frivolous nature take on an edge of irritation. "Didn't you look out the carriage window on our way here? Or did we pass too quickly through that vile, little slum near the Tuileries for you to notice?"

"Oh, pooh. If they spend every *sou* they earn on wine, they can't expect pity." She made an airy gesture with her fingers. "Not mine anyway."

"I'm not talking about the drunkards. What about the children? The women?"

"Most of them are such skilled pickpockets that they probably dine on pâté." Turning back toward the mirror, she fingered the neckline of her gown. "Now do you think I can get away with another half-inch of *décolletage* without giving *maman* the vapors?"

"By all means." Her mouth thinning, Ariane rose and walked to the window. Pushing aside the shade that had been pulled closed to allow the clients to see precisely how their gowns would look in the artificial light of a ballroom, she looked down toward the street. It was full of carriages that were full of fashionable women come to patronize the dressmakers of the rue du Faubourg Saint-Honoré.

"You really think so?" Without waiting for a reply, Justine gestured to the seamstress. "Yes, I think a half inch less will be just right."

Blocking the younger girl's chatter from her consciousness, Ariane stared down into the street, unable to get the sights she had seen on the way here out of her mind. What was she doing here? she asked herself. How could she stand this vapid life that her father demanded of her for a whole season? And for what? As if in answer to her question, a carriage stopped below and Roger de Monnier alit, followed by Chris's tall, broad figure.

He would understand how she felt, she realized. Her pulse began to flutter. He would not be lacking in compassion.

At that moment Chris looked up as unerringly as if he had known exactly where to find her. He did not smile, but for a long moment he stared up at the window where she stood before he entered the building.

She wanted him. Desperately, she reminded herself that there were many things she wanted. Things she had never had difficulty denying herself.

If it were only desire, it would be easier, she thought. But the damnable part was that she liked him. She liked his brashness and the way he made her laugh. She liked the way he made her feel when his eyes softened with tenderness. She sighed now. There was no way to shut that up in a little box and explain it away.

Love. The truth, clothed in that one single, terrible

word, struck her like a fist. As fear crept up her spine, turning her body to ice, she fought to deny it and found she could not. A cry of desperation rose in her throat and she raised her hands to her mouth to stifle it.

How could this happen to her? She had sworn that she would never let herself surrender to emotions that would leave her vulnerable to pain and manipulation. She had always had such a clear vision of what her life would be. She would not allow him to change it. But, a small voice reminded her, he did not want to change it. He merely wanted her in his bed. Temporarily.

She squeezed her eyes shut against the image of his sun-gilded perfection, which beckoned to her, tempting her. But no matter how tightly she closed her eyes, the image burned in her mind like a torch, pulling her closer until they were almost one. Until she felt herself surrendering to him——her body and her heart both.

Suddenly she could no longer stand the overheated room with its soft, feminine scents of perfume and flowers and chocolates. Picking up her pelisse, she headed toward the door. "I have to go now."

"But—"

Ignoring whatever it was that Justine called after her, she shut the door behind her.

Fleeing past the seamstresses, their arms loaded with gowns and fabrics, she had almost reached the door when she heard Chris call her name.

She wanted to keep going, to run and hide from this flood of emotion and fear, but pride had her turning around.

"Where are you going? What's wrong?" Chris asked as he moved toward her.

Her eyes huge, she stared at Chris. Her lips could form no words and she only shook her head helplessly.

"What is it?" His hands slid up her arms to her shoulders. "Has someone hurt you? If—"

"No." Panic swirled up within her at the way his touch had heat spreading through her, and she shifted back, desperate to escape him. "No one's hurt me."

She felt his hands tighten for a moment on her shoulders before he released her, and she almost cried out in a wild, paradoxical confusion of relief and pain. Pulling all her strength together, Ariane looked past Chris at Roger.

"Will you wait for Justine, Roger?" Ariane tugged on her gloves jerkily. "I need to go."

"Is something wrong?"

"No." She shook her head. "I need some fresh air. I'm afraid that my enthusiasm for fashion does not match your sister's."

"I will accompany you." Chris's tone stated categorically rather than asked polite questions.

Unable to do otherwise, she nodded her agreement.

As they stepped out into the busy street, Chris wordlessly tucked Ariane's arm into his. She jolted a little, but did not pull away.

Chris felt Ariane's small tremble and felt absurdly touched, as if she had given him an unexpected gift. The thought that his desire for her had taken on a dimension that he had never experienced before—never wanted to experience—nudged his consciousness. Uncomfortable with the possibility that, for the first time in his life, his feelings had gone beyond his control, he pushed the thought away. Ignoring the cabs for hire, he steered her down the street.

They did not speak as they moved down the street, nor did they look at each other. But each was so sharply

aware of the other that they might have been the only
people in the world. So it was small wonder that neither
one of them noticed the man who alit from a carriage
and, hugging the walls of the houses, began to follow
them.

They covered one block, then two, and gradually Ariane felt the movement and the cool, slightly damp air
begin to soothe her. It would be all right, she told herself.

"How did you know that I needed to walk?" she
asked.

"You were so desperate to get out of there that I
figured you needed to walk off some of that nervous
energy." He looked down at her, scrutinizing the strain
around her mouth. "So tell me then, what is it that is
bothering you so badly?"

"The superficiality of it all." She made a choppy,
impatient gesture. "The fact that half an inch of *décolletage* weighs more than the fact that there are starving
children in the streets a few blocks from the imperial
palace." She stopped and looked up at him. "We have
poverty at home, but I've never seen anything like this
before."

Chris's eyes darkened as he thought of what he had
seen in the poorer streets of Paris. "I'm not sure I have
either."

He felt Ariane's hand relax within the crook of his
arm and he had the feeling that he had passed some kind
of test.

"Is that all that's bothering you?"

"Isn't it enough?"

"I suppose it is."

"Would you tell me if someone had hurt you, Ariane?" Chris asked, after they had walked a few minutes
in silence. "If you were in some kind of trouble?"

How ironic that he would ask that, Ariane thought, just minutes after she had understood, after she had admitted to herself just what kind of trouble she was in, just how much he could—no, she corrected herself—just how much he *would* hurt her. Whether he seduced her or not, in the end she would suffer.

"I want to be sure that you would come to me if you needed help." The urgent need to protect did not sit comfortably with him, but there did not seem to be anything that he could do about it. "I need to be sure."

She heard the urgency in his voice and it puzzled her. "What a strange thing to say, Chris." She looked up and met his eyes squarely. The pain flashed through her, but she steadied herself against it. "In a few months I will be gone from Paris and so will you."

Her words reminded him that he was safe from the desires, the needs that burned within him. An unexpected pang went through him, but he chose to ignore it. "Yes, but until then."

"Don't." She made a choppy gesture. "I don't want your so-called protection."

"That's too bad, Ariane. Because as long as I'm here, I will—"

"Damn you." She stopped and whirled around to face him. "Don't push me!"

"I haven't even begun to."

His voice was mild and he had not moved to close the space between them, but she felt like a cornered animal. Her eyes narrowed as anger and fear rose to form a new emotion all its own. "And what are you doing now?" Her breath was coming faster. "And what is all this rubbish about danger and coming to you for help, when the biggest danger to me is you?" She gasped a little as she heard her thoughts of a minute ago clothed in words.

"What are you talking about?"

"Forget what I said." She raised her hands palm outward.

"No." He caught her hands in his and when she would have turned away, he framed her face with their joined hands. Her eyes were dark and stormy. "Ariane, are you saying that you are afraid of me?"

"Yes." The word slipped out before she could stop it.

Stunned, horrified, he stared at her. "Why?"

She wanted to close her eyes, not believing that she had given herself away like that. Frantic, she cast around for an explanation. Something. Anything.

"Because someday you're going to hurt me."

With a movement so clever, so quick that she could not have escaped him, he maneuvered her around a corner into an alleyway that was barely wide enough to accommodate her crinoline.

"What are—"

"Sh." Stripping off his glove, he placed the pad of his thumb against her mouth to silence her and stayed to caress, to seduce.

She should move away, she thought. He wasn't holding her. He was only touching her with that light, insolent touch of his thumb against her mouth. And yet within moments that touch had drugged her until her limbs were heavy and her blood like warm honey. So she remained very still.

"I won't hurt you, Ariane. I promise." He lifted his hand away from her mouth and began to nestle at the bow of her bonnet. She did not make a move to stop him. "I just want to show you how much pleasure there can be between a man and a woman."

Leaving the velvet ribbons loosely tied, Chris took off the bonnet so that it hung down her back.

Already Ariane could feel his mouth on hers. Her lips parted in welcome, in anticipation, but he did not move to kiss her. Instead he lifted his hand to the curls that were pinned behind one ear.

"How long is your hair when it's not curled?" he asked softly as he rubbed a strand of golden hair between forefinger and thumb.

It took a long moment for the question to penetrate her mind, already made languorous with arousal. "Halfway down my back, I suppose," she finally managed.

He fisted his hand in her hair, a little appalled that just touching her hair had such sharp arousal flaring within him. "Someday I'm going to unravel every single one of your curls with my fingers and then I'm going to—"

Although she was lost in the sensuous haze he was weaving around her, Ariane suddenly knew that they were no longer alone.

Chris saw the change in her eyes, from the dazed arousal giving way to alarm. He shifted aside to look behind him.

And felt the knife slide between his ribs.

Chapter Fifteen

Chris felt a flash of terror that had nothing to do with his wound and everything to do with Ariane.

With all of his strength, he pushed her farther into the alley and turned to fight. But he garnered no more than a brief impression of a rough-featured, pitted face before his assailant rounded the corner of the alley. Chris lunged after him, but the man was already disappearing into the crowded street.

He itched to go after him because he was certain that it could not be a coincidence that his assailant fit the description the detective he had hired to follow Maurice had given him. But he realized his limitations and he knew that his first duty was to protect Ariane. He slid his hand inside his cloak and touched his side, swearing silently as he felt the wetness that was already soaking through his frock coat.

The way Chris had abruptly shoved her back and the rough contact she had made with the wall had taken Ariane's breath away. But she pushed away from the wall and stumbled toward Chris. "What is it?" She touched his arm. "What is going on?"

Oblivious to his wound, Chris whirled around. "Why

didn't you stay back there?" he demanded, his anger fueled by fear. "Do you think I pushed you back because it amused me? How can you be so foolhardy?"

Ariane stared up at him, momentarily stunned—and fascinated—by the fury that turned his eyes to green fire and had his nostrils quivering. "I—"

"What if the man had still been here?" Just that thought alone whipped his anger as a storm wind whips the waves of the sea. He gripped her shoulders and shook her. "Or if there had been a second attacker?"

His rough touch had Ariane's own temper flaring. "Take your hands off me," she said, and glanced down pointedly at one shoulder, where his hand was biting into her flesh. It was then that she saw the blood.

Twisting out of his grasp, she took his hand in both of hers.

"He hurt you." Her anger—and his—forgotten, panic closed her throat. Moving closer to him, she slid an arm around him for support. "We need to get you to a doctor." Everything had happened too quickly for her to be truly afraid, but now she suddenly felt her heart begin to pound.

"We need to get *you* home," he contradicted. "It's only a scratch."

Although his casual tone settled her nerves a little, she made a disbelieving sound. "That's why you're bleeding like a stuck pig."

"I've had worse. Now—" he reached out with his clean hand and pulled her bonnet forward "—put this on." His voice took on an edge as the pain grew sharper.

"Chris—" She paled, instinctively aware of his pain as if it were her own.

"It's all right." He managed to curve his mouth into a semblance of a smile. "I was attacked, but the man is gone now." A new flash of pain had him catching his breath. "I suggest that we find ourselves a carriage and take you home."

She would fight him later, she thought, as she hastily tied the ribbons into a haphazard bow. As they moved out of the alley, she hooked her arm into his, squelching the desire to support him more fully.

He was pale when he let himself fall onto the hard seat of the cab. As he leaned forward to give the driver her address, she put her hand on his arm.

"Where are you staying, Chris?" she asked him, her voice low and urgent.

"It doesn't mat—"

"Don't be a fool, for God's sake." Not wanting the coachman to understand their argument, she continued in English. "Can't you give in with grace?" she asked. "I can make quite a scene and don't believe that I won't."

"The Meurice," he snapped and leaned back. "God, protect me from stubborn women," he muttered as he closed his eyes.

The drive was only a few blocks and when the elegant arcades of the rue de Rivoli came into view, Chris called to the cabdriver to stop.

"I've done what you wanted. Now you return the favor." He spoke briskly to mask the weakness that he could feel rising within him like flood tide. "I want you to get out here. It's one thing to risk your reputation by being seen in my company in public. I will not allow you to risk it by being seen with me in my hotel."

"An interesting choice of words—'I won't allow.'" She shrugged. "I'm not going to waste time arguing with you because I don't know how badly your scratch, as you put it, is bleeding."

She heard his sigh of relief and felt a stab of guilt. She reached up, untucked the veil gathered under the dark green band of her bonnet and lowered it over her face.

"Propriety is served now," she said softly for his ears only, then raised her voice so that the driver could hear her. "Continue to the Meurice, *monsieur.*"

Wanting to be as unobtrusive as possible, Chris had insisted on climbing the stairs without help from any of the hotel staff. Now, as they moved down the long corridor with its plush burgundy-colored carpet, she felt him sway.

"Will you stop being a hero for a moment and wait here while I get your manservant?" A mixture of alarm and exasperation made her voice sharp.

"No need." He winced, not so much at the hot stab of pain that went through him, but at the abominable weakness that seemed to have turned his legs to water. "It's the next door."

He was still fumbling with the key when the door was opened by Sam, the largest man Ariane had ever seen. He took one look at Chris and, without saying a word, swung an arm around him to support him to the sofa. She followed the two men, ridding herself of bonnet, pelisse and gloves on the way.

"What happened?" Sam undid the closure of Chris's cloak and started to pull it away, but Chris grabbed the velvet-trimmed edge and shook his head.

"I was attacked, but the man ran off before I could do anything."

"Was it—?"

Chris silenced Sam with a shake of his head and turned to Ariane.

"Just what do you think you're doing?" he demanded when he saw that she had rolled up one of the sleeves of her gown and was unbuttoning the second. "You've seen me to my bed. What more do you want, for God's sake?" The throb of pain was insistent and he did his best to breathe with its rhythm. "Now put your things back on. Sam will get you a cab downstairs."

"I can help until a doctor can get here." Ignoring his words, she moved closer. "And I don't faint at the sight of blood." Her tone was sharper than she had intended, but the thought that she was somehow at fault was plaguing her.

She leaned forward and touched his hand, which still held the edges of the cloak at his throat. "Chris." Her voice softened. "Let me help."

Chris let go of the cloak and closed his hand around Ariane's wrist.

"Go home, Ariane." His voice rose. "I don't want you here."

She jolted as if he had struck her. She supposed that he was sending her away for her own good, but that did not soften the sting of a harshly delivered rejection. Twisting her hand out of his grasp, she straightened and turned away.

Chris saw the hurt flood her eyes for one brief instant before she lowered her lids and turned away. Before he could defend himself against it, her pain flowed back to him so that he felt it as sharply as if it was his own. How could he feel someone else's pain so clearly? he asked himself. The answer crowded into his mind, but afraid, he pushed it away.

"Ariane, I'm sorry. I didn't mean to shout at you."

"I see." She turned around, but did not look at him. "You apologize for the delivery, but not the content."

Because she felt the tears burning in the back of her eyes, she kept her gaze on the sleeve that she was rolling back down as meticulously as if it were the most important task in the world.

Sam interrupted them with his deep voice. "Maybe y'all can chat later, after I've doctored him up some."

Sam set down the basin of water and towels he'd collected and, bending down toward Chris, peeled away the cloak and began divesting him of his frock coat.

Not sure of her welcome, Ariane approached slowly. "I'll go as soon as I'm sure you're all right."

Chris looked up at her. Her eyes were huge and sparkled with unshed tears—like rain-washed amethysts. For a moment, he just stared at her and then he fell into her magical eyes as if they were a bottomless well.

Ariane saw something flicker in his eyes—something dark and deep. It called to her and, afraid, she looked away.

Sam's softly spoken oath and Chris's sharp intake of breath as his shirt was cut away brought her back to reality. The training she had so often needed to deal with injuries on the estate took over, and with quick, efficient movements she dampened a towel in the water and began to wipe away the half-dried blood, her other hand curved around Chris's shoulder to support and soothe.

For a moment Chris closed his eyes, as Ariane's touch wiped away the pain. But then that feeling of uncontrolled falling returned and he retreated. He did not want this, he reminded himself. All he wanted was to share some pleasure with her.

"Somehow when I envisioned your hands on my body," he said in an effort to distance himself from the feelings that tumbled through him, "I had something else entirely in mind."

"I'm glad you still have your sense of humor." She took a fresh towel and dipped it in the water, grateful for the activity that allowed her to hide the sudden flash of heat that went through her at his words.

"There's nothing humorous about it." Chris slanted a look up at her. "I'm quite serious."

"Be still." She gave his shoulder a warning squeeze as she pressed the folded towel to the still bleeding wound.

"Sam, do you know enough French to ask where you can get some yarrow and arnica?" She addressed him in her precise English. "If we could make a poultice, it would stop the bleeding and prevent infection."

"Got those same herbs in my medicine bag, miss." A broad smile split Sam's face. "Ain't the first time I needed 'em either."

"So you've had to, how did you say it, doctor him up before?" Ariane answered Sam's smile with one of her own.

"Oh, yes, ma'am." His big brown eyes sparkled.

"Will you stop talking about me as if I were a side of beef?" Irritated, Chris looked from one to the other.

"I'm glad that you're feeling well enough to be cranky." Ariane changed the towel again and was pleased to see that the bleeding was slowing to a trickle.

She watched with approval as Sam expertly prepared the poultice and applied it to the wound, fastening it into place with a wide bandage.

"Now that I see that you are in capable hands, I can leave with a clear conscience." Ariane took a step back. She suddenly felt self-conscious in front of this half-naked, bronze-skinned man. The fact that he was wounded and sprawled on the couch took nothing away from his power.

She turned away and walked to where she had left her things. Her movements were more than a little jerky as she busied herself with putting on her bonnet and pelisse.

"Thank you."

She jumped at the sound of Chris's voice so close behind her, and her already fluttering pulse began to pound.

"You shouldn't be moving around." She turned to face him, but it occurred to her that it was an ill-advised thing to do and she took a step back.

"At times we all do things we shouldn't." He smiled and shifted to close the gap she had widened. "But you would know about that, wouldn't you?"

"It's a matter of perspective." Although she managed to speak coolly, his closeness seemed to be cutting off her breathing. She kept her eyes focused on a cabinet that stood to his left.

"Indeed, a matter of perspective." He tucked a finger under her chin, but did not turn her face toward him, finding that he needed her to take that step. "Will you look at me, Ariane?"

There was challenge in his voice and invitation. But it was the hint of an appeal that had her shifting her gaze. She swallowed as her eyes skimmed over the starkly white bandage that slashed through the expanse of golden skin. Her cheeks were flushed by the time her eyes finally met his.

"Will you forgive me for hurting you?" he asked softly. "I wanted to spare you the sight of my blood and I wanted to spare myself."

"Yourself?"

"It's hard on a man's pride when the woman he wants sees him when he is as weak as a babe because, as you so elegantly put it, he has bled like a stuck pig."

"You look quite recovered, so your pride should be comfortable again." But he was still pale beneath the sun-kissed color of his skin, she thought, and had to keep from giving in to the desire to lay her hand against his cheek. "I needed to make sure you were all right. After all, it was my fault that this happened."

"Your fault? How so?"

"If I had not wanted to walk, then you would not have been there."

He considered telling her that it had not been a random attack. That the knife had been meant for him personally. That if the man had not attacked him today, he would have attacked him another time. But he discarded the thought, not wanting to burden her further.

"It was not your fault, Ariane. It was the fault of the man who wielded the knife." And the man who paid him, he added silently. "But it was the expression in your eyes that warned me. If I hadn't moved, the knife would have done far more harm."

"I'm glad." She gave in to the desire to touch him then and lifted her hand to his cheek.

"Ariane—" He found himself searching for words and discovered there were none. Instead he curled his fingers around hers and drew her hand to his lips.

As he watched her, he felt himself falling, and with the last of his strength he pulled himself back. But when he spoke, his voice was slow and dreamy.

"There is a meadow on my land in California. Every spring it is full of irises that are the same color as your eyes."

"I'd like to see that someday," she said, forgetting that when their charade was over, she would never see him again.

"And I'd like to show it to you," he said. "But since

it will have to wait, I'll show you something else in the meantime.''

Slowly, he kissed her fingertips one by one, then he drew her hand down until it rested on his chest, just above the bandage.

His skin was warm and Ariane could feel the strong beat of his heart accelerate as her hand came to rest over it.

''What are you doing?'' she whispered, instinctively jerking her hand as if to escape his grip. His fingers loosened so that they no longer imprisoned her. And her hand stayed where it lay.

''I needed to feel your hand on my skin again,'' he said softly. ''I needed you to touch *me* and not just a body you were caring for.''

She opened her mouth to tell him that she *had* been touching him, but the words died in her mouth as he began to move her hand in small, gentle circles on his skin. His skin seemed to heat beneath her touch and the heat seeped into her skin, into her blood, until it was a living, breathing entity within her.

''Please.'' Her voice was a desperate whisper as she felt herself spiraling into the vortex of the desire he aroused in her so effortlessly, unsure if she was asking him to stop or asking him for more.

''Please what, Ariane? Tell me,'' he murmured. ''I want to please you. I want very badly to please you.''

''No,'' she managed, fighting her way past her own desires. ''Let me go.''

''I'm not holding you fast,'' he said.

Her eyes went to where his hand lay on top of hers. She knew that he was not holding her captive and yet she did not have the strength to pull away. The realization terrified her.

"Please." Her eyes lifted to his again.

Understanding dawned and he felt a small flash of triumph as he lifted his hand away from hers.

"I will accompany you down in a minute." He turned to take the shirt that Sam was holding out to him.

"There's no need." Ariane busied herself with her bonnet and gloves. "I'm perfectly capable of finding a cab on my own. Besides, if it's discretion you're looking for, I'm sure it will cause less of a stir if I am unaccompanied."

She looked at him one more time, but finding that her hard-won control was slipping again, she looked past him at his manservant.

"Make sure he doesn't get into more trouble, Sam." She smiled.

"Yes, ma'am." His smile split his face from ear to ear.

"*Au revoir,* Chris." Quickly, before he could stop her, she moved past him and was gone.

Staring at the door that had closed behind her, Chris rubbed his hand over the place where Ariane's hand had lain. When he finally roused himself and turned around, he almost ran into Sam who was watching him with a gleeful smile.

"Take that foolish grin off your face," he growled.

Sam shrugged and kept on smiling. "When you decide to bite the dust, you do a fine job. Yes, sirree."

"Don't be ridiculous."

"I know what I saw and my eyesight's pretty good."

Chris made a disparaging sound and sent him a glare. "I need my clothes, Sam. I have a call to make." He sucked in his breath as he pulled his shirt over his head. "I wouldn't want my dear brother to think that he has rid himself of me."

Moving a little more carefully, he tucked his shirt into his trousers and began to bind his cravat. By the time he was finished, Sam was standing there, wearing hat and overcoat, a fresh cloak for Chris over his arm.

"Do you have plans, Sam?"

"Startin' now, you ain't goin' nowhere without me."

"Now, Sam—"

"No one's gonna keep me from lookin' out for you," Sam said stubbornly. "Not even yourself."

"Then by all means, come along." Chris grinned and clapped Sam on the shoulder. "Let's see what my brother has to say for himself."

This time, the secretary in Maurice de Blanchard's antechamber took one look at Chris's grim face and did not even try to stop him. And a glance at Sam's massive figure behind him had the young man retreating even farther behind his desk.

Gesturing to Sam to wait for him here, Chris opened the elegantly carved door. As he reached back to send it flying into the doorjamb, he caught sight of Maurice. His brother was standing in front of the window, his arms akimbo, his stance implying that he was well pleased with the world. Chris felt a new wave of rage. Because he knew himself too well to want to exacerbate his temper, he loosened his grip on the door and closed it behind him with a soft click.

"I told you that I was not to be disturbed, Gaston. You should know that having my instructions ignored makes me quite ill-humored."

Chris leaned back against the door. Perhaps he was going to enjoy this after all.

"I fear that this time it is not Gaston who is going to be responsible for your ill-humor."

His mouth hanging open in surprise, Maurice spun around and stared at him.

"Wh-what are you doing here?" Maurice's mouth worked soundlessly for a few moments before he spoke again. "Why—how—"

"You mean, why am I not dead and how do I come to be here?" Chris curved his mouth in a ghost of a smile. "Was that what he told you? That he had killed me?"

His face turned a peculiar shade of greenish-gray and Maurice fumbled for the back of his chair, his knuckles whitening as his grip on it tightened. "I do not know what you are talking about."

Because his wound was beginning to throb again, Chris pushed himself away from the door very carefully and, taking his time, crossed the room. "If that is the case, then perhaps I should enlighten you."

"I am not interes—"

"Shut up and listen to me." Because he wanted to reach across the polished expanse of the desk and haul his brother forward, he flexed his hands at his sides. "My patience appears to be in short supply today."

Realizing that he had little choice but to hear what the bastard had to say and try to brazen it out, Maurice crossed his arms tightly in front of him and remained silent.

"Does a rough-featured man with a pockmarked face ring a bell?"

Maurice's mien remained stony, but a muscle near his eye began to jump.

"No matter." Chris waved his hand. "Let me spell it out for you, just so you understand that I know exactly what you're doing."

"I am not doing anyth—" His voice petered out as he caught Chris's gaze and saw the cold fury there.

"I know that you set Morny to stalk Ariane de Valmont, thinking to annoy me. Why such drastic measures now? Are you so desperate to rid yourself of me?"

"Really—" Maurice adjusted his cuffs and found his fingers trembling "—you are speaking in riddles."

"Your paid assassin tried to kill me." Chris leaned forward. "Is that clear enough?"

"I will not permit you to cast aspersions on my honor in this way." He straightened to his full height and gave his waistcoat a tug over his rounded belly. "I should call you out."

"Feel free." Chris shrugged, although he knew in his heart that, for the sake of their father, he could never cold-bloodedly point a pistol at Maurice. "But do try to refrain from hiring another assassin. I am particularly partial to this life." He started to turn away.

"Oh, and one more thing." He paused. "I was not alone today when I was attacked. If Ariane de Valmont is ever endangered by you again, I will see that you pay for it." He leaned forward a little. "Personally."

He was almost at the door when he turned back one more time. "I hope you didn't pay your man too much for the botched job." The flash of rage in Maurice's eyes told him that he had hit a bull's-eye. "Let that be a lesson to you, *mon frère*." He sent his brother a cocky grin. "Always check whether a job has been done properly before paying for it."

His throat clogged with hatred and bitterness and fear, Maurice watched his father's bastard close the door behind him. The taunting, threatening words echoed in his mind, fueling his rage until he was so filled with it that he thought he would explode.

Chapter Sixteen

Ariane was laughing with pleasure as they slowed their mounts from a gallop to a walk.

"Now, don't tell me that you aren't glad I persuaded you." She leaned over to touch Chris's arm, but thought better of it, when she saw how he shifted away from her. Some of the pleasure went out of her, but she went on brightly. "Wasn't that more fun than those well-mannered trots we've been having along the bridle paths of the Bois?" There didn't seem to be an answer forthcoming, so she continued. "But, of course, even the tamest trot is more fun than salon conversation."

His mood uncertain, edgy, Chris had let Ariane's words flow past him. Now he fixed her with a direct stare. "Speaking of salon conversation, just how badly is Morny harassing you?"

"Harass is a pretty strong word." She gestured with her hand as if she were shooing away a pesky fly. "He's a nuisance, that's all."

"I don't trust him." His mouth thinned.

"Oh, he just thinks he's irresistible." She shrugged. "But then he probably is to most women. He's the second most powerful man in France, after all."

"And power can be seen as an aphrodisiac."

"For some, I suppose."

Chris opened his mouth to ask Ariane what she did consider to be an aphrodisiac, but he closed it again. Something had changed between them that day he had been wounded. Ever since, he had not been able to find his way back to the suggestive banter he had shared with her so easily.

Ariane heard Chris's intake of breath as if he were going to say something, but he remained silent. Looking over to him, she saw that he was frowning again. He'd changed somehow since that day he had been wounded.

Did he feel the change in her, she wondered? Was he retreating from it? Oh, she had tried so hard to keep the feelings inside her, but they had a disconcerting way of coming to the surface at the most inconvenient moments.

"Chris!"

Frowning at the interruption, Chris turned at the sound of Sam's voice.

"It's gettin' mighty dark." He gestured upward with his eyes.

Chris followed his gaze. "Damn. It's going to rain any minute." He looked back at Ariane. "I'm sorry. I should have noticed earlier."

"I'll be all right." Ariane shrugged off his apology. "I've gotten caught by thunderstorms at home often enough."

"A winter storm won't be as pleasant." Chris wheeled his mount around. "There was a signpost for an inn a few miles back. Maybe we can get there before the worst hits."

They had not gone more than a mile when it began to pour.

* * *

The tiny inn was barely visible through the sheets of icy rain. But lights within the small building promised warmth and shelter.

Leaping down from his horse, Chris felt the mud of the courtyard suck at his boots. Moving quickly, he lifted Ariane down from the saddle. Before she could protest, he carried her over to the stoop, where the eaves of the thatched roof gave them a little protection.

Just as Chris took hold of the handle, the door opened and a rosy-cheeked woman appeared.

"Mon Dieu!" she exclaimed. "Come inside quickly." Peering out, she saw Sam and the horses and pointed to the left. "The stables are just around the side." She shut the door against the rain and glanced up at Chris. "Come closer to the fire, please."

"The fire won't be enough. We will be needing rooms and something to wear while our clothes dry."

While Chris talked to the innkeeper, Ariane tossed her sodden pelisse and wilted hat aside and went to stand as close as possible to the welcoming flames in the fireplace. Water from her clothing began to puddle around her feet and her riding habit lay against her skin like an icy blanket. Now that the excitement of their gallop through the pounding rain began to wear off, she started to shiver.

"I'm afraid we only have one room, *monsieur*. We are really only a tavern for the local farmers."

"Then we will take what you have."

"I will prepare the room as quickly as possible."

"Thank you." Chris nodded, his eyes on Ariane, who stood stiffly near the fireplace. "A blanket, please, before you go."

The woman bobbed a curtsy and scurried off, returning moments later with a blanket. Chris took it from her and moved toward Ariane.

"Take off your dress, Ariane."

She spun her head toward him, her eyes wide. "Just because they have only one room is no reason to assume—"

"Now is not the time for modesty," he said irritably. "Or do you think that I intend to take you here in the taproom?" His words were heavy with sarcasm. "You're courting a lung ailment unless you get out of those wet clothes."

He shook out the blanket and held it up between them. *"Voilà."* He smiled, attempting to smooth over his impatient, crass words. "A hundred years ago it was all the fashion for ladies to receive their gentlemen callers while sitting in their bath, with only a screen between them."

Ariane might have argued further, but her practical nature took over. She was freezing and her chattering teeth would make it very difficult to present an effective argument. Turning her back to him, she began to undress with fingers that were awkward with cold.

Chris listened to the rustling, feminine sounds of buttons being slipped through buttonholes, the swish of cloth falling to the floor. The scent of wet wool gave way to the fragrance of skin. As he felt his body tighten, he bit back a sigh. It was going to be a very long night.

Ariane swore under her breath as her icy fingers fumbled on the hooks of her corset. It was incredible what women allowed to be done to them in the name of fashion. The dressmaker *papa* had hired had been horrified that she wore nothing but a chemise beneath her clothing and had threatened to leave immediately if she did not consent to an elastic corset at the very least. She looked forward to burning every single one of the contraptions once she was safely back home.

"Do you need help?"

Ariane's fingers stilled halfway down the row of hooks.

"Can you unlace your stays by yourself?"

Cautiously she peeked over her shoulder, expecting Chris to be looking at her with one of his insolent grins, but he stood there as still as a statue, his face averted, his mouth grim.

Suddenly the utter absurdity of the situation overcame her and she began to giggle.

"Ariane, are you all right?"

She pressed her hands against her mouth in a vain attempt to stem the laughter.

Thinking that she was about to succumb to hysterics, Chris closed the distance between them, wrapped the blanket around her and turned her to face him.

Ariane looked up at him and dissolved again in another gale of giggles.

"Well, would you like to share the joke?" His concern of a moment ago faded as relief warred with irritation. "I'd be grateful for a little amusement just now."

Ariane shook her head. "It's simply too bizarre—the wild ride through the rain, the inn—and then you ask me if I need help unlacing my stays as if you were asking me if I needed—" she tried to gesture, but found her hands trapped within the blanket "—I don't know, a hand to mount my horse or some such thing. It was just too much." She dragged in a breath where laughter still trembled. "I thank you for your concern."

"Then I take it that you do not need help."

"No. I'm not wearing stays." She almost giggled again as the impropriety of discussing her undergarments with a man occurred to her. "I have a real fondness for breathing."

Amused, aroused, as much by her reaction as by the fact that she was half-naked beneath that blanket, Chris gave the blanket a tug so that she fell against him.

"That's too bad," he whispered. "It would have been my pleasure to unlace your stays." His mouth curved. "I'm very good at it."

The amusement she had felt dissipated in the face of his husky whisper and the smile that made all kinds of promises. Ariane tried to shift away, but found that every movement served only to bring her closer. A flame came to life within her and she fought to ignore it.

"Abilities come no doubt from frequent practice." The words were sharp, but the delivery was breathless.

He tugged her closer so that she was flush against him. "Ariane—"

Although the pounding of his pulse filled his ears, he heard the sound of steps on the stairs.

"Here," he growled, irritated both with the interruption and with his own lack of self-control. "Hold this yourself." He thrust the ends of the blanket at her and stepped away.

Just managing to catch the blanket before it slipped away, Ariane wrapped it tightly around herself. Closing her eyes, she exhaled. The situation no longer felt bizarre. And she no longer felt like laughing.

Turning back toward the fire, she heard Chris speak with the innkeeper without really hearing what either one of them said.

"Ariane."

She jumped when he spoke her name.

"We can go up now."

That simple statement seemed so terribly intimate and

the heat shot into her cheeks as she stared at him for a moment. Then she nodded and slowly moved forward.

The room was still chilly, but a fire had been lit. The furniture was simple and sturdy, the linen clean. Satisfied that the room would provide a modicum of comfort, Chris returned to where Ariane still stood just inside the door.

"A bath will be brought up shortly."

She nodded again, unable to say a word. Finding herself half-naked with him in this room that was dominated by the large, white bed seemed to have turned her into a simpleton, she thought. Only when he opened the door again, did she find her tongue.

"Where are you going?"

"To find myself some dry clothes, to get us something to eat and to send Sam with a message to your parents."

"Oh, my God. I'd completely forgotten about them."

"Then it's good that I remembered." Chris smiled. "I'll be back in a little while."

She looked so tiny and bedraggled in that big, rough blanket that he almost reached out to pull her close. Instead he stepped out into the dim corridor and closed the door behind him.

Ariane was floating on the verge of sleep. The innkeeper had put a handful of dried lavender into the bathwater and the fragrant steam had soothed away all her nervousness. Even the opening of the door, the footsteps on the floorboards registered only as some faraway sound that did not threaten.

Chris took the tray from the innkeeper, who had followed him up the stairs, and set it down on the table. He grinned when he saw that Ariane had rigged a makeshift screen by setting three chairs side by side and spreading a sheet over them.

"Ariane?"

The sound of Chris's voice brought her totally awake with such a start that water splashed onto the floor.

"I brought up some mulled wine for you."

Although she was fairly sure that he could not see her, she brought her knees up to shield her body. "Thank you. I'll drink it after my bath."

"You should drink it while it's still hot. May I bring it to you?"

"No!" The word burst out of her and she closed her eyes, embarrassed at the desperate sound of it.

"Ariane, there is no one here to monitor propriety."

His voice had that patiently amused tone of an adult trying to explain something to a fractious child. "So? My behavior is not dependent on the presence of a chaperon."

"Ah, yes, I remember."

Her cheeks burning, she slid down farther into the water, remembering how he had kissed her right under Henriette's nose. She closed her eyes against the image, but that only made the memory sharper. She could almost feel his mouth on hers.

She sat up again, her fingers rubbing her temples as if she could erase that image.

"Has it occurred to you that I would like to bathe in privacy?"

He grinned at the annoyance in her voice. Her eyebrows would be drawn together in that light frown, her mouth pursed just on the edge of a pout. "Has it occurred to *you* that I have a very good idea of what your body looks like?"

"What?"

"Some of your gowns are rather revealing. Besides, I have an excellent imagination."

Ariane made a small sound of exasperation.

Chris waited a moment before he spoke again. "At any rate, my dear, I'm too old to play Peeping Tom games. If I offer to bring you a cup of wine, it is no more and no less than that."

"All right." Hearing the less than gracious tone of her voice, Ariane sighed. "I'd like a cup of wine, please."

As she heard the sound of his steps on the wooden floor, she slid back down as far as she could into the water, stopping only when she felt the warm water splash against her chin.

Chris stepped around the makeshift screen. Although he needed some little control not to indulge himself with a glance downward, he kept his eyes on her face. Crouching at the side of the tub, he held out the earthenware cup to her. As Ariane reached for it, their fingers met and, for a moment, held. Her hand was just a little unsteady, but he felt no triumph as he relinquished his hold on the cup.

Ariane closed her eyes as she savored the spiced, warm wine, taking pleasure both in the taste and the warmth. She drank again and when she opened her eyes, she found Chris's face just inches away. It occurred to her that she should move away, look away. But instead, she kept her gaze on his and felt a heat rise through her. A heat that had nothing to do with the wine she'd drunk. A heat that had everything to do with the fact that the amusement that had been in his eyes moments before had faded, its place taken by an intensity that made her mouth go dry.

"You should have unpinned your hair. It will never dry like this. May I?"

She nodded, her fingers tightening on the cup.

Reaching behind her head, he began to pull out the pins one by one until her hair spilled down behind her like a golden waterfall scented with flowers. He wanted to comb through her hair with his fingers. He wanted to put his mouth to the pulse that beat quickly at the base of her neck. He wanted to take her mouth.

He pulled back a space of a breath before he gave in to the temptation.

"I will let you finish your bath in privacy now." He smiled with his mouth only. "When you have finished, we can eat."

Ariane drained the rest of the wine. Shifting to her knees, she peered cautiously over her barricade. He was sitting at the table, his back to her. Not sure whether to be relieved or disappointed, she stood and began to dry herself.

The splash of water as Ariane stood had Chris jolting as if someone had prodded him with a red-hot poker. She would look like Aphrodite rising from the waves, the water sliding down her slick, fragrant skin. The taste of arousal on his tongue was sharp and urgent.

He fisted his hands against the desire to carry her to the bed that waited and make love to her until he was sated. Surely, he thought, surely if he had her once, just once, this need that was consuming him would fade. Surely, it was no more than the basic desire of a man for a woman, he told himself. Because arousal was already stirring his body, it was easy to believe it.

His gaze fell on the pack of cards, which he had bor-

rowed from the innkeeper, thinking to pass an hour with
a game. His head rose as the idea blossomed.

They had been playing a game all along. What better
way to prove to himself that it was still no more than a
game? A game he would win. And once he had collected
his prize, he would be free.

Something within him resisted the idea, but his half-
Russian blood embraced the plan. It was fate, he told
himself.

Ariane donned the simple white nightgown and wrapper the woman had left for her. Although they covered
her far more completely than any ball gown, she felt
exposed and awkward as she approached the table where
Chris sat.

He arranged cheese and sausage on a plate and placed
it in front of her. He filled both their glasses with wine.

"Aren't you going to say anything?" she demanded.

"What is it that you want, Ariane?"

She propped her chin in the palm of her hand and
looked at him. "I don't know, Chris. If I did, it would
be so much easier."

"Are you afraid?"

"Yes."

The unequivocal honesty of her reply touched him and
his voice softened. "Just what are you afraid of, Ariane?"

"Myself." Her fingers toyed with her glass although
her eyes remained on his. She saw the question in his
eyes and shook her head. "But not the way you think."

"Will it help if I make you a promise? No seduction
tonight. No persuasion."

She gave him a long look before she spoke. "Why
do I have the feeling that there is a trick here?"

"No trick. The chances are even."

"Chances?" Her eyes narrowed. "What are you talking about?"

"I will explain later." He held out a basket of bread to her. "Shall we eat now?"

The bread smelled wonderful and Ariane found that she was ravenous. "Yes," she agreed, "let's eat."

Pushing the remains of their meal to one end of the table, Chris picked up the pack of cards.

"It's early yet. A game to pass the time?" He held up the pack of cards, ignoring the flutter of nerves, the small stab of guilt. "What's your pleasure? Poker, *chemin de fer, vingt-et-un?*"

"*Vingt-et-un.*" Ariane's smile was replaced with a frown. "But I don't have any money. Playing isn't really fun unless you're wagering something."

"Who needs money?" He tossed a small bag that contained small wooden blocks, which were used for markers. "One can play for sport."

There was something in his voice that made her wary. She wished he would look at her so that she could see his eyes. "Yes, but somehow—" she paused and a faint line appeared between her eyebrows "—somehow I do not see you playing for sport alone."

"We could make a wager." He picked up the cards and tapped them on the table. "To make the game a little more interesting."

"A wager?"

"Yes. If I lose, I will sleep there." He tipped his head toward a narrow bed that stood tucked into a small alcove at one end of the room.

"And if you win?" Ariane asked, although she already knew the answer.

He shifted his gaze to her face. "I will sleep with you in that bed."

Chapter Seventeen

"Ah, now I understand your little remark about the chances being even." The sound of her voice surprised her. It was calm and coolly mocking, denying the pain welling up inside her. As if she were truly discussing only a card game.

"I believe I told you once before that I do not play games of chance, only games of skill." She waited for a moment, wanting him to meet her eyes fully, but he did not. "With only two players, the outcome would depend on little more than the luck of the draw."

"You still need skill." Chris's voice was defensive. "Skill to decide how to play and skill to keep the contents of your hand off your face." He leaned forward, finally meeting her eyes. "And even if luck will play a slightly bigger role, aren't you willing, for once in your life, to trust fate?"

"Fate?" Gripping the edge of the table, Ariane rose, her chair scraping loudly on the plank floor. "How dare you? How long have you been planning this?" She pushed away from the table and began to pace. "A ride away from the public paths. A cloudy day with the promise of rain. A convenient little inn.'' She raised a fisted hand. ''Oh, go to the devil.''

''You might remember that the ride away from the public paths was your idea.'' He slapped the cards he was holding back down on the table with such force that they fanned out. ''And since it's a little difficult to purchase a rainstorm, I guess this must be my lucky day.''

He rose then and, rounding the table, came toward her.

''Stay away from me.'' She raised a hand, palm outward.

He obeyed her, but when he spoke, his voice held a mocking note. ''What's the matter, Ariane? A little while ago you were relieved when I promised to neither seduce nor persuade you.'' He watched her lips part as she pulled in a breath and he continued quickly before she could deny his words. ''And now, when it comes down to proving your skill and accepting a bit of luck, yours or mine, you're playing the outraged maiden.''

Ariane stared at him. How could he do this to her? she thought. How could he stand there, so cool, so distant, and offer to play a game of cards for the possession of her body? She wanted to turn away, to let the tears, which she felt burning behind her eyes, come. Instead, a desperate pride had her stiffening her back. No, she thought, she would not let him see that he had hurt her. As she had so many times before, she reached inside herself for the only weapon she possessed against him— anger.

Chris saw her eyes darken. He'd hurt her, he thought. In his headlong attempt to free himself from her spell, he'd hurt her. No matter how much he wanted to be free of this obsession, he did not want to cause her pain. An apology on his lips, he moved forward.

But as he came closer, he realized that he had been mistaken. Her eyes had gone to the almost purple color of a stormy summer sky, but it was not pain that had darkened them, but the blaze of anger.

"You're angry."

"Yes, damn you, I am. Do you find that so surprising?" She threw back her arm in a parody of a gesture of welcome. "Step right up, *monsieur,* and try your luck!" Her voice rose in self-protection because she could already feel the lump growing in her throat. "Win a tumble with Ariane de Valmont on a hand of *vingt-et-un!*"

"Ariane—" He caught her wrist. "Stop making it into something coarse and cheap!"

"Isn't that just what it is?" She tried to twist her hand out of his grasp, but he was holding her too tightly.

"Only if you think that our bargain is coarse and cheap, too. That's what it has been about all along." His voice gentled. "Or have you forgotten?" He drew her hand toward him until it rested against his chest.

"I court you according to all the rules to free you from the unwanted attentions of your would-be suitors and ultimately from marriage, and in return—" He paused and his thumb began to stroke the pulse point of her wrist. "In return, I get to do my best to finesse you into my bed."

"Finesse?" Her pulse was beginning to pound beneath the light stroking, but she told herself that it was anger. "Finesse? You dare to talk about finesse?" She felt some small measure of satisfaction as he looked away.

"You listen to me." She grabbed the front of his shirt with the hand he still held, bringing his eyes back to her face. "Yes, we made a bargain. But why are you trying to force it to a decision now when the season has months to go yet?'' She let her hands fall to her sides. ''You've asked me many times if our bargain still stands. Perhaps I should ask you the same question.''

When he said nothing, she continued. ''Or is it something else?'' Her voice took on a taunting note. ''Have you fallen back on this little card game because you are afraid that you can neither seduce nor persuade?''

The spark of anger leaped high in his eyes. She had gone too far, she thought. In her heart, she knew that the only reason why they were not yet lovers was that he had not pressed hard enough, not pushed her far enough. She thought she could see this mirrored in his eyes and it infuriated her. This time it was she who looked away.

''I'm sorry.''

The softly spoken words had her gaze returning to his. ''I didn't want to hurt you.''

All the arrogance, all the anger were gone from his eyes, but she found that she would have far preferred that to the gentle compassion she found there. If there was anything she did not want, she thought, it was his pity.

''You haven't hurt me,'' she lied. ''You've insulted me.''

''You're right and I apologize for making the suggestion. It was rude and callous.'' He lowered their still joined hands and released her. ''Let's just forget it.''

''Yes, it was rude and callous. And no, we will not forget it.'' Her mouth thinned. ''I've never stepped back from a challenge. We're going to play.'' Her chin rose. ''And I'm going to win.''

Returning to the table, she sat down and, gathering up the cards, began to shuffle them with easy expertise.

"Ariane—"

"Why don't you divide up the markers." She brushed a glance over him that did not quite reach his face, before her eyes returned to the cards. When he was seated opposite her, she looked at him again. "Is thirty hands agreeable to you?"

Her voice was so calm, so cool that he could almost make himself believe that he had not hurt her.

"Yes," he said, ignoring the guilty ache that was burgeoning in his heart like some dark, evil flower. "That's quite agreeable."

They played in silence, dealing in turn. If they wanted another card, they signaled with a tap of a finger. If they chose to stand, one raised finger signaled their wish. If the dealer wished the other's bet to be doubled, two fingers gave the signal.

They watched the other's face, the other's eyes. Each one was disappointed.

Markers changed hands and changed hands again. When they had finished the twenty-ninth game, Ariane held fifty markers against Chris's thirty-two.

Chris shuffled and dealt the cards for the last hand. One card facedown for Ariane. One card facedown for himself.

Each one lifted a corner of their card.

Ariane pushed forward five markers. Chris pushed forward twenty.

For the first time since they had begun to play, Chris spoke. "Double your bet."

Ariane jumped at the sound of his voice. Unnerved, she pushed forward another five markers.

Chris dealt two more cards. For Ariane the queen of diamonds. A ten of spades for himself.

For the first time since they had begun to play, Ariane felt a little of her tension ease. She knew that he could still win, but the chances were much higher that it was she who held a better hand than he.

"*Vingt-et-un*," he said softly and turned over the ace of spades. "You owe me double your bet." He paused. "Unless, of course, you, too, have an ace."

In the quiet room, where the only other sound was the crackle of the fire, Ariane perceived his voice as a roll of drums.

She froze. Then carefully, very carefully, because she was fighting the overwhelming need to fling the card in Chris's face, she turned over the king of hearts.

"It would seem that you have won." She stared down at traitorous cards, still not quite able to believe that with the very last hand he had beaten her—by one point and only two markers.

"It would seem that I have."

Her head snapped up. She was ready to hiss and scratch like an angry cat at the least suspicion of mockery, but his eyes held no derision, not even that faint amusement that she had often seen there. Instead they regarded her with a kind of serious friendliness, as if he were going to inquire kindly how she was feeling. It occurred to her that that warmly sympathetic gaze was surely as false as a napoleon made of gilded bronze instead of gold and it enraged her even more than mockery would have done.

"You snake," she hissed and looked down to where his cards lay. "You dealt the last hand. You must have chea—"

"Don't."

Ariane found herself silenced more effectively by tha

one softly spoken word than by a shout. She stared at the cards, as if she could magically change them.

"Look at me."

Her gaze remained stubbornly on the cards.

Chris leaned back in his chair and blew out a long breath. He had been prepared for fury. But he had not been prepared for this. And he had not been prepared for how much her words could hurt him.

"Ariane, I would like you to look me in the eyes and tell me that you truly believe I cheated. If you do, I will ride back to the city immediately and send a carriage for you." He paused and pressed two fingers to the bridge of his nose. "And tomorrow I will leave Paris."

Leave Paris. The words reverberated in her head until they were a deafening roar. She would be safe then, she thought. And she wanted that. Didn't she?

Raising her head, she looked at him. "No, Chris." She felt the anger drain from her, leaving her in a state of lassitude, as if she had been depleted by a fever. "No matter how I would like to believe that you've cheated, in my heart I know you didn't."

"Ariane." Her hands still lay near her cards and he covered them with his. She tried to pull them back, but he tightened his grip.

He looked down at their joined hands and at the cards that lay under them.

"Look at your cards. Can they be a mere coincidence?" He smiled. "The king of hearts and the queen of diamonds together?"

She said nothing. This time, when she pulled back her hands, he let her go.

Chris watched her rise and walk to the side of the bed. For a long moment she stood there looking down. Then she slipped out of the wrapper and nightgown so quickly that he only got a glimpse of her body before she ducked under the quilt.

His nerves were jumping, he realized. He had wanted her so badly all these weeks. And now that he was minutes away from having her, he felt as nervous as a callow boy with his first woman.

He filled a glass with wine and lifted it to his mouth. But instead of drinking it as he would have wanted to, he set it down without tasting it. He'd won, he reminded himself. He'd won fairly, through skillful betting and good luck. He'd won and he deserved to enjoy his winnings.

Rising, he turned down the lamp so that it only gave a faint glow and began to undress.

Chris slipped under the cover and, propping himself on an elbow, looked at Ariane. She lay very still, her eyes closed. He said nothing, but continued to watch her. Her eyelids flickered, but she did not open her eyes. He heard her breathing accelerate. He saw a pulse beneath her ear leap.

Pushing aside the coverlet just enough to expose the slope of her shoulder, he allowed one finger to glide down the soft skin. Then, because he could not resist, he lowered his head and followed the path with his mouth. He felt rather than heard the slight catch of her breath, her faint tremble, and lifted his head, not quite sure if it was desire she was feeling or fear.

"Look at me, Ariane."

His voice coaxed gently, but she squeezed her eyes shut even more tightly. She did not want him to see what was surely reflected in her eyes. There would be fear there—and hurt and that tickle of anticipation that had sprung to life when his lips had touched her skin.

"Please, Ariane. Open your eyes and look at me."

Finally, she lifted her eyelids and met his gaze.

He saw the first sparks of desire in her eyes and he knew that a few touches, a few kisses would have her melting in his arms. But because he also saw the questions and the insecurities and the fears, his mouth remained serious as he cupped her cheek in his hand.

"Do you want this?" he asked softly.

"It does not matter what I want." Her voice was sharp, clipped. "I lost a bet. The price was to sleep with you and I will pay it."

He smiled then, charmed by the way she managed to tilt her chin at him defiantly although she was lying naked in his arms. Regretting now that he had allowed her to simply undress instead of uncovering her body slowly, inch by inch, he lowered his head and brushed his mouth lightly against hers.

"A debt of honor. Is that it?"

"Don't you dare make fun of me." Because she felt the tears pricking at her eyes, she turned her head aside. She would die before she let him see how much it had hurt her to undress and get into bed like a woman bought and paid for. Couldn't he have seduced her as he had promised to do in the beginning, she thought, and made it a little easier for her?

Because he had seen the shine of tears in her eyes and because he understood pride, he did not try to make her face him again. Instead, he propped his cheek against his hand and prepared to wait.

Ariane lay there, the tension like a fist in the pit of her stomach, and waited for him to touch her. She could feel his eyes on her—watching, always watching—but still he did not move. Finally, unable to stand the tension any longer, she looked at him.

"Well, are you going to do it?"

"Am I going to do what?" He teased, his mouth tilting up at her tone that was such a contradictory mixture of timidity and insolence.

"Are you going to sleep with me?"

"Yes. I'm going to sleep with you."

His velvet voice flowed over her skin like a kiss and Ariane felt herself soften, as if her body were already yielding, accepting. She closed her eyes, afraid that he would see the surrender in her eyes.

"But not the way you think," he continued.

Her eyes flew open. "What do you mean?"

"Close your eyes and relax, Ariane. I said I would sleep with you in this bed and that is just what I'm going to do."

"Is this some kind of a trick?" Her eyes narrowed. "That's not what you meant before."

"No," he admitted ruefully, "That's not what I meant before."

"Why?"

"Despite what you might think, I have no interest in taking you against your will just because you lost a card game. I want to make love to you—very badly in fact." He paused. "But I can wait."

He touched his knuckles to her cheek. "When I make love to you, Ariane—and I will—I want you soft and pliant from the very first moment. I want you to want me as badly as I want you." His hand dipped to trace the line of her lower lip. "I want you to surrender yourself because you cannot bear it to be any other way."

Ariane wondered if he knew how laughably easy it would have been for him to have her just that way.

"Will you sleep with me, Ariane?" He let his hand drift downward, down the line of her neck, down the graceful slope of her shoulder. "Will you let me hold you while you sleep?"

She felt her body warm, her muscles grow lax at the thought of lying in his arms. "Yes," she whispered.

"Sleep now." He reached across her and, gathering her against the curve of his body, he pressed a kiss into her hair.

Warm skin met warm skin. Ariane shivered—and knew that it was not with fear but with pleasure. Then he hooked his arm around her waist and pulled her fully into the curve of his body. Her breath caught as she felt the press of his aroused sex against her. Before she could resist the temptation, she shifted against it, testing the hard-soft texture, testing, too, the tingle of excitement within herself.

Chris stifled a moan of pleasure. Anchoring his arm more firmly around her, he fervently hoped that she would not move with that unconscious provocation again. If she did, he was not certain if he would be able to answer for his actions.

He had always been a considerate lover, but for the first time in his life he was trying to be completely self-less with a woman. Oh, he knew that he could seduce her into surrender. He knew that he was skilled enough to kiss and caress her until she begged him to take her body. But that was no longer enough.

For the first time in his life, physical desire, no matter how complete, no matter how great, was not enough.

There'd been a time when he might have seduced her, back when she was no more than a lovely young woman with fabulous violet-colored eyes. But even then he'd wanted her beyond all measure, beyond all reason. Now that he was—he stopped, but because he was tired of lying to himself, he continued. Now that for the first time in his life, he was in love, he could only wait until she came to him. Until she showed him that she wanted him. Until she showed him that her need was greater than her fear.

Chris surfaced from a deep, dreamless sleep into that half-aware, misty region where one drifts like fog over water. He heard a sound—a sigh, a moan—but did not heed it until he heard it again.

"Ariane?" His murmur was husky, slurred with sleep.

She gave no answer, but made a soft, kittenish sound.

Like a butterfly's wing, the sound skipped over his skin with a light tickle. He burrowed his face into soft, fragrant hair and smiled, although he did not realize it.

As he drifted closer to wakefulness, other sensations began to tease him. The satin skin of her back pressed against his chest. His hand pillowed against soft, lush flesh.

Instinctively, he turned his hand palm upward. As if she had been waiting just for that, she shifted and her breast filled his hand as perfectly as if the two were made for each other. The aroused crest pressed into his palm in an insistent caress that brought him yet another step closer to wakefulness.

Even in half sleep he was aware of that first tug of desire in his belly. His every breath filled him with her scent. Her skin was like a caress upon his.

Her breast was imprisoning his hand. His fingers flexed against the softness and he almost moaned aloud at the pleasure of it. It was madness, he knew, to torment himself further. Even as the thought entered his still sleep-dazed mind, he tucked his thumb inward and stroked over the crest. It hardened in concert with his own body and he repeated the touch, once and then again.

She moved in silent approval of his caress, her derriere rubbing against his belly. Unable to resist the invitation, he arched his hips so that his sex pressed against her thighs. Yielding to the pressure, she parted her legs. He slipped between them and came fully awake.

He pulled in a deep breath, then another one. The fragrance of flowers that mingled with the scent of arousal—his and hers. Carefully, he began to shift away from her, but her thighs closed around him to keep him captive.

"Ariane?" he whispered. "Are you awake?"

Her reply was a murmur that might have been his name.

"You're killing me." He pressed his face against her hair, but there was no relief. Instead a new wave of need tightened his every nerve.

He slid his other hand under her and filled both hands with her breasts. She moaned again and, wondering if she had come awake, he stilled, not wanting to frighten her.

"Ariane?"

"Mmm." She lifted her head just a fraction. "Is it morning already?"

"No." He nudged her hair aside and brushed an open-mouthed kiss over her shoulder. "Not yet."

"Good," she murmured and turned her head back into the pillow. "I'm having this lovely dream." She sighed and pressed her bottom more firmly against his belly. The movement had his sex sliding forward against her slick dampness and, instinctively, she began to move, rocking against him.

He could only stand this much. On the very brink of taking what she offered, Chris pulled back. Throwing aside the covers, he rolled to the side of the bed to lie on his back, his body hot and throbbing. But there was no escape.

Making a sound of discontent, Ariane followed him, instinctively searching for the warmth, the pleasure she had lost. Nuzzling her face against his side, her leg slid up his thigh.

"Ariane, I beg you—"

Perhaps because the alarm in his voice penetrated her sleep-hazed mind, her head fell back a little. Her eyelids fluttered briefly, then opened. And her leg continued its journey along his.

Desperate, Chris twisted to face her fully, his hand closing over her thigh to stop her progress. She kept moving. His hand slipped from her thigh to lie against her belly.

The heat of her center was drawing him. Then she moaned and arched toward him. His hand slipped further. And he was lost.

"Ariane." His whisper was urgent—a question, an invocation.

Her eyes were dark, cloudy with desire. She said nothing, but her fingers closed around his hand.

"Do you want me to stop?"

Her eyes widened, but she still did not speak. Her legs parted—just a fraction. His hand slipped further—just a fraction. She quivered and, shifting onto her back, she opened for him.

Surrendering, he slid his hand between her legs and began to touch her.

His fingers glided over her hot, slick flesh. He did not need to search out sensitive points, for every place he stroked seemed to have been waiting for his touch. Her hips began to move in counterpoint to his caresses. Her breath began coming in quick, hard bursts. Her eyes grew unfocused with pleasure and fell closed again.

The needs of his body were insistent, but he knew that this first time was for her. Only for her.

Her hips stilled and he felt the muscles in her thighs tense in anticipation. His body was pulsing with the desire to surge into her, but he did not think of that now. Instead his fingers continued to trace circles of exquisite lightness. Then he heard her breath catch and hold. One more touch and then another. When he felt her slick flesh begin to throb against his fingers, he went still and watched as the climax swept over her.

Ariane opened her eyes and saw Chris leaning over her. She wanted to reach up and touch him, but she could not move. Her body was pulsing with a pleasure so acute that it was but a breath away from pain and she pressed her thighs together against it. What a lovely, erotic dream, she thought, and smiled. Then her eyes closed again and she slipped back into a dreamless sleep.

His heart was racing as if he had run for miles. For a long time, he watched Ariane as she slept. Then he lay down, his body still hard, his fingers still damp where they had touched her. Pulling the covers over them both, he waited for dawn to break.

Chapter Eighteen

He had fallen asleep after all. But it was a light, restless sleep that fled the moment Chris felt Ariane stir beside him. He was lying on his side facing her, his hand splayed on her midriff. Unable to resist, he stretched his fingers to touch the soft undercurve of her breast.

Warm and pliant, she moved beneath his hand, as if she, too, could not resist. When he felt her stiffen, he knew that she had come awake. Before she could move away from him, he slid his hand downward and curved it around her waist.

Ariane's first conscious perception was a weight against her middle. The weight shifted and a hint of pleasure trickled through her as something touched her breast. Still hazy with sleep, she moved toward, against it. Her mind sifted through the jumble of thoughts inside her head.

She had had a dream, she remembered. The most incredible, erotic dream. Just remembering it set off a tingle in her belly. Moving against it, she encountered that delightful pressure again. As the realization that that pressure came from Chris's hand slipped into her consciousness, she stiffened against it. But before she could move away from him, he had slid his hand downward and curved it around her waist.

Although he was holding her captive now, somehow the touch was less threatening than the other and, allowing it, she remained still.

"Did you sleep well?"

The sound of Chris's voice had the memory of the night before, of the card game intruding. She'd been angry with him, she remembered. She still should be. But somehow she could not summon up the energy for it. Her limbs felt heavy, but pleasantly so. And she felt a closeness to Chris, as if sharing a bed and the vulnerability of sleep had been a greater intimacy than the mating of two bodies would have been. No, she thought. It was a shame to waste energy on anger.

"Yes, I did." Her voice was so husky that she barely recognized it.

"Pleasant dreams?"

Just as the memory, lush and seductive, flashed through her again, leaving heat in its wake, so his breath that feathered over her ear as he spoke had a small, voluptuous wave of sensation traveling down through her. The wave ended as an ache at the apex of her thighs and was a delicious temptation all its own.

Had she talked in her sleep? she wondered. Could he know what erotic dreams had filled her night? Even now she could feel her body soften as she remembered how he had slid his mouth over her skin in the dream. How he had touched all her secret places until her body had overflowed with an indescribable pleasure.

She tipped her head to the side and looked at Chris for the first time that morning. His mouth was curved with just the bare trace of a smile and there was an odd look in his eyes, at once expectant and knowing.

"What of it?" she demanded.

"Don't get all huffy on me. I'm just making conversation." He smiled fully. "So are you going to tell me about your dream?"

"It's none of your business." She gave him her best haughty look, but she found that it was difficult to retain your dignity when you were naked and in bed with a man.

"A pity." He touched a finger to her cheek. "It must have been a wonderful dream."

Her heart leaped and she sent him a sharp look. "Why do you say that?"

"Just a thought." He smiled. "Your eyes went all soft for a moment." Then he lifted one shoulder in a shrug. "Why don't I tell you about my dream, then?"

"Perhaps I don't want to hear it." She made a face at him, but that slow, lazy smile of his had already charmed her.

"Ah, but you're a captive audience." He increased the pressure of his hand against her middle just a little to remind her, at the same time, bending to brush a kiss onto her shoulder.

"You and I were close." He lifted his hand to cup her face and turn her so that she faced him fully. "As close as two people can be without being joined." He lowered his head to taste her mouth. "I touched you. I tried not to, but I could not resist." He took another taste. "You opened yourself to me—" this time he dipped his tongue into her mouth "—like a flower opens to a bee come to sip its nectar." He took the kiss deeper and deeper still.

This was seduction, she thought. These slow, almost lazy kisses accompanied by honeyed words that evoked her dream so uncannily. She was drowning, she thought.

Drowning in the memory of her dream. Drowning in the pleasure he was giving. Drowning in the pleasure he was offering.

A stray thought, no, the fragment of a thought, had her surfacing from that pool of pleasure. He had described her dream so precisely. How did he know—? But then he was kissing her again, drawing her further.

But the thought returned—more insistently this time—and she struggled to free herself from the pleasure as a trapped bird struggles against a net.

"What are you saying?" Her pulse leaping, she shifted to her side. "Are you saying that you made love to me while I was asleep?" Vivid color flowed into her cheeks as she fought to sit up. The covers fell away, but she did not think of her nakedness now.

"You weren't asleep, Ariane," Chris defended himself. "You wanted me to touch you."

"No, I was asleep," she insisted. "I was dreaming."

"Ariane—" He reached out to grasp her shoulders, but her arms flew up to knock his hands away.

"How could you do that?" she demanded, her hands fisting. "How could you pleasure yourself upon my body?"

His nerves raw, his body still aching with unfulfilled desire, his control began to slip. "I watched you move. I heard you moan." His hands circled her arms now with such a fierceness that she did not try to dislodge him. "I felt my fingers slide over your wet flesh until you trembled."

Her eyes were huge with shock that was laced with a beginning arousal, but he did not stop. "Giving a woman pleasure is an aphrodisiac, Ariane." He drew a deep breath. "Yes, I pleasured myself. But the ultimate pleasure was yours alone."

He needed something from her, he found. Because he needed it more than he needed his pride, his voice held a plea when he spoke again. "You don't have to pretend. Or lie." His hands gentled. "There was nothing shameful in what we did."

Ariane stared at him. Could he be telling the truth? Her question had an edge of desperation. The memory was sharper now, clearer. Her body was already half-aroused by his words. But her mind still denied it. She could not have given herself to him so easily, she cried silently. Or could she?

"It was a dream," she whispered stubbornly as if saying the words could make them true. "I was asleep."

Her insistent words lashed out at him as if she were wielding a whip, the pain taking him by surprise. This was why he hadn't wanted to fall in love with her, he reminded himself. He'd been afraid of this vulnerability that left him without defense against her.

Then it occurred to him that perhaps he was not completely without defense after all. He still had one weapon.

"And now?" he asked softly. "Are you awake now?"

She had been prepared to have him shout at her. But his mild tone took her by surprise. Unsuspecting, she nodded. "Yes, I'm awake."

He moved so quickly that she did not have time to make a sound. Then his mouth was on hers as he bore her down into the mattress, his hand covering her breast. Her body arched as she tried to twist out of his grip.

His sex pressed into the indentation beside her hipbone even as his mouth plundered hers. For a moment longer she struggled, before she surrendered to the flames. When she arched again, it was not escape that she sought. Her hands tunneled into his hair and fisted there as she answered his kiss.

He took his mouth down. Down to where the blood pulsed beneath the delicate skin of her neck. Down to the curve of her breast that fluttered from her racing heartbeat. All subtlety, all gentleness forgotten, he cupped it and took the peak into his mouth.

His head lifted at her moan. He'd hurt her, he thought, as he fought to surface from the madness. But then her hands in his hair tightened, bringing him back to her breast.

As his mouth teased and tasted, his hand raced down to find her. She was as hot and wet as she had been in the night. And as open. Desperate to give pleasure—and to take it—he pressed forward to find her center.

He was trembling with the need to plunge into her. Balanced on the razor's edge, he raised his head.

"Ariane, look at me."

She barely managed to lift her eyelids that were heavy with passion.

"Tell me what you want."

She moved against his hand in a wordless plea.

"Say it."

Ariane was long past any rational thought. Her world consisted only of emotion and sensation. His eyes held hers with a power that left her as breathless as his caresses. There was nothing of that familiar, springwater coolness in his eyes now. They were hot and fierce—the eyes of a warrior.

Unable to resist, her lips moved with the words he demanded of her. "I—I want you to make love to me."

"I made love to you before. Is that what you want?" His hand pressed closer. "Or do you want more?"

Surrender, she thought. It was surrender he wanted.

But she couldn't think now. Her body was a coil of desire poised on the edge of pleasure. She wanted. She needed. The last barrier fell away. "I want—"

He watched her. "What?" he whispered. The tip of one finger slipped into her, teasing, moving. "What do you want me to do?" His hand retreated and her body arched as she followed him.

She would go mad, she thought. Surely, she would go mad. But even as her body clamored wildly for relief, she did not dare to reach out and take it.

But then her heart spoke—a single word—and her fear fell away. This was the ultimate permission to take what she wanted, what she needed so badly.

"Take me. I want you to take me." She arched toward him again. "Please, Chris."

Her breathless words almost pushed him over the edge. He wanted to bury himself within her, but instead he shifted over her and only nestled his sex at her center, his touch provoking her—and himself.

But the moment came when he could wait no longer. The blood was pounding in his temples as he fitted his body to hers. Pounding.

The pounding grew louder and louder still. That was not just the sound of his pulse, he realized. But that moment of awareness was easily pushed away in his intentness on Ariane. Ever so slowly, he pushed his hips forward, once and then again.

As he lowered his mouth to hers and prepared to fill her body, the door crashed open and shouts and curses filled the room.

They sat at the long plank table in the taproom—the Comte de Valmont on one side, and Ariane and Chris, wearing clothing that was still a little damp, on the other.

"I would like to hear your excuses, Ariane." The large glass of cognac, which the innkeeper had pressed upon him, had gone a long way toward calming the Comte de Valmont's nerves, and only the unnaturally high pitch of his voice betrayed his earlier frenzy.

"I have none, *papa.*" She looked her father directly in the eye. "And since I am a grown woman, I don't see why I should have need of any."

Her body was still aching with that frantic arousal, but her mind and her heart were numb. It was as if she had been robbed of something she had wanted very badly, and yet, at the same time, she understood just how narrowly she had escaped the surrender she feared above all else.

"How dare you?" The Comte de Valmont half rose from his chair. "Don't you realize how badly you have compromised yourself? And you, *monsieur*—" He turned to Chris.

"Leave him alone, *papa,*" she interrupted. "There is nothing to be upset about." She raised her hand to silence her father when he started to speak. "No one but the people in this room knows that we have spent the night here, and I am still a virgin." Her mouth twitched with a parody of a smile. "Technically, at least."

"Damn you, we had guests when your message came!" Valmont shouted. "By now, the news is all over Paris."

"Good. Then I hope that now you will understand the folly of what you wanted, *papa,* and we can go back home in peace." Under the cover of the table, her hands linked tightly. "I have had quite enough of Paris."

"No, no, it is I who has had enough." Valmont's voice rose dangerously. "You have led me around by the nose long enough, Ariane. You will marry him and I will not take no for an answer.''

For a moment she felt as if the breath had been knocked out of her. But even as her heart leaped with sudden joy, her mind fought to quash it.

"I told you, *papa,* that I would choose my own husband. And you accepted that.'' Her breath began to shudder. "You gave me your promise.''

"You *have* chosen him, Ariane.'' Scowling, he leaned across the table, but his voice softened as he looked into his daughter's eyes. "In that bed you chose him.''

Desperate, she tried to think of excuses, of reasons, but her mind could not summon up a single one.

"And you, *monsieur?*'' Valmont turned to Chris. "You told me once that you would marry her. Were those empty words as well?''

"I will marry Ariane.'' The words rose to Chris's lips with an ease, a matter-of-factness that stunned him. Strangely enough, no regret, no bitterness sprang up to mar the moment. And if there was fear, it was because in the past hours he had come to know just how much power to hurt him Ariane wielded.

Chris's words sent a chaos of thoughts tumbling through Ariane's mind. She would not have this. She did not want this. *But you love him,* an insidious voice inside her whispered. *Yes, that's exactly why I cannot marry him,* she shouted back at the voice. *Not only will I lose my independence according to the law, I will lose it in fact. I will become his pawn, his plaything to do with as he wills. I will become just like my mother.* Paralyzed into utter stillness, she stared at Chris.

"I will marry her, but not against her will. I want that understood.'' He turned to Ariane. The look on her face stole his breath away and left him with the feeling of having just taken a fist in his stomach. She was looking at him with something resembling horror, as if he were a monster.

She felt nothing for him, he realized. Nothing but the lust of the moment. He waited for the pain to subside, as it surely must. But it did not. As he had always done, he cloaked his pain in the arrogance of generations of aristocrats and turned back to Valmont.

"I would speak to Ariane in private, *monsieur le comte.*"

Valmont jumped up. "I need some air." He hurried outside and began to pace in the courtyard that was still muddy from yesterday's rain.

"I can well imagine what you have to say, Ariane, but I would ask you to hear me out before you do." His gambler's life stood him in good stead now, permitting him to keep his eyes blank and his voice steady. Permitting him to function as if he were not raw inside.

Ariane raised her eyes to Chris's face and her head snapped back as if he had slapped her. He was looking at her as if she were a stranger with whom he had some tiresome business to discuss.

He felt nothing for her, she realized. Nothing but the lust of the moment. She waited for the pain to subside, as it surely must. But it did not. As she had always done, she cloaked her pain in the arrogance of generations of aristocrats. She gave an almost imperceptible nod, allowing him to speak.

"I think that neither one of us can dissuade your father from forcing this marriage. I also believe that this is not the tragedy you envision." He scratched at a drop of wax on the plank table and began to roll it between his fingers.

"I have no interest in your property, nor your dowry. Nor do I have any wish to tie you to a marriage you do not want." He spoke quickly. "We will marry to appease your father and after a proper interval, we shall obtain a divorce if you so wish."

He was offering her what she wanted—her freedom. Why then did his words feel like whips lashing at her? And if she took what he was offering, how would she survive this proper interval he was talking about?

"There is no such thing as divorce in France." Her calm voice, which gave no hint of the feelings that were rocking her, surprised her.

He released the breath he had not realized he had been holding and his blood turned to ice. "An annulment then."

Her fingers tightened at his easy agreement. She turned in her chair so that she faced him fully. "So you are suggesting that we make another bargain?" She paused for a moment. "Our first one was not notably successful. Can you give me one good reason to say yes to this one?"

She faced him. Her body was stiff and straight, her voice was flat, her eyes calm. How could it be, he asked himself, that she could look at him with such indifference when but an hour ago she had been pliant with passion in his arms?

"Because, Ariane," he said slowly, "you have no choice."

His words rang in her ears like the tolling of a bell. It was true, she thought, she had no choice. Not anymore. Once, weeks ago, she had had a choice. But then she had made that one decision. *Papa* had been both right and wrong. She *had* chosen him. But the choice had been made not an hour ago in the bed upstairs, but weeks ago when she had chosen him for her charade. Or perhaps even before that.

She was so still that Chris wondered if she had heard him. He drew breath to speak again, when his eyes happened to drift downward. Her hands were linked so tightly that the skin of her knuckles was white. Then, abruptly, as if she had become aware of his gaze, they loosened and he saw the marks her nails had left on the backs of her hands. Hope burgeoned and he leaned forward and covered her hands with his.

The simple pleasure of the warmth of his hands over her icy ones swept through Ariane. Because she was afraid that he would see in her eyes what she was feeling, she lowered her gaze to her lap.

What would it be like, she wondered, if she could turn her hands over to link them with his? What would it be like to look forward to a marriage that would be real and not merely a cold, brief formality? But she did not want that, she reminded herself a little desperately. She wanted her freedom. She needed it.

She raised her gaze to his. Chris felt hope wither and released her.

"So we exchange one charade for another," she said tonelessly.

"It would seem so."

"And do we have rules this time? Promises that will be kept?" Her voice sharpened. "Or do I have to take my chances like I did last night?"

"I am open to your suggestions." He leaned back and crossed his legs.

Incredulous at his facile words, his nonchalant stance, Ariane stared at him. When she spoke, her voice was rich with sarcasm. "That's generous of you." Rising, she strode over to the fireplace, gazing into the flames for a moment before she whirled around to face him.

"Just what does that mean?" she snapped. "I make suggestions and you are free to accept or refuse them? Is that it?"

Except for those painfully twined fingers, this was the first time she had shown emotion since they had risen from the bed. Chris felt something ease within him.

"You can make all the rules you please, Ariane. I only have one condition."

"And what might that condition be?" Her caustic tone hid the flutter of anticipation in her belly.

"You and I are the only ones who will know of this agreement. For everyone else this will be a marriage in fact. Neither one of us shall be made to look the fool."

"What do you care? In a little while you will be gone from Paris and so will I."

"It doesn't seem to be worthwhile to do a charade unless you go to the trouble of doing it right."

"Just what does that entail?" she asked slowly.

Chris raised an eyebrow. "You have not just left a convent, Ariane."

"You mean that you intend to sleep with me." Her heart was beginning to race again. It was fury, she told herself.

"I will share your bed, Ariane. Whether or not you *sleep* with me, will be, as always, your decision."

"You're gambling again, aren't you? You're gambling on your charm, on your *finesse*." She spat the last word. "You're gambling that if you sleep with me an annulment will no longer be possible."

His only answer was a shrug.

"All right. I accept your condition, with one of my own. Six months from the day of our wedding, you will take the steps that are necessary to dissolve our marriage." She crossed the room and stood directly in front of him. "No matter what has happened in the meantime. Do you understand me? No ifs, no buts, no excuses." She could feel her heart breaking as she burned the bridge in front of her. "Do I have your word?"

"You have my word." He paused. "In fact you shall have better than my word."

Rising, he went to a table where an inkwell and quill lay beside several sheets of cheap paper. Not bothering to sit down, he dashed off several lines in his generous script and returned to hand it to Ariane.

They were still looking at each other over the sheet of paper when the door opened and the Comte de Valmont stepped inside.

"Well?" he demanded.

Carefully Ariane folded the piece of paper and tucked it into her sleeve. Then she turned toward her father. "I will marry Monsieur Blanchard, *papa*." Without a glance at Chris, she went outside and stepped into the carriage.

Chapter Nineteen

He was getting married today. Chris stared out of the window down into the rue de Rivoli. Married! He shook his head. At times, he was still not quite sure that he believed what was happening. What he himself had done. And yet at the same time, he accepted it. More than that, he was certain that it could be no other way. The Gallic part of him, so precise, so orderly, had battled with and lost to his Russian soul, which had been so ready to accept, no, to embrace its fate.

Fate, he mused. Yes, he accepted that Ariane was his fate. And because she was his fate, he had no intention of resigning himself to the conditions she had set. It was the biggest gamble of his life.

He'd have six months to prove to her that he did not want her to give up anything—not her independence, not her property, not herself. Six months to prove to her that it was not a divorce or annulment she wanted, but a life with him. Six months to make her believe that he loved her too much to ever intentionally hurt her.

He rubbed his hands over his face as he remembered just how coolly she had looked at him as she had set her conditions for their marriage. No, damn it, he would change her mind. The alternative was just too terrible to consider.

Ariane stood in the middle of her bedroom, observing the bustle, listening to the babble of voices around her with detachment, as if they concerned her not at all. And in fact she could almost pretend that all this was happening to someone else.

Two seamstresses knelt at her feet, making last-minute adjustments to the rosettes fashioned of swan's feathers that held back the draped satin folds of the overskirt of her wedding gown. Behind her, two maids argued about how best to remove a spot that had suddenly appeared on one of the satin gloves. Henriette scolded a chambermaid for spilling the *tisane* that she had had brewed especially for Ariane. Justine flitted around her—fluffing the veil of silk tulle here, giving a tug to a sleeve there, keeping up a steady stream of meaningless chatter. Her mother merely fluttered around her, sometimes waving ineffectually with a lace handkerchief and occasionally uttering a piece of motherly advice that went unheard.

Yet another maid slipped into the room. "The carriage has arrived," she announced. "It is covered, simply covered with white roses," she added, her voice breaking with excitement.

"Tell the count that we shall be down shortly." The Comtesse de Valmont waved her handkerchief at the girl. "Go now."

"Why don't you tell him yourself, *maman*." Ariane spoke for the first time in an hour. "I'll be down in a few minutes."

"Are you sure, child?" Marguerite pressed her hands against her chest. "I will gladly stay if you need me."

"It's all right, *maman*. Truly."

"Before you left for the church I wanted to—that is, I felt I should—perhaps you and I could—" The countess's voice petered out, as she looked at this child of hers whom she had never quite understood.

"Don't worry, *maman*." Ariane managed a creditable smile and patted her mother on the arm, feeling more the parent than the child. But then she always had.

Suddenly, as if speaking after that long silence had activated some center of nerves, Ariane found that she desperately needed a moment of quiet. She twitched her voluminous skirts out of the seamstresses' hands and turned around, holding out her hands for the gloves the maids were still squabbling over.

As Henriette shooed the servants out, Ariane turned to Justine. "Would you do me a favor and see if *maman* is all right? She was excessively nervous."

"Of course." Proud to be given such an important responsibility, Justine hurried to do Ariane's bidding. At the doorway she stopped and turned around again, never noticing her friend's impatient sigh.

"This is all so terribly romantic." Caught up in the romance of a hasty wedding, attributed by all to unbridled passion, she had completely forgotten her reservations about the man polite society still called *le beau sauvage* and had fashioned him into the perfect romantic hero. "Are you utterly, ecstatically happy?"

Ariane thought of the heaviness that lay in her heart and the fear that had kept her awake most nights during the past two weeks, but she managed to curve her mouth into a smile. "Of course."

Justine gave a little, excited whirl. "I'll tell them that you'll be down soon."

As the door clicked closed behind Justine, Ariane suddenly felt immeasurably tired and slumped a little.

"Is there something you want to talk about, *ma petite?*" Henriette took Ariane's hands into hers.

Ariane shook her head. "I'm all right."

"I know you're going to be all right. You're much too stubborn not to be." Henriette gave her charge's hands a squeeze. "But that's not what I asked you."

"No. There's nothing."

Ariane freed her hands and turned away, before Henriette, who knew her better than anyone, saw the truth in her eyes. She had never been one to seek advice or comfort from anyone, but she could have done with a bit of both at the moment. Damn Chris, she thought, for making her promise that no one would know the details of their agreement.

"All right," Henriette said. "If you don't want to talk, then I will."

Ariane raised a hand to silence her, but Henriette pressed on. "I know that you did not want this marriage, although I do not understand why. Perhaps you're too stubborn to admit it, but you feel something for him. More than you want to." She moved around Ariane's wide skirt and tucked a finger under the girl's chin so that she was forced to look her in the face. "And he feels something for you."

Oh, yes, Ariane thought bitterly. *He feels what all men feel when thinking with what was between their legs instead of with their heads.* Because there was nothing she could say, she lifted her shoulders in a shrug.

"I've seen how he watches you. How his eyes follow you around. And you." She reached out and gave Ariane a gentle shake. "You look at him as well. But only when you think no one is watching you."

Ariane stiffened. She would have to be even more careful, she thought. She had to forbid herself all feeling and cut it out of her heart.

"Don't close yourself off to your feelings, child. Not every woman is fortunate enough to feel something for the man she marries."

There was a knock at the door and Justine peeked inside. "Are you ready?" She giggled. "Your father is pacing like a lion in a cage."

"I was just about to go down."

Ariane felt tears pricking at her eyes as she turned and gave the old servant a hug. "Thank you, Henriette. For all the years."

The older woman gave a small sob. "Will you remember what I said, *ma petite?* Will you allow yourself to feel?"

Ariane nodded and a panicked feeling rose to clog her throat. This was just what she could not allow herself. For the next six months, she could not allow herself to feel anything at all.

Surreptitiously, Ariane touched her thumb to her wedding ring. The most obvious, the most outward symbol of marriage. Of bondage. A link in a chain. A manacle. Why did it feel so right then?

Something drew her gaze and she turned slightly to look beyond the shoulder of the woman who was speaking to her. He was looking at her, his eyes watchful, brooding. The eyes of a gambler, she thought, revealing nothing but a seemingly unlimited reservoir of patience, prepared to wait out or to bluff his opponent. She wanted to look away, but those eyes held her. She murmured something, she knew not what, in response to what the countess was saying.

Then something changed, at first so subtly that she did not notice. His eyes warmed, then grew heated. And she understood that the challenge was still there. She understood that their original bargain still held.

Chris let the door of their suite in the Hôtel Meurice fall shut behind him. Leaning back against it, he closed his eyes. He'd watched her. All day he had watched her for a sign that she might be ready to forgive him for marrying her, but he'd been disappointed.

He had time, he told himself. Plenty of time. But the patience he had always prided himself on was wearing very thin. How would he deal with it, when she lay beside him every night, where he could see her, hear the rise and fall of her breath, smell her fragrance? He would deal with it, he assured himself. He would have to.

Opening his eyes, he watched Ariane roam around the room.

She was so exhausted that she could barely stand, but still Ariane was compelled to move. She wandered through the large sitting room, barely noticing the exquisite furniture, the fine carpets. But she did not dare to stop. If she did, she would remember that she was married to Chris now. That he still wanted her. That they were alone. That only her will lay between herself and surrender.

She could feel him watching her, she thought as she trailed her fingers over the carved back of a sofa. For a moment she was tempted to turn around quickly and meet his eyes. What would she see there? Would it be that friendly, casual charm that had been there for most of the day? Would she see that patient watchfulness that had surprised her this afternoon? The challenge? Would she see desire? Or would she see whatever it was that Henriette had insisted was there?

Turning around, she met his eyes. For a fraction of a moment she thought she saw something flicker in them—warmth or concern or perhaps something else. But then he shuttered them so quickly, so totally that she decided she must have imagined it after all.

When she turned around, Chris thought for a moment that he saw something in her eyes—a need, a question. But then it was gone, replaced by that edgy resentment that had been there ever since she had agreed to marry him.

As he pushed away from the door, he gave a tasseled bellpull, which hung next to it, a tug.

"I made arrangements for a maid to come up to prepare your bath and help you undress. Is that agreeable?"

His tone was detached, but the words themselves sounded so intimate that Ariane felt herself flushing.

"Thank you." Feeling off balance and foolish, she breathed a sigh of relief when he turned away from her and moved toward a small table that held a tray of several decanters and glasses.

But the relief did not last more than a moment as he turned around and came toward her. No longer distant, his eyes held a seductive warmth. A warmth that told her that he remembered that they had already shared a bed. That she had begged him to make love to her.

Even as the memory had her body softening, it occurred to her that now that they were married, he could take her if he wished. It was his right to do so and she would not be able to stop him. Oh, God, she thought. She would not want to stop him.

"Would you like some sweet Porto wine?"

She didn't want the wine, but she took the glass, glad

to have something to do with her hands. Glad to have elsewhere to look than into the eyes of the man she did not want to be in love with.

"Cheers." He touched his glass lightly to hers. For a moment it lay on the tip of his tongue to make a little toast to the next six months, but the words died on his lips as she tilted her face upward and looked at him. Her eyes were huge and dark with fear. No, he thought, it wasn't merely fear, it was absolute panic.

The look in her eyes stunned him, reminding him yet again how much she could hurt him. He continued to look at her, forgetting the drink in his hand, forgetting what he had been going to say, forgetting even to ask her why she was looking at him like that. Then he heard a knock at the door and knew that it was too late to ask.

He had long ago heard the maid leave the suite, but Chris stayed in the smaller bedroom on the other side of the sitting room, staring into space. What was he going to do? he asked himself. He'd gambled for the highest stakes, but he'd lost before he'd even begun. How was he going to bear it, if she looked at him again as she had an hour ago, her eyes full of panic? He could have dealt with anything else. But how was he going to deal with fear?

The clock had long since struck one. He rubbed his hands over his face. If they were both lucky, he thought as he rose, she would be asleep by now.

But when he opened the bedroom door, he saw that she was sitting up in bed, her arms encircling her drawn-up knees where she had rested her chin.

"I thought you would be asleep." Because the sudden desire to hold her was so strong, his voice was abrupt. "Aren't you tired?"

"Yes." Tilting her head upward, she forced herself to look him straight in the eye. "But I can't run away from you forever. We have to live with each other for six months, after all."

"Is that what you were doing?" Keeping his silk dressing gown on, Chris sat down on top of the covers on his side of the wide bed. "Running away from me?"

Crossing her arms, she tucked them under her chin. "I feel like a complete coward. I haven't really spoken to you in two weeks."

"Have you wanted to?" he asked softly.

She bit back the answer that rose to her lips. "We have to talk to each other sometime," she hedged.

That certainly put him in his place, he thought, tasting the bitterness. Taking refuge in irony, his eyebrows rose. "I'd quite given up hope on that."

"What did you expect?" Her voice sharpened in defense against what she saw as mockery. "Did you think I would just surrender and pretend everything was going just the way I wanted?"

Chris smiled then for the first time since he had entered the bedroom. "Never in my wildest dreams did I expect you to surrender, as you put it. Nor would I want you to." He paused. "This isn't a war, Ariane."

"You could have fooled me."

He shook his head. "Have I ever asked you to change? Have I ever said that I want you to be any different than you are?"

"Maybe not in so many words, but—"

"Not in any words," he exploded, all pretense to equanimity gone. "Not words. Not actions." Swinging his legs up on the bed, he moved closer to her. Her eyes darkened with the same panic that had been there an hour before and he felt the pain move through him again.

He fought to keep the pain out of his eyes. "Why are you looking at me like that?"

Mortified that she had not been able to better hide her feelings, she lowered her eyelids. "I don't know what you mean."

"Damn it, you're looking at me as if I were some kind of monster. As if you were petrified of me." He leaned toward her. "How do you think that makes me feel?" His hands itched to touch her and he curled them into fists to keep them still.

"Am I supposed to apologize for being afraid?" She raised her eyes to his.

"Afraid?" He frowned. "Why are you afraid of me? Have I ever hurt you? I've let you make all the rules. What more do you want?" He shifted closer, lifting his hands to touch her. But when she shrank back from him, his hands fell back down on the bed.

She had believed they could have a quiet, civilized conversation. This was not what she had envisioned, she thought, as her own temper rose.

"Oh, yes, you've let me make all the rules. Rules you have no intention of honoring." When he started to interrupt her, she held up a hand to silence him.

"I saw how you were looking at me at the wedding, with all of that gambler's patience of yours."

He almost smiled at her sullen tone. "And that offended you? Did I promise not to look at you? Not to be patient? Our agreement concerns what will happen six months from today. Up until then, everything is open." His voice softened. "Will you tell me why you were afraid of me?"

His voice was so gentle and mellow that Ariane forgot that he was a threat to her. "When you brought me the wine, it occurred to me—'' She stopped. It would not be a good idea to share her fears with him.

"What occurred to you?" he pressed.

She sighed. "That it would be within your rights to take me now. No matter what we had agreed on. No matter whether I wanted it or not."

Pain slashed through him, but the heat of anger was not far behind to cauterize the wound.

Because he wanted to shout, his voice was mild. Because he wanted to curse her, he chose words of a dagger-sharp irony. "The trust you bear me touches me beyond belief."

"I—" A shake of his head, the flash of his eyes cut her off.

He reached out, wanting to twist the thick golden braid that hung down one shoulder around his hand and haul her up against him. Instead he took hold of the long satin ribbon that fell from the neck of her nightgown of virginal white and twined it once around one finger.

"If I make love to you, it will be only if you ask me. Do you understand me?" He gave the ribbon another tug. "Only if you say the words."

Her heart leaped and began to race, but when she spoke, her voice was cool and haughty. "And so lock myself into this marriage by destroying the only grounds I would have for an annulment? I would be mad to do it."

His mouth curved in a bitter smile. "You will still be free. Don't you remember the promise I made? No matter what happens between us, I promise to perjure myself and swear that this marriage has not been consummated, if you so desire it." He gave a brief, mirthless laugh. "Don't worry. You can have your annulment, no matter what."

"Is this how you would lure me?" She passed her tongue over lips that had gone suddenly dry. "With pleasure that will have no consequences?"

"I do not lure you, Ariane," he said softly. "I offer and you are free to take or to reject as *you* will." He paused. "It has never been any other way, and if you were being honest, you would admit it."

One more tug of the ribbon and she would be close enough to kiss. Instead he unwound the ribbon from his finger and held it up between them with finger and thumb before he let it flutter downward.

She was tempted to take what he offered. But she knew that if she gave in—even once—she would never be free of him again. She would become a captive. If she surrendered to him, she would become just like her mother—a woman who was no more than an appendage of the man she loved above all else. A woman with no life beyond what her lover chose to give her. A woman prepared to bear any hurt, any violence, because she loved too much.

Her eyes still on his, she shifted back. "Perhaps talking isn't such a good idea, after all. Maybe we'll do better by daylight." She slipped down under the covers and doused the light by her bed. "Good night."

Chris stripped off his dressing gown and got into bed. He turned off his light and lay down, his back to Ariane.

"And stay on your side of the bed," he growled. Then he willed himself to sleep.

Chapter Twenty

It wasn't working, Ariane thought, as she turned over for the hundredth time. She just could not sleep. Every time she thought she was getting drowsy, the mattress would shift beneath Chris's weight and she would be wide-awake again. Giving in to the impulse, she turned to face his side of the bed.

A thin line of light slipped between the drapes, allowing her to see that the covers had slid down to his waist. His back was as smooth as if it were made of marble and her hand crept toward him, wanting just a touch. Then, suddenly, he murmured something unintelligible and she pulled her hand back just in time to keep it from being captured under him as he rolled over onto his back.

He grew restless. His breathing quickened, as if he were running. He muttered something, then moaned. And grew more restless. When he started to thrash around, Ariane sat up and softly called his name.

For a moment he seemed to respond to it, but then he began tossing even worse than before. Frightened now, Ariane slid closer to him. When she heard him cry out her name, she thought that he was coming awake and she reached out to touch his shoulder.

In response to her touch, he cried out, a guttural sound. Then he flung his arm out, the side of his hand striking her throat viciously enough to make her gasp for breath. Jackknifing up, he opened his eyes.

She was staring at him, her hand pressed to her throat. Dragging in a ragged breath, Chris ran a shaky hand through his damp hair as the terror of the dream vied with the terror of having hurt her. It took a long time for him to find his voice.

"Did I hurt you?" he finally asked.

Unable to speak, she gave a shake of her head.

"But I hit you." He wanted to reach out for her, but there was fear in her eyes again and he dug his fingers into the blanket. "Where?"

Snapping back from that panicked numbness where the blow had plunged her, she whispered, "My—" her voice stumbled "—my throat."

"Oh, God, I'm sorry." Raising his knee, he dropped his forehead on it.

The lines of his body seemed to grow slack with dejection and, unable to resist, Ariane reached out and touched a tentative hand to his shoulder. "Are you all right?"

He raised his head and looked at her, his eyes full of self-disgust. "I strike you so that you can hardly speak and you ask me if I'm all right?" He shook his head. "What are you? Some kind of saint?"

"A saint?" A smile touched her mouth. "I'll remind you of that occasionally."

He rubbed his hands over his face, then tunneled them into his hair. Fisting them there cruelly, he waited for the physical pain to drive the terror of the dream away, but it mocked him, dancing closer instead. Images of himself racing after Ariane and having her disappear were suddenly more real than reality itself.

As she watched him, Ariane felt the love that she had been fighting so desperately for the past weeks inundate her, flowing through her, until it filled her so completely that she almost cried out with the bittersweet pleasure of it.

In that moment she felt only his need, which was radiating from him like waves of icy cold. She slid closer to him.

"It's all right now," she whispered. "The dream is gone." She laid her palm against his back.

Her touch destroyed the last of his control and Chris turned his upper body into her and lowered his head to that soft fragrant curve where her neck met her shoulder.

For a long time they stayed like this, not moving, not speaking, taking comfort and giving it, breathing in the other's scent. Other needs surfaced, and desires, and both afraid of not keeping the promises they had made to themselves and each other, they moved away to opposite sides of the bed.

It was a long time before either one of them slept.

Never much of a dancer, Maurice de Blanchard sipped champagne punch and watched the couples swirling on the polished dance floor of the great mirrored ballroom at the Tuileries.

His gaze landed on his father's bastard and his pretty new wife. His little plan to have Morny seduce the chit hadn't been successful. And his attempt to rid himself of the bastard had been a dismal failure. But, he thought a little desperately, perhaps this outcome would be just as well.

He watched how the bastard's gaze remained on his wife's face, not straying for a moment. As long as he was so besotted, he thought, surely he would not take time to get involved with Crédit de Paris affairs.

When he saw the Duc de Morny coming toward him with a scowl on his face, he tensed.

"You will arrange it, Blanchard." The Duc de Morny stroked his dark, bushy mustache as he watched Christopher Blanchard and his wife.

He had long forgotten that this seduction had begun as no more than a favor to Blanchard. It had become intensely personal and it irked him no end that he had been reduced to having the woman he wanted deposited in a chamber for his use just like the emperor. However, there was no help for it. He'd waited far too long as it was, he mused grimly. Now the American had taken the innocence that should have been his.

"But, b-but," Maurice de Blanchard stuttered, "h-how do you expect me to do that, if you did not—" He stopped abruptly when Morny turned toward him, the dark eyes that could be so warm and charming gone ice-cold. "I mean, I'm not a man to persuade a lovely woman to accompany him to some far-off room. A newly married woman at that." He frowned at the blond couple on the dance floor.

Morny continued as if Maurice had not spoken. "I will give you an hour, Blanchard. That should be quite sufficient. There is a room—" He bent closer and rapped out his instructions.

Chris followed Ariane with his eyes as she strolled arm in arm with Justine on the other side of the ballroom.

He and Ariane had spent a few days in the country, where they seemed to be able to talk again without continually taking potshots at one another. And though his nightmares had returned almost nightly, even that had given him cause to hope, for in its aftermath Ariane had lain close to give him comfort.

Surely, he thought, surely she must feel something for him. Surely—

A footman at his elbow interrupted his train of thought. With a bow he handed him an envelope. He read the note inside.

I have important information for you. In the garden at the east staircase.

Chris frowned. "Who gave you this?" he demanded.

"I do not know his name, *monsieur.* A small man with dark hair."

Maurice? Absently Chris dug into his pocket for a coin. What did Maurice want? He glanced to where Ariane still stood talking to Justine. Ten minutes, he thought. He'd give him ten minutes. Turning, he made his way through the crowd.

"You haven't told me anything." Justine pouted. "Tell me, what's it like to be married to a man like that?"

Ariane hedged. "A man like what?"

"A man—you know—so large and strong." Justine had the grace to blush.

"You're just going to have to wait until you've angled that young count of yours to find out."

"Oh, how can you be so cruel? Please, Ariane." She gave her friend's arm a little shake. "Just a hint. A little one." She pushed out her lower lip. "*Maman* won't tell me anything until the day of my wedding."

"It's not something you can describe." Ariane felt her heartbeat speed up. "Please don't ask me to."

"Is it terrible then?" Justine's dark eyes grew large.

"No," Ariane said slowly, thinking of that morning in the country inn that now seemed so long ago. What if— "No, it's not terrible. But I'm sure it's different for everyone." She shrugged. "Like comparing apples and oranges."

"Oh, pooh. You just want to treat me like a child."

"Just because I don't want to share all the intimacies of my life with you, Justine, does not mean I am treating you like a child." She sighed. "Even when you're acting like one."

Justine's bow-shaped mouth opened in a round O of indignation. "And you're being mean." Whirling around, she hurried away.

Ariane lifted a hand to rub her temple as she followed Justine's progress. Where had that come from? she wondered. And what irony that Justine wanted to know what she could not have told her even if she had been willing to do so.

"*Madame.*"

Ariane looked up to see a tall footman in a powdered wig and sumptuous livery of blue and silver.

"Your husband requests your company."

"My husband?" She looked across the ballroom to where she had last seen Chris just a few moments ago. "Where?"

The footman bowed. "If you will follow me, *madame.*"

Ariane glanced again across the ballroom and turned to follow the footman.

* * *

They were so far away from the ballroom that the music was no more than a distant echo. As they turned into a narrow, poorly lit corridor, Ariane stopped, suddenly uneasy.

"Just where are we going? Where are you taking me?"

"We are almost there, *madame.*"

"Who gave you the message for me?" she demanded. "Are you sure it was my husband?"

Before the footman could answer, a door opened.

"Chris?" She moved past the servant.

"Welcome, my dear." The Duc de Morny stepped into the corridor. "I'm pleased that you could come."

Stilling for a moment, she only stared at him. Then she whirled to flee, but the footman was standing there, taking up most of the narrow space. She tried to push past him, but he blocked her way.

"You wound me."

She felt hands descend on her bare shoulders and slide down to circle her upper arms.

"Come, my dear." The voice had lost most of its mellow charm. "I don't think you want to annoy me any more than you have already."

She pulled in a breath to reply, but his hands tightened, the fingers biting into her flesh hard enough to make her cry out. He stepped back, taking her with him.

On the threshold, she saw the bed that dominated the small chamber. He had had her brought here to rape her! The realization exploded in her mind like a bomb. Twisting within his grasp, she began to fight him.

His hands were brutal, but she managed to get free. Throwing herself forward, she pushed past the footman, but hands grasped her skirt and dragged her back. Silk ripped, but she did not hear it. She fought, her fisted hands flailing around her like windmills, but she was no match for two strong men. And still she fought.

She gasped with pain as her fist made contact with bone. The shout of rage was loud in her ear. Then everything around her began to fade as hands closed around her throat.

When she next became aware of her surroundings, Ariane found herself crumpled in the corner of what seemed to be a couch. Although her first impulse was to jump up and try to flee, she forced herself to remain still. Lifting her eyelids just a fraction, she saw Morny standing at a table, rubbing at his waistcoat with a napkin. There didn't seem to be anyone else in the room now, but logic told her that the footman was probably guarding the door.

Think. She had to think. She fought to concentrate, but she only tasted the fear.

Through her slitted eyelids she saw Morny toss the napkin down on the table and look in her direction. She would play dead, she thought. Just like an endangered animal. She saw him begin to move toward her and although every fiber of her body wanted to flee, she forced herself to remain still and limp.

She could feel him standing above her. She could hear his breathing.

"Wake up," he bellowed. "Wake up, damn you." Bending down, he gripped her upper arms and half-lifting her from where she lay, he shook her.

Ariane managed to remain limp, letting her head loll back, ignoring how the muscles of her neck stretched painfully. She even managed to swallow a cry when he flung her back down and her head struck the wooden carving on the back of the couch.

She heard him swear and allowed a long breath to whistle past her lips. How long could she keep this up? she wondered. Surely, Chris would start looking for her. Surely he would find her. But she remembered the long way she had walked behind the footman. How would he ever find her in this warren of staircases and corridors?

She heard the gurgle of liquid being poured. Through her slitted eyes she saw him turn back toward her, a wineglass in his hand. He emptied the contents of the goblet.

There was the sound of breaking glass as Morny pitched the goblet aside.

Terrified, she watched as he slowly bent over her. When he hooked his hand into the neckline of her gown, the last of her control skittered away and she gasped. Then he jerked his hand down, ripping silk and lace.

Ariane opened her eyes and screamed.

Chapter Twenty-One

Chris stepped outside and walked briskly halfway down the staircase. There was no one at the bottom of the stairs and he looked back the way he had come, but there was no one there either—only the long facade of the palace, blazing with so many burning gas jets that the night was turned into day.

Leaning back against the stone balustrade, he reached into his pocket for a cigar and matches. The match flared and even as the fragrant smoke rose around him, he found that he was too edgy to enjoy it.

Impatient, he descended to the bottom of the staircase and glanced under it. No one. Hearing a sound, he whirled around, but there was nothing there. But the sound was still there. It was in his mind, he realized, nudging him. Not a sound precisely, he thought, but an echo.

Another man might have brushed it aside, but he stopped to listen. Then, without warning, he felt that telltale prickle between his shoulder blades. For a split second he had a clear image of Ariane's face, followed by the same pure terror he knew all too well from his nightmare.

Pitching the cigar away, he took the stairs two at a time.

Maurice de Blanchard gnawed at his lower lip as he watched his father's bastard elbow his way through the crowd, apparently unmindful of the indignant stares and comments that came his way. Damn it, he thought, the fellow hadn't stayed down there nearly as long as he'd counted on. He probably should have been there to occupy him with some tale, he thought, although he knew perfectly well that he could never have done it. Just the thought alone had his bowels turning to water.

He passed his little hiding place and Maurice cautiously moved forward. He felt as though he had stumbled into a second-rate farce, he thought. First, playing the pimp for Morny by sending all the participants false messages, and now, hiding behind doors and potted plants to keep an eye on the soon-to-be cuckolded husband and make certain that Morny had enough time for his dalliance. Not that Blanchard was likely to find them in that far-off room, Maurice comforted himself.

Well, he thought as he wiped his damp palms on his coat, perhaps it was worth it after all. He smiled, wishing that he would be able to see the bastard's face when he found out that Morny had used his wife.

It was madness to try to find her in this crush of people. Although the urgency within him pushed him to run, to shove people aside, Chris slowed his steps. Blocking out the music, the babble of voices around him, he tried to focus his concentration on Ariane, but he heard nothing, felt nothing, but the pounding of his own heart.

Then that prickle between his shoulder blades returned. Stopping completely, he drew his concentration together until it was focused on one single point like a magnifying glass. Then he spun around and saw his brother.

Maurice turned to flee, but Chris plowed through the crowd, pushing people aside as if they were tin soldiers. Reaching Maurice, he grabbed him by his coat and, with his own momentum, propelled him facefirst against the nearest wall.

Maurice cried out in terror, barely managing to turn his head aside to prevent his face from being smashed against the wall.

"Where is she?"

The fear had translated itself into nausea that was clogging his throat, making it impossible for him to speak. Maurice only gave a small shake of his head.

"Where is she?" Cloth ripped as Chris pulled him away from the wall and sent him crashing back.

Maurice whimpered as his temple hit the gilt molding. "Please, don't."

"Listen to me." Chris bent close. "If you don't tell me where she is, I will kill you here, now, with my bare hands." His grip tightened. "Don't think I won't." Keeping one hand against Maurice's neck, he took his arm with the other and twisted it cruelly.

"You have five seconds. Then I'll teach you what it sounds like when a bone snaps." He increased the pressure.

"A-all right." Maurice swallowed desperately. "Let me go now. Please." His voice rose in a wail.

Chris's grip eased—marginally. "Where?"

"I'll show you."

Pulling Maurice back from the wall, he kept a grip on

his arm. "Go."

As if in a trance, Maurice began to move.

"No!" The sound of her clothes being ripped away from her body told Ariane that the time had come to fight. Her fingers stretched into claws, she went for his eyes. She was beyond terror, beyond panic now. She was fighting for her life.

Morny yelped and fell back a step as one of her fingers found its way into his eye.

The small retreat gave her the opportunity she needed and she scrambled up. Her eyes darting around the room, she looked for something—anything. A possibility to flee. A weapon. But there was nothing.

Moving as quickly as her crinoline allowed, she put the small table between her and Morny, but there was nowhere to go. No matter what she did, her back was, literally, against the wall.

Morny lifted his hand to rub his eye. He was in no hurry now. She was conscious and she would feel whatever he chose to do to her. And he planned to do a great deal.

"There's no place for you to go, my dear." His voice was almost pleasant. "And you can scream all you want." His hand traced an elegant gesture of invitation. "The only one to hear you is the footman outside."

His calm tone, paired with the feral, greedy look in his eyes, made her skin crawl. She wanted to say something, to bargain, but the wall at her back reminded her how useless that would be.

She jerked when he moved, flattening herself even further against the cold wall. But he did nothing more than move toward the table that stood between them and pour himself a glass of wine. He was toying with her, she thought. Like a cat with a mouse. And still she was grateful for the moment that delayed what was to come.

He stood there, sipping the wine in silence. But his eyes never left her.

Oh, God, she thought with all the desperation of hopelessness. Why hadn't she let Chris make love to her? At least then she would have given her virginity to the man she loved. Now she would have nothing. Suddenly all her reasons for not allowing herself to yield to him seemed so petty, so unimportant.

"Would you like some wine?" Morny asked as conversationally as if she were a guest.

"Yes," she whispered. Anything, she thought. Anything to delay the inevitable.

He refilled his glass and reached across the table. "I apologize." He shrugged. "It would seem we only have one left."

She stepped away from the wall and took the glass from him.

"Drink quickly, *madame*. I find that I have tired of waiting."

The crystal was cool against her fingers. Cool and heavy. She raised the glass to her lips, but before she could taste the wine, she saw him move.

Slowly, confidently, Morny rounded the table that stood between them. Ariane felt her breath begin to shudder. A few more steps and he would be close enough to touch her. Her hands flexed, reminding her of the glass she held.

With instinct sharpened by desperation, she struck the goblet against the edge of the table, but there was no sound of breaking glass and she struck it again. This time she was rewarded and she tightened her fingers around the stem.

"You don't really think that that will help you, do you?" Before she could answer, he continued. "And here I was almost ready to forgive you for your earlier impetuosity."

Lunging toward her, Morny went for her arm, but she was quicker.

His cry and the blossoming of red along the underside of his chin told Ariane that she had scored a hit.

With a bellow of rage not unlike that of a wounded bull, he dived forward.

Again Ariane struck and again, not knowing whether or not her aim was true.

They grappled like two wrestlers, so immersed in the battle that they heard nothing. Not their ragged breathing. Not their grunts of exertion and pain. Not the sound of the door being broken down.

Chris tumbled into the room, barely managing to stay on his feet. Beyond terror, beyond rage, he leaped forward. Surprise was on his side and as he gripped Morny, the man released Ariane and tumbled backward against him. Chris staggered back, then with a savage cry, he flung Morny aside, almost regretting the ease with which he had done it.

When he turned back to Ariane, his throat closed with horror at the sight of her. Her breasts half-bare, both her torn gown and her skin smeared with blood, she stood swaying, glassy-eyed, the hand holding the broken goblet still raised to strike.

"Ariane."

She looked at him then, but her eyes still showed no recognition.

He spoke again, "Ariane, can you hear me?" He was

afraid to move closer and perhaps frighten her even more.

She shuddered then and slowly her gaze focused and filled with panic.

"Careful." Her voice was little more than a hoarse croak. "Behind you."

Chris whirled around just in time to send his fist into Morny's middle. With a grunt, the older man stumbled back. Chris followed him, the pain humming up his arm as his fist connected with Morny's jaw.

Morny staggered, but pulled back his arm to fight. Chris barely flinched at the punch, perhaps because the rage that filled him left no room for anything else. Using his fists as if they were weapons instead of parts of his body, he pounded them into Morny. Even when Morny was pressed up against the wall, Chris continued to pound his fists into him.

"Chris, stop. Please. You'll kill him."

The voice penetrated the haze in front of his eyes. He stopped, his fist barely an inch from Morny's nose. His hands still balled tightly, he watched Morny slide down the wall, collapse on the floor and begin to retch.

He shifted toward Ariane, who still clutched handfuls of his coat in her hands. His stomach lurching, he looked at her. He wanted to reach out and touch her, to assure himself that she was all right, but he was afraid she would get that panicked look in her eyes again.

"Did he hurt you?" he asked, feeling like an inadequate fool.

"No." She shook her head. "I'm all right."

"You're bleeding."

Ariane let go of his coat and looked down at herself. The horror of the past minutes was still there, yet in an odd way it had receded so that she could almost believe all this had happened to someone else.

"It's his blood, I think." She looked down at her hands, but they were empty. "I cut him." Her voice rose in an abrupt giggle. "With a broken wineglass."

Had he ever felt so helpless? Chris wondered. He stood there, his hands at his sides, wanting desperately to touch her, to hold her, but was afraid.

Ariane's eyes lifted to his. "I want to go home." She felt the last of the strength that was still keeping her upright drain out of her. Her head grew light and the weakness wandered downward. "Will you take me home now?" She felt her knees give way and, slowly, she began to crumple.

Chris caught her in his arms, almost grateful that her physical weakness had made his decision for him. Only when he moved out into the corridor and saw Maurice cowering against the wall, did he remember.

"Blanchard."

Maurice jerked his head up, his eyes huge with fright.

"If there is so much as a breath of scandal, you will answer to me. And don't think you can run."

His voice was expressionless, yet the underlying menace was so palpable that Maurice could feel the cold sweat breaking out of his pores.

"I will find out wherever you go, if you do.

"Show me how to get out of here without wading through crowds," he added, turning to the footman.

The footman nodded, recognizing both the threat and the determination.

Cradling his precious burden in his arms, Chris followed him.

Ariane shifted against the pillow to accommodate a bruise on her shoulder. She had not seen Chris since he had carried her into their apartment. He had not spoken to her except to ask her if she wanted him to send for her mother or Henriette, but she had declined, not wanting to deal with the inevitable questions. Then he had turned her over to a maid, whom he had summoned, and disappeared.

Did she repulse him? she wondered. Did the fact that Morny had touched her, had almost raped her, disgust him? Was that why he had not come to bed yet?

Well, she thought, if tonight had taught her anything, it was that life was too short to spend in useless self-torment. If Chris no longer wanted her, she preferred to know it now.

Throwing back the covers, she slid out of bed. As she reached for her robe, she bumped into a table, rattling the porcelain tea set that still stood there. Lifting her arms to put on her robe, she winced.

"Ariane? Are you all right?"

Turning toward Chris's voice, she let the robe settle on her shoulders. "I was just going to look for you."

"Did you need something? Shall I ring for the maid?"

"I don't want the maid. I was looking for you."

Oh, God, Chris thought. She was so small, so pale. He took a step inside the room. "Can I get you something? Wine? A glass of water? A sleeping draft?"

Ariane gave a shake of her head. "I was just wondering—" she paused, worrying the inside of her lower lip with her teeth "—if you were coming to bed?"

"I thought I would sleep in the other room."

"I see." Although she wanted to weep, she tilted up her chin. She would not beg, she thought. "Good night then." Shrugging off her robe, she tossed it on the chair and turned toward the bed.

"Ariane?"

"Yes, what is it?"

Her tone was tart, and even as that assuaged the worst of his fears, he also heard the thickness of tears.

"I assumed you wouldn't want to be anywhere near a man tonight."

"I cannot imagine that you would lump yourself in the same category as him. So *I* must assume that you don't want to be near me." The horror and the misguided shame rose to clog her throat. "Oh, God, I feel so filthy." She let herself fall on the bed and, hugging herself, doubled over with the pain of it.

"Don't say that, Ariane." Within moments he was beside her, but he still did not touch her.

"I scrubbed and scrubbed myself, but I still felt filthy." Tears filled her eyes and spilled down her cheeks. "Will I ever feel clean again, Chris?" Her breath began to shudder. "Will I?"

Carefully, as if she were made of the most fragile glass, Chris put his arm around her.

It was not until she felt his arm curve around her shoulders that she realized just how much she had been waiting for his touch. As relief, mixed with the remainder of fear and shame, flowed through her like a river, huge sobs began to shake her small frame.

Chris held her closer and closer still until he finally shifted her onto his lap so that he was cradling her against him like a child. Gradually the tears and sobs subsided until she lay quiet and spent against him.

He pressed his face against her still damp hair and breathed in her fragrance. He had beaten the nightmare, he thought. The nightmare had become reality today, but he had won.

Ariane felt Chris shift, the movement rousing her from

the trancelike calm that had come in the wake of the tears.

"Don't go," she whispered.

Still cradling her against him, he shifted so that he lay back against the pillows. "I'm not going anywhere, love."

Her breath caught as that single word cascaded through her like a crystal-clear waterfall. It didn't mean anything, she chided herself. He was just being kind and gentle. She'd denied it for a long time, but she had always known that he was a kind, gentle man.

As she moved against him, her curves teasing his body, stirring it, Chris almost groaned aloud. He was an animal, he rebuked himself. How could he even allow himself to desire her tonight?

Carefully, keeping her away from his body, that had gone from the dull ache of desire to full arousal within the space of a breath, he shifted her to lie against his side.

"Will you sleep now?" He tucked a loose strand of golden hair behind her ear.

"Not yet." Wanting to keep him close, she curled her fingers around his hand. When she felt how he tensed, she looked down. Despite the dim light, she could see that his knuckles were discolored and scarred with reddish lacerations. Immediately she loosened her grip.

"I'm sorry," she whispered and lifted his hand to her lips.

Unbearably moved, Chris watched her. Even as he felt a new flash of desire, the sight of her pressing her mouth against his hand, soothing his hurt when hers was so much worse, had his heart filling. If he had not already loved her, he would have loved her now.

"Chris." She murmured his name against his hand as

she would have murmured words of love if she could have done so.

"Tonight, when he had torn my clothes and I had no place to run—"

"Don't, Ariane." He traced his hand down her cheek and tucked it under her chin to bring her face up to his. "Don't think about it anymore."

"Let me say this, Chris. While I still have the courage."

There was apprehension in her eyes and, against his better judgment, he nodded. "All right."

"I was beyond fear, beyond panic. But I felt regret. Regret that I hadn't let you make love to me." She moistened her dry lips with a quick swipe of her tongue. "Will you make love to me now?"

Chapter Twenty-Two

Chris stared at her. How could she ask him that tonight of all nights? He shook his head, as much in disbelief as in refusal.

"I would be a barbarian, if I made love to you tonight. Tomorrow morning you would hate me." His voice darkened. "And you would be right to do so."

"I know what I'm saying." She spoke quietly, without heat.

"Ariane, please. In a day or two, when you're better." Desperation colored his voice. "Tomorrow if you want. But not tonight."

"Tonight, Chris." She held his gaze, willing him to see inside her. Willing him to see all the needs she had too much pride to put into words. Willing him to see all the reasons she was afraid to voice. "Now."

He heard the needs in her voice. He saw them in her eyes. How could he fight them and his own needs as well? His own needs that for weeks and weeks had filled him to overflowing. Unable to look at her one moment longer and resist, he turned away and sat up, tunneling his fingers into his hair.

Ariane watched him and understood. He had touched

her, she thought. He had held her, as if he truly cared. As if she had not been soiled and defiled by what had happened tonight. It was less than she needed, but it would have to be enough.

"It's all right, Chris. I'm sorry I pressed you." Even as she said the words, she knew it wasn't enough. Pain whipped through her with such violence that she almost cried out. She wanted to curl up against it, but he had turned around and was looking at her again.

"What?"

"I said it's all right." The pain was almost more than she could bear and as a defense against it, she spoke carefully, slowly. "I understand."

He gave a shake of his head. "What are you talking about?" he demanded. "What do you understand?"

She was weakening, she thought. A moment longer and she would dissolve in tears and would not have even a remnant of her pride.

"It's not important. I think I will sleep now."

"No!" When he saw her jolt at the loudness of his voice, he took a deep breath. "No," he said as quietly as he could. "I want you to tell me what you meant just now."

"Aren't you going to leave me anything?" she whispered, feeling her eyes fill with tears. "Aren't you going to leave me even a little bit of pride?"

Needing to move, to do something to combat her weakness, she would have gotten out of bed to pace. But because he was in her way, she rose to kneel on the bed. But there was nothing of the supplicant in her.

"I told you tonight that I felt filthy. That he made me feel filthy." Feeling a chill, she lifted her hands to rub her upper arms. "It stands to reason that you feel the same."

"Is that what you think?" Chris shifted onto his knees and faced her.

He searched for words, but found only the image of how she had looked when he had found her. "Your eyes were blank with shock in that room. Shock from what he did, from what he almost did." Fury rose again at the memory, so strong he could almost taste it. "He marked your skin." He lifted his hand to the neckline of her nightgown where the bruised skin showed, but he did not touch her. "Your lovely, soft skin." He shook his head. "How could you think—?" He shook his head again.

"I was afraid to touch you." He looked at his hands. "Afraid that my touch would remind you."

Ariane felt the pain fall away from her. "Do you want to touch me?"

"Always."

"Show me."

He shifted closer, but not too close, still afraid that he would frighten her. With his fingertips only, he framed her face and lifted it to his.

Her mouth beckoned, invited, her lips already parting for his kiss, but he only skimmed his mouth over hers. She moved, seeking to recapture his mouth, but he was already tasting the soft, fragrant skin below her ear.

Desire was pumping hotly through his blood, but Chris kept his touch light, his mouth gentle. His breath fanned her skin as he caressed it with his lips, occasionally allowing himself a taste.

Ariane was floating in a warm, silken pool, the universe melted down to this moment with this man. Her skin began to hum where he touched and tasted and she shifted closer, eager for more.

But Chris would not be hurried. Even when he heard

her breath catch, even when he felt her pulse begin to race, he did no more than feather his mouth over her face, her throat. When he felt Ariane grip the front of his silk dressing gown to bring him closer, he knew he had been waiting for this invitation.

He brought his mouth to hers. Her lips were soft, so soft, so welcoming that the instinct to plunge his tongue past them and taste the secrets of her mouth was almost uncontrollable. But because he understood that it had never been more important for him to bridle all the desires that were pounding through him, he did no more than nuzzle them.

His hands moved up to cup her neck, the fingertips touching her hair, and she stretched, flowing into his touch like a cat. Pleased, his mouth curved and he allowed himself a taste, outlining her lower lip with his tongue before he drew back. She made a small, impatient sound and her eyes opened.

Ariane could see the glow of desire in his eyes, but it was a fire that was carefully banked.

"Aren't you ever going to kiss me?"

"I thought that's what I was doing." His eyes were amused. "Why don't you show me just what it is that you want?"

"Are you saying that you want me to make love to you?"

"No." He lowered his head and, moving his head back and forth, stroked his mouth over hers. "Wherever you lead, I will follow and then, if you want it, we will make love to each other."

Ariane sighed, not sure which was more arousing— his mouth just barely touching hers or his words. She understood now what he was doing and if she had not loved him already, she would have loved him now.

Lifting her hands to his face, she held him so that he was still, his mouth pressed lightly against hers. Her eyes on his, she slid her tongue between his lips.

Just as he had promised, he followed where she had led. His tongue met hers in the slow dance of beginning arousal. Slowly, with exquisite care, he curled his tongue around hers, probing, tasting, inviting her to take more.

Her hands slid down to his shoulders and wound around him, bringing him closer. The tip of his aroused sex butted against her belly. She stilled. And so did he.

Chris waited, barely breathing. Her hands wandered downward, gliding down the silk he wore until they reached his hips. Her fingers tightened, then dug even more insistently into sinew and muscle.

For a moment Ariane paused, not afraid precisely, but unsure. Then she drew him closer and closer still until his erection was pressed fully against her. Her thighs began to tremble as a languorous, delicious weakness crept through her.

"I think—that I would like to lie down," she whispered.

"Hold on to me," he commanded and wrapping his arms tightly around her, Chris lay down against the pillows so that Ariane was sprawled on top of him.

"That wasn't quite what I meant." Her nervous laugh changed into a sigh as she felt his sex flex against her belly and she found herself wishing that there were not all these layers of silk and batiste between them.

When his arms loosened and fell away from her, Ariane propped herself up on her hands and looked down at him. His arms were bent at the elbow, the hands turned palm upward. He lay perfectly still, as if he were surrendering to her.

Surrender. Was that what he was doing? she asked

herself suddenly. His body perhaps, she answered her own question. Only his body.

And you? a voice inside her head demanded. What are you surrendering? She pushed the question away. She would not think about that now. Not now.

Chris tensed as he watched the play of emotions in her eyes. There was doubt there and questions, but beyond that he could only guess at the thoughts going through her mind.

"Ariane?" He swallowed. "Do you want to stop?"

"Stop?" Afraid that he would see the love in her eyes, she lowered herself back down and nestled her face into his shoulder. "No. I don't want to stop." Her hands crept over to his so that they lay palm to palm quietly for a moment before their fingers laced tightly. "I don't know what to do."

He laughed softly. "Of course, you do." His smile died. "Or did you mean that another way?"

"Another—?" She smiled into his shoulder. "No."

His thumbs insinuated themselves between their joined hands to stroke her palms. "Just do what feels right, love," he whispered.

Ariane felt heat flash through her and pressed her mouth against his chest where his dressing gown had fallen open.

Chris moaned as her mouth touched his skin, thinking of all the delicious things they could do to each other. How much time would they have together? he wondered. Then he forgot everything as she moved against him.

"Help me, Chris," she whispered. "Teach me."

Her breath whispered over his skin like moonbeams. He wanted to draw the moment out forever, but he knew that he was already at the end of his tether.

He unlaced their hands and stroked down her back to

her thighs. Gently, he nudged them apart so that her legs slid down on either side of him.

Her body shifted over his so that his sex was pressed against that crevice where he would fit so perfectly. His breath whistled through his teeth as his hips arched for a moment before he controlled the movement.

When she sat up, the friction, the pressure increased and Chris knew that he was not going to last long enough.

"You see," he managed, "you're doing fine without my help."

Even as he said the words, his hips arched again and Ariane felt his sex begin to pulse beneath her. His head thrown back, he groaned with his pleasure, but his eyes stayed on hers.

She felt the dampness seep through his dressing gown and her nightgown. She felt the still aroused flesh press against her.

"What happens now?" she whispered.

"Whatever you want."

Her lips curved in a secret little smile and she tugged the cord of his dressing gown from where it was wedged beneath her knee. Suddenly nervous, her heart began to pound so wildly that the fabric of her nightgown moved with it. Ducking her head down, she carefully untied the knot. Then she shifted away so that she was kneeling at his side.

That combination of boldness and shyness was incredibly appealing and Chris felt his arousal soar as he watched her. Keeping his eyes on hers, he shrugged out of the robe and wiped away the residue of his passion with the wine-red silk. Tossing the dressing gown aside, he picked up Ariane's hand.

"What do you want?" His thumb played over her knuckles.

"Will you kiss me? Really kiss me?"

He pulled her down so that she lay half across his chest. Tunneling his hands into her hair, he took her mouth. This time it wasn't the easy, subtle, teasing kiss of before. Now his tongue was merciless—questing, thrusting, as if presaging the movement of his body within hers.

Ariane surrendered to the kiss. He filled her mouth, his tongue possessing her. She felt the ache start between her thighs, and swell until she pressed her hips into the mattress in an attempt to relieve it. But there was no relief and she moaned.

Chris was already half lost in passion again, but her moan penetrated the haze.

"Have I hurt you?"

"No." The denial came out on a sigh. She shifted again against the ache.

He understood, and although his instincts drove him to cover her body with his, to take her quickly and thoroughly, he knew that nothing that happened tonight could be marred by even a trace of submission.

Wrapping his arms around her, he rose to his knees, taking her with him.

"Ariane."

His breath caressed her mouth as he spoke her name and she parted her lips, expecting his kiss. But instead, his mouth traveled downward, brushing her skin with damp kisses that had her tipping her head back with pleasure.

He lingered over the hollow of her throat, sampling the skin that pulsed with the blood coursing beneath it.

Then his mouth drifted down to loiter along the neckline of her nightgown while his hands traced over her breasts.

Ariane could feel herself melting as his mouth tasted its way over her skin. But when she felt the warmth of his breath against her breasts, she went spinning onto yet another plane of pleasure. But he only gave her a moment to savor that warm caress before he took the aroused crest into his mouth.

Her hands fisted in his hair as she cried out softly. She looked down. His skin was a dark gold against the white of her nightgown, that contrast wickedly arousing. Then he released her breast and looked up at her.

His eyes on hers, he flicked his tongue at the crest while his hands traced their way down her sides.

Fascinated as much by the sight of Chris at her breast as by the sensation of his tongue rubbing the thin fabric over her, Ariane let the pleasure roll through her in waves. His eyes remained on hers as his mouth teased her, that contact arousing her as much as the other.

As he played with her breast, Chris slid his hands underneath the nightgown that had ridden up over her knees. Slowly, his thumbs drawing gentle circles, his hands drifted upward, closer and closer to the heat that drew him.

Ariane stilled, almost forgetting to breathe. In a moment, she thought, he was going to touch her, there, where the ache was centered. But he did not. He continued to tease her with his mouth and hands, but he offered no relief.

Chris looked up at her. Her earlier pallor was gone. Now her skin was rosy with the flush of passion and he smiled.

He lowered his head to brush a kiss over her fingers. "Perhaps you would like to cool off and undo some of those buttons.'' His hands slid down to her wrists, leaving her hands free to do as she willed.

Chris watched pearl button by pearl button slide through the buttonholes. The white fabric fell open, just enough for him to see how badly her skin was marked.

Ariane saw how his eyes darkened, how his mouth thinned. Not wanting anything to mar the moment, she sought to distract him. Freeing her wrists with a gentle twist, she captured Chris's hands instead. Her hands over his, she smoothed the fabric aside until it barely clung to her shoulders. Then she released him.

''Are you going to make me do all the work?'' The words were playful and more than a little breathless.

But he did not take her invitation. Instead he bent forward and nudged the fabric with his mouth, over one shoulder, then over the other. Gently, he worked her hands through the ruffles at her wrists and let the gown fall around her so that she knelt in a pool of white.

Still watching her, he moved away and half lay, half sat against the pillows piled at the head of the bed. Then he held out his hand to her.

''Will you lie with me now, Ariane?''

She placed her hand in his and let him draw her to his side. He slid one arm around her to hold her close. With the same care, with the same reverence that a musician brings to his beloved instrument, he began to touch her.

His hand whispered over her skin like a summer breeze, touching, teasing, until Ariane thought that the pleasure could be no greater. But she was wrong. His fingers slipped between her thighs to seek her secrets. She began to tremble as the pleasure grew, wave upon wave.

''Chris, please,'' she whispered.

"What is it?"

"I want you." She dragged in a breath. "Inside me."

"Are you sure?" He caught her gaze.

"Yes."

He pulled her over him. "Then take me." Gripping her hips, he lifted her so that she knelt over his body. Then, taking her hand, he slid her fingers around his sex. "Take me inside you now."

She stilled—shocked and tantalized and seduced by the pure voluptuousness of the moment. But the urgency, the need, the desperation grew stronger. She fitted him to her body, moaning with pleasure as the tip of his sex slipped into her.

"Give me your hands," she whispered.

He held out his hands and she laced their fingers together. Then, her eyes on his, she surrendered. Surrendered her body. Surrendered her heart. And slid down so that they were one.

Chapter Twenty-Three

Ariane had never felt such utter contentment. She had not even known that such contentment could exist.

She lay propped up against the feather pillows, Chris's face pressed against her breasts. Her fingers played lazily with his soft, thick hair as the wonder of the past hour drifted through her. He shifted against her and the light scrape of his cheek against her skin had a flutter of desire blooming within her like a flower that opens at the first ray of sunlight. She willed him to move again, but he lay still.

Chris had never felt such utter contentment. He had not even known that such contentment could exist.

His face was nestled against Ariane's breasts, where the flowery fragrance that seemed to be part of her skin had mingled with the sexual scents of arousal and satisfaction. He breathed in deeply, enjoying the lazy stirring of desire.

He moved slightly, not because he was uncomfortable, but because he wanted to feel the soft slide of her skin against his face. The sheer pleasure of the sensation flowed through him like a warm river, tempting him to rub his cheek against her again. But suddenly he stilled, conscious that his skin was rough and that her skin was like the finest satin.

Then he felt her heartbeat change beneath his cheek. Felt her move against him, stretching so that her body pressed closer to his. He took a lazy taste of her skin. And then another.

Ariane felt fresh desire curl through her—gently, like a wisp of smoke. Would he make love to her again? she wondered. Touch her again with those clever fingers, which knew exactly where the pleasure was greatest? She wanted to ask him that, but when she spoke, she said only his name.

"Chris?"

Her voice was soft and dreamy, but it startled Chris out of that hazy, luxurious idleness that was just beginning to edge into arousal. My God, he thought, he had been about to make love to her again. He really was a barbarian.

He shifted back and, propping himself up on an elbow, looked down at Ariane.

Her skin still carried a hint of the color passion had put there, but he could see the pallor beneath. Damning himself again, he shifted further away and pulled up the counterpane to cover her.

Ariane saw the frown in Chris's eyes and felt tension gather in the pit of her stomach. So the anxiety was already starting, she thought bleakly. Anxiety at the thought that she had somehow displeased him. Now that he had made love to her, now that she had surrendered to him, was she ever going to be a person in her own right again?

Chris saw the last traces of pleasure fade from her eyes.

"Is something wrong?" Because he wanted badly to touch her, he fisted his hands to keep them still.

"Shouldn't I be asking you that? You're the one who's frowning."

"I'm frowning because you're pale and tired." Giving in, he touched a finger to her cheek. "And I—" he leaned down toward her and touched his forehead to hers "—I am a breath away from making love to you again."

The memory of the pleasure, the memory of that wonderful closeness they had shared in the aftermath of that pleasure almost had her reaching for him. But the fear was stronger.

"Will you let me hold you?" he asked softly. "I want to hold you through the night."

"Yes," she whispered, her heart filling. "Yes."

Chris gathered her close. Long after her breathing had evened in sleep, he lay awake and wondered if someday soon she would reproach him for making love to her when she was needy and vulnerable.

Chris awoke, his body heavy with desire. He looked down at Ariane. There were shadows around her eyes, but a night of sleep had brought back a trace of rose to her cheeks. She shifted a little, her flank rubbing gently against his.

He could make love to her now, he thought. She would move with him until they were both lost in the pleasure they could give each other. Edging away from her before the madness took him and he gave in to his needs, he rose and went to stand at the window.

Surfacing from sleep, Ariane rolled over and buried her face in the pillow. She stretched and reached out for Chris, but found only an empty spot, still warm from his body. He'd be back, she thought drowsily and curled up to dip back into that dreamy state that hovered between wakefulness and sleep.

The next time she woke, the spot beside her had cooled. Sitting up, she saw him standing at the window. He was tense, she thought. Even from here she could feel the waves of tension emanating from him. Was he regretting what had happened? she wondered. Was he remembering that another man had had his hands on her?

Pulling one of the coverlets around her, she slid to the edge of the bed. She rose to go to him, but she stopped before she had taken a step.

Suddenly, all the doubts returned, more urgent, more pressing than they had been the night before. Last evening, everything that had happened had been as essential as breathing so that she had had no choice but to do as she must. But now she understood just how much of herself she had given away.

She was losing herself, she thought. She could not afford to surrender any more power to him than she already had. If she went to him now, in the light of day, she would be giving herself up completely.

But then the love within her heart swelled, swamping her, and she moved toward him.

Chris heard the rustle of sheets, and turned around. Ariane stood at the edge of the bed, the coverlet of pale blue silk, which she had fashioned into a makeshift covering, trailing to the floor. One shoulder bare, her hair tousled, her eyes still heavy with sleep, she was the picture of provocative disarray.

Ariane stopped in the middle of a step as he turned around to face her. His gaze, heated, possessive, moved over her, and her heart leaped against her rib cage. For a moment love and fear warred against each other. Fear won and her hands tightened on the coverlet.

As he slowly crossed the room toward her, he saw her gaze skitter away and felt the hope he had felt a moment ago fade. He stopped several steps away from her. "How do you feel?"

"Fine." Her gaze skimmed over his face, but her eyes did not meet his.

"Are you sure?"

She nodded. "Yes." Color flooded her face as the memories of the night before swept over her. "I'm fine." Chiding herself for being a coward, she forced herself to meet his eyes.

He had been afraid of what he would see in her eyes. There was none of the condemnation or the regret there that he had feared, but he felt no relief. The distance, the remoteness there struck at him like a knife. He could have fought against the other. But how could he fight against this?

What if he told her? he asked himself. What if he said those three small, terrible, irrevocable words? Surely now, after last night, she would be able to accept them, to believe them. But his courage failed him.

"Would you like breakfast?" he asked instead.

"No, no, I don't want anything." She shook her head and turned aside. If only she could be home, she thought. Surely she would be safe there.

Chris braced against the pain that lanced through him. "Not anything, Ariane?" The words were out before he could stop them. "Isn't there anything that I can give you?"

"I want to go home." Her thought of a moment ago found its way to her tongue. "Will you take me home, Chris?"

As she turned to face him again, he saw her wishful look, like a child at Christmas. Slowly, the last bit of hope died within him. "I'm sorry, Ariane. I would fulfill your every wish if I could, but I can't give you this. Not yet."

"Why not?"

"I have business to take care of in Paris."

His tone was bland, but Ariane saw the spark of fury in his eyes before he controlled it. Suddenly everything was forgotten, but the fear clogging her throat.

"What kind of business?" She wanted badly to reach for him, to touch him. But she had already been so weak, she thought. She had already given him too much.

"Business too important to be put off." Unable to look into her eyes, he turned away.

"Don't, Chris," she pleaded softly. "Don't try to take revenge on Morny. Promise me you won't."

He slammed a fist into his palm. "I should have killed him last night."

"He didn't hurt me, Chris. Not really." Unable to stop herself, she closed the distance between them and laid a hand on his arm. "Please, stay away from him."

"I can't do that."

"His power is second only to that of the emperor." Her fingers curved around his arm and tightened. "I don't want anything to happen to you."

"Nothing is going to happen to me." Treacherous hope was blossoming within him again.

There was something in his eyes, Ariane thought as he turned to face her again. Something that reached out to her. Something that touched her.

What if she told him? she asked herself. What if she said those three small, terrible, irrevocable words? No, she thought. She had to leave herself something. If she said the words, she would surrender whatever she still held of herself. No matter how much she loved him, she could not allow herself to surrender herself completely. Still, she needed to say something. To give something to him. And to herself.

"Chris—" She paused, unsure of her words.

"No." He brushed his thumb over her lips to silence her. "Don't say anything." He did not want to hear whatever it was she had been going to say. He replaced his thumb with his mouth. They had this, he thought. At least they had this. Then he took her mouth and didn't think at all.

"You want me to do what?" Monsieur Leclerc stared at Chris, allowing his spectacles to slide to the very tip of his nose.

"You heard me. I want those shares—" Chris tipped his chin toward the thick bundle lying on the desk "—put on the market as soon as possible."

"If you wish, I can certainly accommodate you, but—"

"I do wish it," Chris said sharply, raising his hand for silence when Leclerc would have interrupted him again. "However, that's not all I want."

"I want the news spread in the financial community that these shares are being sold because the Crédit de Paris is nothing but an elaborate swindle. I want Blanchard and Morny to be completely discredited." He slammed a fist into the palm of his hand. "Completely."

"You overestimate my power, Monsieur Blanchard." Leclerc remembered to push his spectacles back into place. "I am but a broker."

"And I know how fast news travels, especially if the

messenger is trustworthy. My wife tells me that you are the best broker in Paris."

Leclerc acknowledged Chris's words with a nod. "To do justice to your wife's opinion of me, may I point out that if I proceed as you wish, you will not realize anywhere near what the shares are worth now. At first the shares will be snapped up, but as soon as their value starts going down, you won't be able to sell them even at a fraction of their present value. Are you certain you want to do this?"

"Quite certain."

Leaning forward, Leclerc continued, as if Chris had not spoken. "I've seen these things happen, *monsieur*. Once the shares start going down and confidence is lost, they won't be worth the paper they're printed on."

"Yes, yes." Chris gestured impatiently. "But the most important thing is that Blanchard and Morny be exposed as the frauds they are."

"I'm a broker, Monsieur Blanchard, and I can only do so much." He tapped his fingertips against each other. "If you are really serious about doing this, you might think about enlisting the help of a journalist."

Chris laughed. "I don't believe that there is actually a newspaper that would print anything against Morny."

"Try Jouvet at *Le Spectateur*. They even print articles that Victor Hugo sends in from his island exile."

Chris rose. "Thank you for your advice."

"You are telling me nothing new, *monsieur*." Jouvet ran a hand over a face that was lined despite its youth. "Every shopkeeper, every widow with a few paltry francs wants to partake in this golden age." He gestured tiredly. "And there are plenty of vultures to accommodate them. The Crédit de Paris is only one of them."

"Why haven't you exposed them before then?"

"We navigate on the razor's edge as it is. I never know if I will wake up in prison. Or dead."

"And if you have proof of a sort?" Chris leaned closer. "For instance a major shareholder throwing his shares on the market because he found out that the projects are all spurious?"

Jouvet straightened, his eyes suddenly sharp. "How many shares?"

"Four million francs worth."

The journalist whistled. "Whose?"

"Mine."

"Why?" Jouvet demanded. "Are you so rich or so foolish?"

"Neither. I want everyone to know that Blanchard and Morny are charlatans." He paused. "I want people to know that Morny has grossly misused his power to line his pockets."

"All right." Jouvet did a quick tap dance on the table with his fingers. "As soon as you put your shares up for sale, I will write the exposé on how our leaders are defrauding us." He smiled for the first time. "The crash of all the Crédit de Paris investors losing their hard-earned francs should be loud enough to keep me safe from reprisals."

"What do you mean?"

"You are not only delivering an excellent story, *monsieur,* but protection as well. All those investors with just a few paltry shares will howl and gnash their teeth and I will be their champion." He rubbed his hands together. "When will your shares be on the market? Today? Tomorrow?"

"What?" His mind was spinning.

"When will you put your shares on the market?" Jouvet's voice showed an edge of impatience.

"I will—I will let you know."

"But it will be soon, won't it?"

Chris nodded. "Yes, soon."

"I shall look forward to it." Jouvet's step was jaunty as he walked away.

Long after Jouvet had left, Chris sat staring into his glass of brandy, the man's words reverberating in his mind.

"Oh, thank God you're back!" Everything but her relief forgotten, Ariane ran toward Chris. "Where've you been?"

"I had business to take care of."

"I see." She looked into his cold, distant eyes and took a step back. "I am not supposed to know." The terrible thought that he had bloodied his hands for her had her throat closing. "Perhaps it is just as well."

Turning away from him, she paced to the other end of the room. Needing to keep her hands busy, she began to aimlessly rearrange the writing utensils on the desk.

The same distress that had darkened her eyes yesterday would be there now, Chris thought. "It has nothing to do with your not being supposed to know," he said carefully. "It's not that important."

"I'm not a fool, Chris. You come in here with eyes as cold as ice and then you try and tell me that it wasn't important."

He shrugged in acknowledgment of his helplessness. "I didn't want to disturb you."

"Ah!" She turned around to face him. "So it was important enough that it would disturb me?" Her voice rose. "Do you think you have to pack me in cotton wool?"

"I didn't want to remind you—"

"You don't have to remind me." She met his gaze. "Every time I close my eyes I remember."

Chris felt the murderous rage flare again. "I should have killed them." His voice was harsh with self-reproach. "I should have killed them both."

"You didn't hurt them?" Ariane took a step toward him.

Miserable, misunderstanding her question and her wide-eyed gaze, he shook his head. "I should have. Can you forgive me?"

The relief Ariane felt was so great that she buried her face in her hands.

"Ariane?" He closed the distance between them, but did not touch her.

She raised her head. "I thought you'd killed them."

"I'm afraid I can't oblige," he said stiffly. "All I did was set up a pathetic little revenge that will do little more than hurt their purses."

"Didn't you hear anything I said this morning, Chris? Don't you remember that I asked you to stay away from Morny?"

"Yes, but—" He paused. "Did you really mean it?"

"I've been going mad all day imagining the most horrible things," she whispered and reached out to link her hands with his. "Thank you."

He shook his head. "For what?"

"For not bloodying your hands." Stepping closer, she met his eyes and held them. "And for wanting to."

Chris looked into her eyes. If he allowed himself, he could almost believe that she felt something for him beyond desire and a certain affection.

Now, Ariane thought. Now, when there was something in his eyes that called to her, she could tell him what was in her heart. "Chris, I—"

Chris slid his hand up to cup her neck and, lowering his head to hers, he silenced her with his mouth. He could pretend, he thought. This way he could pretend that she had been about to say what he wanted to hear so badly.

Chapter Twenty-Four

How many people would lose everything they owned? Chris stared into the darkness as if he could find an answer there. How many people would be ruined on his whim, just because he wanted to take his pitiful revenge on Morny and bring him down a notch? Someday soon all these fraudulent speculations would become common knowledge, he argued. Then they would lose everything anyway. At least this way some good would come of it.

Good? an insidious voice inside his head sneered. What good? Oh, Morny and Maurice would be in the middle of a scandal for a little while. Their reputations would be a little muddied. But it would blow over and they would still be powerful enough to perpetrate yet another fraud.

He leaned forward and, propping his elbows on his knees, rubbed his hands over his face. What should he do? he asked himself. He swore silently. Did he have a choice?

"No," he murmured. He had none. Not if he wanted to look himself in the eye for the rest of his life.

The door opened and a narrow band of light fell across the room.

"Chris?"

He looked up, for a moment, but found that he was too tired and let his face drop back down into his hands.

"Go back to bed, Ariane," he muttered.

When the cushion beside him dipped under her weight and her arm slid around him, he jolted.

"What is it, Chris?" she asked softly. "Tell me about it. Maybe I can help."

"You can't." He almost groaned as her hand stroked down his back. "Go away. I don't want to talk about it."

"All right then, we won't talk." Shifting back, she pulled him toward her.

Taken by surprise, he tumbled against her, his face coming to rest against her shoulder. When he would have straightened, her arms tightened around him.

"Sh, it's all right."

His chin lay against the swell of her breast, the tempting softness sending that first ache of arousal through him.

"No, it's not all right." He struggled up.

"You're wrong, Chris. It is." Her heart was so full of love that for the moment there was no room for logical thought, or for doubts and fears. She reached up to touch his face. "Last night I needed you. I think that tonight you need me."

"Is that what this is all about?" His eyes cooled as he pulled back from her. "Gratitude for services rendered?"

She battled the hurt, but still, it welled up in waves.

Knowing that she would not be able to keep the pain out of her eyes, she lowered them.

"Or was it gratitude last night as well?"

"If you think that was the way it was—" she stared down at her tightly linked hands "—you are doing both of us an injustice."

"Then how was it, Ariane?" he demanded, all the needs and frustrations and fears making his voice rough. "Tell me."

She shook her head. "I don't know what to say." No, she thought, that was a lie. The words of love with their honeyed taste lay on her tongue. All she had to do was speak them. But the moment passed and the words remained unsaid.

Chris laughed harshly. "Neither do I."

Tears pricked at her eyes. "What's happening to us?"

"Real life." He grasped her shoulders and gave her a little shake so that her gaze skittered up to his. "Real life is happening to us, Ariane. All we did before was play too many games, make too many bargains."

She looked into his stormy eyes and her heart overflowed with so much love that everything else receded.

"Shall we pretend there are no bargains then?" she asked softly.

"But there are."

"Just for tonight. Tonight let's just be what we are."

"And what are we?" His voice was husky.

"A man and a woman who want each other." She swallowed. "Who need each other."

"Do you need me?" Again he felt that unreasoning, insane hope surge within him.

"Yes, I—" Again the words trembled on the tip of her tongue. "I need you."

It wasn't nearly enough, he thought. Not nearly. But he would take it.

His hesitation had all the doubts swirling up. All the fears. "You made me beg last night, Chris. I'm not going to beg again."

"Should I beg then to even the score?" He laid his hand at the base of her throat. "I will if you want me to." He lowered his head toward her, but instead of taking her mouth, he let his lips trace a path along the line of her jaw.

"Will you let me touch you?" His breath tickled her ear. "Please?" Slowly, his hand slid down to nestle at the top button of her nightgown.

Her answer was barely more than a wisp of sound.

She shifted toward him as his hand slipped past the thin linen to cup the curve of her breast. Softly, she sighed with pleasure, then sighed again when his hand did not linger.

He let his lips roam downward toward her mouth, but did no more than let them brush over hers. Skimming her nightgown up, he slid his hand along her thigh, and further still until his fingers were just a breath away from the heat.

"And here?" he whispered against her mouth. "Will you let me touch you here?"

Her answer drifted over his lips like a summer breeze. He shifted his hand so that the tips of his fingers slid over her already damp flesh. But he had barely touched her when the pressure of his fingers was gone and this time, she moaned in protest.

Suddenly he was kneeling in front of her, his hands pushing her nightgown up still farther.

"Will you let me taste you, Ariane?"

She stared down at him. His face was taut, his nostrils trembling with passion just barely held in check. She moved her head, not sure if she was saying yes or no.

"Please." His hands slid upward, gently widening the cradle of her thighs. "Please."

Incapable of speech, she arched her hips in answer. The heat of his breath flowed over her and she was certain that she would go mad. And then it was not only his breath touching her, but his lips and his tongue.

He felt her begin to tremble. Rising then, he gripped the back of the sofa on either side of her head.

"Touch me, Ariane. I'm begging you."

His robe had fallen open and her eyes on his, she curled her fingers around him.

He let his eyes fall closed as the sharp pleasure flashed through him.

Then he pushed himself back and scooped her up into his arms.

In the center of the soft bed, passion swept them toward the peak. And in that very last moment as the final burst of madness pushed them over the top, whispered words of love vanished unheard.

Ariane lingered over her breakfast of hot chocolate and oven-warm croissants. The slant of the sun told her that it must be past noon and she felt a little stab of guilt at the self-indulgent life she'd been leading for the past days.

The world beyond this room seemed to have ceased to exist. She spent the nights making love with Chris and during the days he left her alone to sleep and eat whatever delicious tidbits were sent up from the legendary kitchens of the Hôtel Meurice.

Leaning back against the pillows, she let her eyes fall closed. Saturated with the pleasures of the flesh, she brushed her palms down her body. As her hands came to rest on her belly, her eyes suddenly flew open.

What if she was with child? The thought had her breath turning into a solid mass in her throat. It was not improbable, given the intensity with which they came together night after night.

Oh, God, please make me be with child. The thought slipped into her mind so seamlessly that it took a long moment for awareness—and terror—to strike. Sitting up abruptly, she spilled the contents of her tray over the bed with a clatter of porcelain. She pressed her hands against her face as if she could bodily push the thought out of her mind, but it took root and spread until it seemed to fill her brain to the exclusion of all else.

There was a light knock and the maid entered with a salver piled with mail and newspapers.

"Oh, *madame,* is something wrong?" She rushed forward and dropping the salver on the bed began to pick up the contents of the breakfast tray.

"No," Ariane managed. "I'm all right." She drew in a deep breath. "Leave me alone now."

Casting her a doubtful look, the maid scurried out.

Forcing herself to relax, Ariane leaned back toward the pillows again, but stopped in midmovement when the headline of a newspaper, which had fallen open, caught her eye.

Crédit de Paris Declares Bankruptcy, the headline screamed. Stunned, she stared at it for a long time before she picked up the paper and began to read the text underneath.

"The business world was shocked to learn that the

Crédit de Paris has declared itself bankrupt, stating that most of the projects it has invested in have failed. Crowds of angry investors, fearful that they had lost their life's savings, gathered in front of the offices in the rue de Saint-Marc.

"But they learned that there is fortune in misfortune and that chivalry and honor are not mere words. Marquis de Blanchard, the owner of the bank, stated that he and the major shareholders, among them the Duc de Morny and General Cavaignac, will reimburse the small investors out of their personal fortunes."

She read the text twice and then a third time. This had to be Chris's doing, she thought. Somehow he must have forced them to do this. She felt a flash of pride and love. They would never have done this freely.

Now Chris had lost his fortune. She bit her lip. Now he had nothing left but his land. The magnitude of what he had done dawned on her. She had to go to him. She had to tell him—

Hearing the sound of a door closing, she slid out of bed and ran through the dressing room and into the salon.

Chris met her gaze across the room. "I see you've read the latest news." He flicked his chin toward the newspaper she held and tossed a portfolio onto a table.

Whatever she had been about to say as she had run into the room was silenced by his flat, almost unfriendly tone and Ariane stared at him for a long moment before she spoke. "Yes, but I'd like to hear about it from you."

"If you've read the newspaper, you know all the essentials." He walked to a cabinet and poured himself a hefty measure of brandy.

"And what is your part in this?"

He sent her a brief glance over his shoulder. "What difference does it make?"

"You must have forced them to do it. I know you did."

His only response was a shrug.

"Oh, Chris." She went to him and, putting her hands on his arms, she laid her forehead against his back. She felt him stiffen, but he did not shift away and she remained pressed against him.

What manner of man would do something as noble as this? she asked herself. Surely, a man so honorable would never misuse her. Would never hurt her carelessly or willfully. Surely, she could let herself love a man such as this.

Suddenly, her breath caught in her throat, as a thought occurred to her. "Are you going to—" Her words stumbled. "Did *you* promise to reimburse the small investors as well?"

"And if I did?" He moved away from her. Tossing back the brandy, he poured himself another. "Listen, I don't want to talk about it."

"Well, I do." Anger flared that he would shut her out. "I have a right to know what's going on. I'm your wife."

He'd wanted and waited for her to see herself as his wife, but not like this, he thought. Not like this. Feeling raw and cynical and hopeless, he turned to face her.

"Yes, Ariane, you are my wife. For six months." He saw her head snap back as if he had struck her. "Ariane—" He reached out to touch her, but she stepped away beyond his grasp.

"Meaning that I have no right to know, is that correct?" She tamped down on the hurt. "Maybe not, but

I'm asking you to tell me." She paused, waiting for him to speak, but he remained stubbornly silent. "How are you going to get the money to reimburse investors?"

"Don't worry, madam wife." His voice was heavy with sarcasm. "I'm not planning to use your dowry." He saw her eyes darken, heard her sharp intake of breath. "Wasn't that what you were afraid of?"

Something filtered into her eyes. Something soft. Something warm. Because he wanted that softness, that warmth so badly, his voice was harsh when he spoke again.

"Wasn't it?" he repeated.

"No, Chris." She shook her head. "That wasn't something I was afraid of. In fact, it never occurred to me until you mentioned it."

"Why not?"

"Because you are an honorable man."

"Really?" He laughed cynically. "When did that amazing realization strike you?" he demanded. "I can think of a dozen different times when you thought quite the opposite."

"Why are you doing this?" She had seen him angry before, but she'd never seen him so caustic, so bitter. "Why are you playing the devil's advocate now?"

"Because it's over, Ariane."

"What do you mean?" she whispered.

"Yes, I blackmailed them into doing it. Yes, I shall do my part to repay the investors. Yes, I have gotten a loan against the sale of my land in America. You are married to a poor man now, Ariane." He lifted his hands and let them drop. "A pauper."

"I don't—"

He held up a hand to silence her. "Don't worry. I won't hold you to the six months of our agreement."

"I want—"

"You can go back to your parents and we will dissolve our marriage. I don't expect you to stay married to a man who can't even afford to pay the hotel bill."

"Chris—"

"Don't worry about me, Ariane." Because the tenderness in her violet eyes hurt so unbearably, he turned away. "I'm a gambler and I know that you win and you lose. I'll be all right."

"What if I'm pregnant?"

He swiveled to face her again, his eyes resting on her for a long moment before he spoke. "Are you?"

"I don't know." She paused. "But I could be."

"We'll think of something." He began to pace as twin feelings of joy and terror warred within him. "We'll—"

"I don't want you to sell your land, Chris." She put her hand on his arm, stopping him in the middle of a step.

"I don't have any choice."

"But you do." She took a deep breath. "I want you to use my dowry to pay this."

"What?" Slowly he turned around to face her fully. "Are you mad? If I did that I would make your worst fears come true." Even as he spoke, that mad hope was surging within him again.

"I'm asking you to."

"No!" He pulled away from her and paced to the window. "No!"

"All right," she said calmly. "Then consider it a loan."

"I won't do it, Ariane. I can't."

He heard her move away, heard the floor creak softly as she left the room. Letting his head tip forward, he pressed his forehead against the cool glass. It was truly over, he thought. Because she was kind and good, she had offered him yet another bargain. Because he was honorable, he had refused it.

"Chris?"

He stiffened at the sound of her voice so close behind him.

"Will you look at me?"

Slowly, he did as she asked.

She stood there, very straight and fragile in her white nightgown, her bare toes peeping out from under its hem, holding out a piece of paper toward him.

"Do you remember giving me this—this voucher?" she demanded.

Feeling as if his heart were in a vise, Chris stared at the piece of paper where he had written his promise that day at the inn just a few weeks ago.

"Well," she continued before he had a chance to answer, "I'm calling off the bargain."

She tore the paper in two, then tore it again and again. Then she opened her hands and let the pieces flutter down to the floor.

"I offered you a loan a few minutes ago, but you refused." He opened his mouth to speak, but she raised a hand to silence him. "Perhaps you didn't like the terms. Perhaps I can make the terms more acceptable."

"What do you mean?" He felt his heart begin to pound against his ribs.

"Would paying back the loan over the next fifty years or so suit you better?"

"What are you saying, Ariane?"

"I do have some conditions, though," she continued. "There will be no annulment and no divorce." She smiled. "There will be children."

Chris felt something melt inside of him—that icy fear that had encased his heart.

"I love you, Chris." She closed the distance between them, but did not touch him. "But I was so afraid."

"And now you're not afraid anymore?"

"No." She shook her head. "I'm still afraid." For a moment the smile trembled on her lips. "But my love is greater than my fear."

He framed her face with his hands. "I was afraid, too. I knew that if I let myself love you, your power over me would be boundless. I knew how vulnerable I would be."

"Then we are well matched," she whispered.

"I love you, Ariane." He feathered his fingers over her mouth. "I love you." He leaned down and pressed his mouth against hers. "You won't regret taking the risk, I promise you."

"I'm willing to gamble on you. On myself. On us. Does that make sense?"

"Perfect sense."

"I suppose that I'm a gambler at heart, after all."

Chris smiled down at her. "I never doubted it." He traced the line of her cheek. "What happens now, love?"

"You promised once to show me a meadow full of irises."

"No, Ariane, I remember your eyes when you spoke of your home." He frowned. "I know how you love it."

She silenced him with a finger against his lips. "Yes, and I love you more."

"And I love you, Ariane." His arms went around her, lifting her up off her feet. "If I surrender my heart to you, will you keep it and guard it?"

She tilted her head back and looked into his eyes. "Forever," she said softly.

Epilogue

As the carriage bearing her parents and Justine back to Paris disappeared in the dust and bustle of the quay, Ariane leaned her head against her husband's shoulder.

Chris bent down toward his wife and felt a flash of guilt as he saw the tears on her cheeks.

"Oh, love," he whispered and wiped the wetness away with his fingers.

"I'm not sad." She shook her head. "Not really."

"Sure?" he said doubtfully. This was the third time in as many hours that he had seen tears on her face.

She nodded. "Let's find our cabin. I have something—" She paused. "Let's find our cabin."

They had almost reached the gangway when the figure of a woman in a dark blue gown caught Ariane's eye. The woman took a step forward and faltered.

Chris felt Ariane's hand tighten on his arm. "Is something wrong?"

She did not answer for a long moment. "Chris," she finally said. "That woman looks like your aunt."

Chris looked in the direction she indicated and swore under his breath. Why had she come here? he asked himself. Had she come here to remind him that she despised him? Had she come to shame him in front of his wife?

His first reaction was to pull Ariane quickly up the gangway, but he stopped himself. He was done with running from his ghosts, he thought. Perhaps it was fitting, he thought, that his ghosts had come to see him off. Slowly, he turned and went toward her.

"Madame la comtesse." He sketched an exquisitely polite bow. "As you can see I am about to leave Europe." He gestured toward the ship. "So I will no longer be a source of embarrassment to you. *Adieu.*" With another bow he turned away.

"Christophe."

The sound of his baptismal name had him turning back to face her.

"I have come here to thank you."

"What?" His eyes narrowed. "Why?"

"I found out what you did from Charles's w—from my sister-in-law. You acted as an honorable man should and forced your brother to do the same." She stood very straight, her hands bearing down heavily on the handle of her parasol. "I thank you for averting dishonor from the Blanchard name."

He had resented, perhaps even hated, this woman for so long, Chris thought, but now all the old animosities seemed to dissipate. Was it really so easy to forgive? he asked himself.

"And I thank you for coming here to tell me that," he said softly. "It cannot have been easy for you."

She inclined her regal head in a sharp nod. "I can never condone what Charles did, but I was wrong to revile you for sins committed by your parents. Will you accept my apology?''

"Yes." Chris understood pride and he understood how much these words had cost her. "And I thank you for your words.''

Something in her face softened then. "*Bon voyage, then, and—*" she paused "*—au revoir.*"

"*Au revoir.*" Chris bowed and, tightening his arm around Ariane's, turned to lead her toward the gangway.

When the door of their cabin had closed behind them. Ariane tossed her bonnet aside and slipped her arms tightly around Chris.

"I'm so glad, love," she whispered. "Now there are no more ghosts to burden our new life.''

"I did not know how much those words would mean to me until I heard them." He tipped her face up to his. "Do you think me a weak man for wanting them so badly.''

"No, not a weak man." She smiled. "A man with a heart." She pressed her face against his chest. "Chris?''

"Yes, love?" he murmured, threading his fingers through her hair.

"Come Christmas, there will be three of us." She smiled as she felt the thump of his heart against her cheek. Tilting back her head, she looked at him, her smile dying as she saw the panic in his eyes.

"I want to give our child everything. We're not rich anymore. How can I—"

"Sh, love." She silenced him with her fingers against his lips. "We're rich in all the ways that count.''

"I love you, Ariane." Chris sighed, wondering how

he had ever lived without her. "More than I can ever tell you."

"Would you consider showing me?" She smiled a knowing, feminine smile and reached up to hook a finger into the knot of his cravat.

Picking her up, he carried her toward the bed.

Much later, Ariane cuddled against Chris's side in a haze of repletion and drowsiness.

"I don't understand," she murmured, "that I could ever have been afraid of surrendering to you."

"You don't have to surrender, love." He played with the ends of her hair. "You never have to surrender."

"No." She tipped her head back. "Just my heart." Reaching up, she stroked a finger over his cheek. "Just my heart."

* * * * *

Harlequin® Historical

A clandestine night of passion
An undisclosed identity
A hidden child

RITA Award nominee

Miranda Jarrett

presents...

THE SECRETS OF Catie Hazard

Available in April,
wherever Harlequin Historicals are sold.

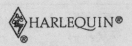

Not The Same Old Story!

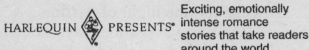

Exciting, emotionally intense romance stories that take readers around the world.

Vibrant stories of captivating women and irresistible men experiencing the magic of falling in love!

Bold and adventurous— Temptation is strong women, bad boys, great sex!

Provocative, passionate, contemporary stories that celebrate life and love.

Romantic adventure where anything is possible and where dreams come true.

Heart-stopping, suspenseful adventures that combine the best of romance and mystery.

LOVE & LAUGHTER Entertaining and fun, humorous and romantic—stories that capture the lighter side of love.

You are cordially invited to a

HOMETOWN REUNION

September 1996—August 1997

Bad boys, cowboys, babies. Feuding families,
arson, mistaken identity, a mom on the run...
Where can you find romance and adventure?
Tyler, Wisconsin, that's where!

So join us in this not-so-sleepy little town and
experience the love, the laughter and the
tears of those who call it home.

WELCOME TO A
HOMETOWN REUNION

Daphne Sullivan and her little girl were hiding
from something or someone—that much was
becoming obvious to those who knew her. But
from whom? Was it the stranger with the dark
eyes who'd just come to town? Don't miss
Muriel Jensen's *Undercover Mom,* ninth in a
series you won't want to end....

Available in May 1997
at your favorite retail store.

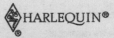

MIRA Books is proud to present
the newest blockbuster from

DEBBIE MACOMBER

*"If I want to get married and have a family
(and I do!) it's time for a plan! Starting now."*

—Excerpt from Hallie McCarthy's diary

This Matter of Marriage

The Problem. Hallie's biological clock is ticking, she's
hitting the big three-0 and there's not one prospect for
marriage in sight.

Being an organized, goal-setting kind of person, however,
Hallie has…

The Solution. One full year to meet Mr. Right, her Knight in
Shining Armor.

But the dating game is always the same. One disaster after
another. Fortunately, Hallie can compare notes with her
neighbor, Steve Marris. He's divorced and in the same boat.
Hmm…too bad Hallie and Steve aren't interested in each other!

Available in April 1997 at your favorite retail outlet.

MIRA The brightest star in women's fiction

Look us up on-line at:http://www.romance.net   MDMTMM

LOVE *or* MONEY?
Why not Love *and* Money!
After all, millionaires
need love, too!

How to Marry a MILLIONAIRE

Suzanne Forster,
Muriel Jensen
and
Judith Arnold

bring you three original stories
about finding that one-in-a million man!

Harlequin also brings you
a million-dollar sweepstakes—enter
for your chance to win a fortune!

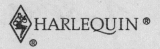

HARLEQUIN ®
®

It's hot...and it's out of control!

BLAZE

Beginning this spring, Temptation turns up the *heat*. Look for these bold, provocative, *ultra*sexy books!

#629 OUTRAGEOUS
by Lori Foster (April 1997)

#639 RESTLESS NIGHTS
by Tiffany White (June 1997)

#649 NIGHT RHYTHMS
by Elda Minger (Sept. 1997)

BLAZE: Red-hot reads—only from

HARLEQUIN® *Temptation*

Bestselling Medieval author of
KNIGHT'S RANSOM

Suzanne
Barclay

Continues her exciting
Sommerville Brothers series with

Knights
Divided

Watch for the spectacular tale of a valiant knight accused
of murder and a beautiful woman who takes him captive!

Don't miss this searing story, available in March,
wherever Harlequin Historicals are sold.